EXPOSURE

a love story

TRACY EWENS

EXPOSURE

a love story

Book design by Maureen Cutajar
www.gopublished.com

ISBN: (print) 978-0-9976838-4-4 | 0-9976838-4-8
ISBN: (e-book) 978-0-9976838-5-1 | 0-9976838-5-6

For Katlyn.
Because you make awkward and hiking boots look cool.
I love you.

Chapter One

Meg Jeffries wasn't wearing underwear. She wiggled a bit in the backseat of the taxi as if to confirm she was now fifteen minutes from her apartment and all but naked under the rainbow fabric of her favorite skirt. If she asked the driver to turn around now, she would be late, and that was not an option. Not today. As traffic on the Bay Bridge slowed, she thought about stopping somewhere along the way but realized she no longer knew the city where she'd grown up. Fashuation, the trendy boutique her older sisters adored when they were teenagers, was now a dry cleaner. Meg leaned her forehead against the cold glass of the window. *Nothing is the same.* In more ways than just her underwear. Besides, she sat up, willing her insecurities away, she was not asking the balding driver who reminded her of a gruffer version of her grandfather if he knew of a place to pick up some panties.

If she'd started working out as she'd promised herself last week, there might have been something in the oversized bag she carried everywhere. Maybe some bike shorts or bathing suit bottoms. When she'd researched the gym up the street, she had noticed they offered water aerobics. There was even a coffee shop en route from her apartment. Normal people worked out and drank coffee, and Meg was giving normal a real concerted effort these days.

Searching the gym's website, she'd landed on the page that described four different membership packages when an e-mail came in from one of her colleagues. It included a link to an article and a rolling eyes emoticon. She'd read the Op-Ed piece it linked to arguing that climate change was "natural" and "simply something for the bleeding hearts to worry about." It had pissed her off enough to close her browser and fire off a two-paragraph e-mail to the paper responsible for the article. Not that she hadn't heard the same drivel hundreds of times before, but it still hit her anew every time. So, instead of picking a plan and joining a gym, she'd put Vivaldi's Concerto in G Minor for 2 Cellos on repeat and made zucchini muffins.

Two rent payments into her new place, and it turned out the only "normal" thing she could manage was baking. It was a bit of an obsession. Since her neighbors were gluten-free vegans, that left a lot of baked goods for late-night snacks. Another contributing factor to her present state of undress, she thought as the taxi took a sharp left and threw her into the door where a wad of dried chewing gum was squished into the miniature ashtray. Perhaps if she'd joined the gym instead of shoving carbs in her face and sending angry e-mails to people who simply didn't care, she would emerge a civilized adult. A woman with a schedule and flat abs. A professional with the basic reassurance of undergarments before she attempted to speak in front of an audience.

It was that damn green skirt. The one that was too tight now that she was in the middle of a love affair with her oven and had discovered the falafel joint around the corner from her apartment. Both were to blame. She'd had on perfectly respectable panties until the green skirt, combined with the panties, made her ass look like it was in four sections instead of two. So, she took off said panties, hoping for a smoother look, but after several more tugs and grunts decided she looked ridiculous in green corduroy and went with her favorite skirt instead. Not only did it have an elastic waist with a silky tie, it was every color of the sunset. That was why she'd bought it four assignments ago. The skirt billowed out and made her feel pretty. Last time she'd worn it was on the plane home from her last shoot in Canada after spending three weeks photographing the gray wolf.

God, what she wouldn't give to be back with the wolves, or any-thing on four legs for that matter, instead of pulling up in front of the Moscone Center naked as a jaybird, to use an Uncle Mitch expres-sion. She certainly wasn't naked, but when the valet opened the door of the taxi, a breeze danced along Meg's skirt, and she sure felt a little exposed.

"No one knows," she said more to herself, but the valet with the gauges in his ears looked up.

"Sorry?" he asked as he patiently continued holding the door.

Meg grabbed her bag and her GoMacro protein bar. She'd decided to skip lunch after pinching her way into clothes that used to fit, but in the end decided she might need a little snack later. She wasn't sure what kind of food would be served at this event, so she brought her own.

"Nothing. I'm a little... nervous." Meg turned toward the valet as the cabbie rounded the front of the taxi for his money.

"Does this look okay?" She glanced down at herself and was cer-tain no one could see the important piece of clothing she'd left behind.

"Yeah, I like the skirt."

"Thanks. I bought it in Morocco."

"Seriously?"

"They have spectacular bazaars there. Have you been?" Meg stepped aside, letting him close the taxi door while she fished through her bag for her wallet.

"To Morocco? Um... no. I'm still saving to get down to San Diego for my sister's wedding."

Meg caught herself again in that eternal state of jet lag. She'd been home three, almost four months now, but somehow she still felt disjointed, as if she was floating in an existence in which no one else could relate. There were times she'd run into other photographers on assignment, and it was standard to ask where they'd come from or which remote corner of the planet they were off to next. Working for *National Geographic* had been the escape hatch from a boring life that Meg had shunned for as long as she could remember. Now that she had changed directions, she was beginning to wonder if that hatch swung both ways.

"Right. My sister is getting married too. That's common ground."

The guy nodded and watched as another car approached.

"Well, do you have a frequent flyer account? Sometimes you can catch huge deals." The cab driver was glaring at her now. Meg opened her wallet.

"I'll keep that in mind," he said. "Are you here for the climate thing?"

"Yes, I'm presenting... something." Meg handed cash to the taxi driver and looked down at her jumbled papers.

The valet reached over as the cabbie handed him something before speeding away. The next car in line pulled forward.

"You might want to put the other one on if you're going to be in front of people." He handed her an earring.

Meg instinctively touched one ear, found the dangling stone, and moved to the other one, which of course was bare. An earring was a simple thing, but she felt out of control. She had been up to her waist in rivers, tracked mountain lions, and dove into icy waters all for the perfect shot, but this looking presentable business was intense.

"Thank you." She slid on the earring.

"No problem." He rounded the next car to open the door for the driver. "Knock 'em dead. Try to... what's that they say? Oh, yeah. Picture them all naked." He handed a ticket to a slender balding man, climbed into the car, and was gone.

Was that a joke?

Could he see through her skirt? Meg shook herself free of her absurdity and stepped past the automatic doors into the beige and sparkly lobby of the convention center. Eighty percent solar, she remembered reading on their website. It was a beautiful building, made even more so because it was gentler to the earth than most massive venues. Meg liked gentle.

Taking a deep breath, she straightened and followed the signs pointing to the Symposium for Climate Wellness Initiative. Kind of a ludicrous name, Meg thought, but they'd invited her to talk about the shrinking habitats of polar bears. Their name didn't matter and neither did her panties, she reminded herself.

Underwear or no underwear, this cause was her "wheelhouse," as Amy, her new agent, had said, tossing her shiny hair and crossing her perfect legs while sitting behind her perfect desk.

Lord, I have an agent now.

Meg rounded the corner near a bronze statue of three dancing figures.

Are you nervous? Her sister Anna texted before Meg had a chance to take the picture. It somehow felt like she knew Meg was in a mini-state of panic. Meg began typing a response. *Not yet, but I don't have any under...*

What the hell was she doing? It's not like Anna could help her or bring an extra change of clothes the way their mom used to when one of them had an accident in preschool. This was the real world, and Meg was a grown-up for Christ's sake. Besides, as much as Meg loved her sister, Anna would not understand forgetting underwear. She was poised and orderly, and Meg was, well, not. That didn't mean she had to share every detail of her disarray.

Nope. I'm great, Meg texted back with a smiley face and tossed her phone into her bag. It would be so like her to get distracted right outside where she needed to be and miss the whole thing. Did lying through text message count? Meg had a feeling it did, which went against her "no lying" policy, but technically she was great. Great might be an overstatement, but she was at least good.

She kept reminding herself to focus. This was serious business. She needed to find a way to make a living, or she'd be stuck taking pictures of fruit for lifestyle magazines or cranky families at one of Murphy's Portrait Studio's ten locations.

Abstract images lined the hallway as Meg followed the sign pointing toward the main auditorium. She didn't recognize the photographer's name, but the images were manually processed. It had been awhile since Meg had been in a darkroom. She could experiment with some city images and work in paper now that she was back. Maybe she could teach.

Now you're losing it, some rational part of her brain muttered. It was right. She knew how to take photographs, which didn't mean she had any clue how to show someone else. Besides, she'd pissed off enough people in her photo workgroups at Berkeley. A classroom of Photography 101 kids didn't need some bitch crushing their dreams right out of the gate. Anna had a way of reaching students, seeing things through their prism. Meg only saw things through one lens — her own. That sounded harsh even to her own ears, but the truth was she'd spent most of her adult life arguing with only herself.

Everything had shifted now, admittedly her own doing. A few short months ago, she was washing her shirt each night in a river, and now she was about to stand in front of thousands of "activists" and share the scary truth about the bears she loved more than most people.

No wonder she forgot her underwear. There needed to be a reentry period for this kind of stuff. She'd planned on taking it easy, dipping into her savings if necessary, but then last month's *National Geographic* cover came out and Amy said she was "hot, hot, hot."

"If you ever want to make a living as a 'normal person,' you'd better seize the day," Amy had added.

Meg sure as hell never wanted to be normal growing up, but she did feel a pull toward something more. Random family breakfasts, a can opener that wasn't part of a multipurpose tool, full-size toothpaste. Meg returned home to put down roots, but as she pulled the doors open to whispers of backstage conversation, she wasn't so sure she was cut out to be among the humans.

Westin Drake rolled over in bed to escape the harsh light of morning. Through a haze of bite-sized memories from the night before, he first realized he was desperately thirsty. Reaching toward the nightstand for a bottle of water, he noticed the glossy photograph and demo his date had slipped him after she introduced herself at the Save Something fundraiser. She had pretended not to know who he was and did a damn good job of it, he had to admit. She'd taken the seat next to him, talked a lot about herself and how she'd come to be involved with the nonprofit, even sprinkled in a little bit about her family back home in Georgia. West bought it hook and line. He'd spent the evening dancing with her and eventually had Vince drive her home. Outside her house, she'd said, "I don't usually do this, but you're incredible. What did you say you did again?" West had invited her back to his hotel and kissed her. She was gorgeous and at least played smart. Well, until she reached into her bag and handed over her promotional materials. He had no idea why he bought the bullshit. Maybe he foolishly thought things would be different now that he'd moved from LA to San Francisco, or he wasn't too bright, as his oldest brother would say shortly before smacking him on the back of the head when they were growing up.

Whatever the reason, West had found himself in the same situation he swore to avoid, but this time he made a few more cocktails and decided if she was going to use him, he was going to use her right back, right there on his hotel suite couch.

Yeah, that routine usually sounded better in his head, but the truth was he only played a badass womanizer on the big screen. In what little reality he had left, West wasn't wired to be an asshole. Which was why even though he'd taken April, the aspiring singer, to bed and even though she'd screamed out his character's name instead of his—twice—he'd still held her and agreed she could stay the night.

West closed his eyes, guzzled some water, and not for the first time in his life kicked himself in the mental balls. Why couldn't he be one of those guys who had rules? Boundaries when it came to his bed—who was allowed in it and for how long?

The answer, while he hated to admit it given his current situation, was simple. He'd had female friends growing up, and brothers who would kick his ass if he started acting like an idiot. Then there was his mother, who called him every Monday on her way home from her Jazzercise class even after he moved to LA. The truth was, he liked women, often with their clothes on.

The one asleep in the king-size bed of his hotel suite at the Fairmont San Francisco with "Free Samples" emblazoned across her ass in sequins had shared something with him last night. Sure, it was purely physical for both of them and opportunistic on her part, but she showed her true colors after he kissed her. He still unzipped her dress, so he was a willing participant. The universal rule was that nothing good ever starts with a lie, but West was weak and male, and he took her to bed anyway.

So, as mind numbing as he was sure the conversation over a room service breakfast would be, he would smile and offer her more coffee. They would eat and then he'd hand her off to the sainted concierge West called "Towner." She would ensure April was delivered safely and discreetly home. West knew no other way to treat people.

He had tried for aloof badass ever since women began throwing themselves at him solely based on his movies or an absurdly air-brushed picture of him in a car he'd never drive. West had wanted to be that guy at different points in his life. It looked much easier, especially during the years he spent climbing out from under the shadow cast by his brothers, but he had long accepted that a clear conscience was worth more than anything.

With all that swirling around in his still-dehydrated brain, he re-solved to order breakfast once again, sign anything that wasn't skin, and feign interest in her music career or her desire to start a celebrity event-planning business as a backup.

West quietly pulled back the covers and made his way to the shower.

Moments later, towel at his waist, he grabbed his phone vibrating in the jeans he'd thrown over one of the gold upholstered armchairs the night before. He should have left the phone right where it was, but instead, he swiped the screen.

"Where the hell are you?"

"Good morning, Hannah. Are we talking physically or mentally? I've been thinking about Malta. Have you ever been?"

His manager said nothing, but her breathing had become a lan-guage all its own. West was fluent.

He gave in. "I'm home, I mean at the hotel. Why? Where am I supposed to be?"

More breathing. "Symposium for Climate Wellness Initiative. Annual event. Ring any bells?"

West remembered because of the stupid name. He looked at the clock on his phone. Right as he realized it was already 11:30, April rolled over, stretched, and gave him the woman-waking-in-a-big-bed grin.

"Shit." He turned to face the bedroom door, willing April to get her bedazzled ass out of bed. There would be no luxuriant farewell today.

Hannah Leighton continued breathing through the phone. "Yeah, shit is an understatement. You're introducing Megara Jeffries. It's a big deal, West. *National Geographic*. You said doing new vodka-flavor unveilings and night club openings were not considered community service, remember? 'I have a conscience. I need more,'" she mocked in a baby voice.

West closed his eyes. He had said that.

"Do you remember that?"

"Not quite in that voice, but yes."

"And since I'm your kick-ass agent, I reached out and showed these hiking-for-fun bleeding hearts that you would be a perfect spotlight for them." Her voice was much louder now. "She's been on the cover of *National Geographic* twice for crying out loud."

"Right." West tossed the red bra hanging from the doorknob and the piece of material pooled on the ground near it toward the bed. April's outfit had passed for a dress last night, but in the harsh light of almost afternoon and his agent's amplified breathing, it looked more like a Halloween costume. He kept that last observation to himself, glancing at April, who apparently had not met Hannah, or she wouldn't be crooking her finger in a gesture that invited West back to bed. He shook his head and pointed to his phone in an animated panic. April's eyes grew wide as she blew her blond locks out of her face, scooted out of bed, and eagerly nodded as if she were privy to an important crisis. She held her finger to her mouth and tiptoed into the bathroom.

Before the guilt in his stomach bloomed, Hannah was back in his ear.

9

"West?"

"I will... How much time do I have?"

"Thirty minutes."

"Where?"

"Moscone Convention Center."

"I'll be there."

"Tamara sent you clothes. Did you get them?"

West considered the living room and noticed the wardrobe bag hanging on the front closet door.

"Yes. I'll be there and in whatever is in that bag. Need to go."

West hung up before more breathing erupted into more yelling.

"Baby, are we late for a photo shoot or something?" the husky voice spilled from behind the bathroom door.

We? West ran a hand over his face, hoping to erase every choice he'd made since yesterday morning's Kinesis workout, but the sandpaper feel only reminded him that the clock was ticking. He called down to Towner.

Alice Towner was a saint. West already knew that, but he would now need to add wizard since less than fifteen minutes later, he climbed into a waiting car after kissing April on the cheek outside the service elevator and assuring her he would share her songs with some of "his people." Christ, he was a good actor.

Once again, he awkwardly offered Towner some folded bills.

"Thank you, but I brought my lunch today," she said in a voice that usually had West sitting up straighter.

"You should try that little deli next to the dry cleaner. It doesn't look like much, but they have scrumptious chopped liver," Towner said before closing West into the quiet of the black sedan. She offered some version of the lunch comment every time he tried to give her money in a voice that reminded him of his Aunt Margaret. Not the tone, but the wisdom behind it.

Twice a year, once the day before Easter and then again during the Christmas season, his mother's sister came up to Petaluma from "the big city." She giggled a little every time she used that label for San Francisco, as if she was the first person to think of it. The van from

Bayview Care Community pulled in at three o'clock sharp. She insisted on it so she and West would have plenty of time to be "seated and prepared" at the backyard picnic table for tea at exactly four. When West was little, he cringed at being forced to wear the bow tie she had given him at Christmas and having to pull out the wooden bench for her as if they'd arrived at the Ritz. By the time he was a teenager, it was an eye-rolling intrusion into his all-important social life.

Aunt Margaret, no nicknames for her, died when West was a senior in high school, and the strangest thing happened. He missed her, missed tea and time with her he would never get back. She'd helped him grow up, knocking every chip off his adolescent shoulder with a simple story or a pouty face. She'd been his friend when the comparisons to his brothers became too much. She'd kept his secrets and trusted him with hers. West didn't know how significant Aunt Margaret was until she was gone. Life seemed to work that way.

He'd thought about having tea a few times after she died to keep the tradition alive, but something far less important usually got in the way. He had never met anyone like her until a few days after he checked into the Fairmont.

He'd been surrounded by photographers while trying to make his way into the lobby. Towner burst through the crowd of cameras, her winter-white bob perfectly quaffed, exclaiming, "Mr. Drake needs to get inside. Please stand back. His dear sister is in labor." The piranhas had parted on an "aww" and allowed West to pass. He didn't have a sister.

As Towner escorted him to the service elevator and explained that he could use the side alley for his "comings and goings," West had thanked her and discreetly handed over a folded hundred-dollar bill. Her help was well worth the money, but she had instead pushed up the brim of her glasses, shaken her head, and showed West a picture of her newest granddaughter. That was it, a picture, some random conversation about when peaches were in season again, and a handshake. It was the beginning of their relationship. Towner informed him less than a week later that she did not want to be called Ms.,

Miss, or Mrs. She was sixty-eight and none of those titles fit any-more, so she said. West, who was raised to respect his elders, couldn't bring himself to use her first name, so they settled on Towner. "Like Madonna," he had told her. He occasionally still tried to tip her, especially when he called on Towner to deal with his less-than-proud moments, but she never took the money.

He smirked at the thought of the hotel concierge being his only true friend and decided his Aunt Margaret would certainly approve.

The driver notified West they would arrive at the convention cen-ter with five minutes to spare, which was good news. He didn't want to listen to Hannah if some *National Geographic* rising star had to walk on stage alone. Like that would be a huge loss. The woman took pictures in freezing water, or with bears. She was obviously more than capable of walking on a stage. He had asked Hannah for more substance, but he'd secretly hoped she would stop sending him to publicity things altogether when he moved from LA. He should have known better; Hannah had selective hearing.

"These groups are happy to have you. And why wouldn't they? You're pure star power, hon," she had said last month when she set the event up and was far less pissed at him than she was on the phone.

Closing his eyes and resting his head back on the leather seat, West wondered how many more of his fifteen minutes of fame were left.

Chapter Two

*M*eg had talked her way out of and into a lot of situations. It was a necessary skill if a woman wanted access to places and the ability to capture images most people only saw on a nature channel. She'd grown up raising her hand, but if she wasn't acknowledged, she spoke her mind anyway. Her mother used to say her restlessness came from being the youngest in a family of four girls. That might be, but now and then the oldest, Hollis, exerted her superpower too, exactly like she had last Thanksgiving.

"We need you home," she had said, never one to mince words and even more bitchy now that she was eight months pregnant.

"I am home." Meg gestured to the living room.

"Not what I mean, smartass, and you know it. Mom had eye surgery three months ago, did you know that?"

"No." Damn her. Meg often wondered if Hollis was riddled with guilt herself. She was a master at bringing it out in others.

Her big sister quirked a perfectly waxed brow in that way that made Meg feel stupid.

"Well, she did. Now you can ask her how she's feeling. And you weren't at Sage's wedding, or mine for that matter. Doesn't that bother you?"

"It's my job. No one asked me if I was going to be available for those weddings, and I can't..."

"Leave the animals?"

"Oh, screw you. I'm sorry you've had a meltdown and discovered your softer side thanks to your way-too-kind-for-you husband, but the rest of us still work. I don't need this right now, Hols. I'm home, and I don't have another assignment until after the new year. I will talk with Mom and find out why she's not telling me things."

"That's temporary. You're all about keeping it real, little sister, so I'm telling you how I feel, how we all feel. You are missing out on our family, and while your pictures are stunning and your success is brag-worthy, we miss you and we need you."

"Bullshit. No one has ever needed me. You guys want the whole family picture now that you've paired up and gone all Hallmark Christmas special on me."

Hollis played a little violin with her fingers, shook her head, and returned to the rest of the family in the living room for pie. Meg had been so frustrated—she wasn't sure if she was pissed or guilty. She'd eventually settled on a mixture of both. That was the same year Anna had blurted out her love for Dane, and Meg was again caught in a blizzard of emotions as the life she'd left behind all those years ago shifted one step further away.

The sister closest to her, the one who loved her even in her disarray and flights of adventure, was in love and it would be no time at all, Meg knew even back then, before she too would be off and married.

Meg had brushed the whole thing off by the time her plane landed in Canada at the start of the year, but her mind had been clouded. She woke before the sun a few months ago with a sense of almost paralyzing loneliness. The predawn sky from her tent in the Great Bear Rainforest of British Columbia was deep violet. It was a morning she'd experienced more than her fair share of times, but that time, her heart began to race as if she'd recently received bad news. For the first time since she was eighteen, her self-imposed solitude rang empty.

She lay back on her sleeping bag with a sense that all the lives that were important to her had learned to live without her, that they were going on and would continue despite her existence. Meg had felt pangs of longing for home before, but they were easily dismissed. This was different. This made her cry.

When the feelings didn't subside despite her usual distractions, she realized she wanted to be home for the first time ever. She took her last shots of the Spirit Bear, turned in her images, and spent a few weeks in the home where she grew up. Her mother kept making her waffles, and her father hugged Meg until she couldn't feel her arms. She was their baby, the last to leave and the last "singleton," as her dad exclaimed one morning over breakfast.

"It makes sense that you are home now. I think you're ready for a change. Thirty is right around the corner and you've sown your oats."

Meg had twisted her face in confusion at the awkward reference. She often wondered where her father came up with this stuff but assumed it must have been handed down through the generations of quirky Jeffries men.

"My oats, huh?"

"Yes. You've been out there roaming around with the animals, and now you're ready to make your own nest or cave or den. You know what I mean."

"I'm sure I don't, but it all sounds good, so I'll let you have it. I'm happy to be home, and yes, a rental den or cave has appeal. Let's start with that." Meg had opened her laptop that morning, again somehow knowing it was time.

Her father ruffled the top of her head, as he often did when he was emotional or not sure what to say, and they'd gone apartment hunting that afternoon.

As of this morning, she had a couch and a dresser for her bedroom. She was well on her way to a full nest. With or without underwear, she was still Meg Jeffries—the wild one of the Jeffries clan.

And yet, the mere act of speaking eluded her when the stage manager explained where she would be standing and that something was going to lift her above the crowd. She had a million questions and wanted to protest, insist she could walk onstage, but all that defiance

came out as a passive smile, and she did something she rarely did—
she followed directions.

Standing in darkness speckled with only a few filtered lights, Meg
knew she'd only allowed herself to be led because she was scared. The
first time she used a guide in Kenya, she listened more than she spoke
and followed his exact instructions. She had never captured images
of big predators before and her stomach danced the entire month
and a half. It had been exhilarating and palm-sweating scary at the
same time. Her palms were sweating again as she stood on some grate
in the convention center as if she were about to be ejected from a
cannon in front of a roaring crowd, but she was nowhere near
exhilarated. She was terrified.

Second guessing why she'd left the comfort of a job she knew and
loved and doubting her ability to be anything more than a photographer in the field, Meg tried to remember which slide was first in her
presentation. The stage manager's whisper cut through the darkness.
He explained that the man introducing her was running late and her
cards had been placed on the podium as she requested. Meg was
three-quarters of the way to convincing herself things would be fine
when she remembered the green skirt and the rest of her morning.

Did he say up and over the audience?

West was questioning Tamara's choice of pants for the afternoon. He
tended to leave the "look" to her, but he wasn't sure he'd ever worn
red pants before and unless his next job was hosting one of those
talent shows that was all the rage these days, he'd be sure to tell her
this was his last pair. As the car inched through traffic toward the
convention center, all he could think about was the shit he was
inevitably going to get from his three brothers back home if they
happened to see any pictures of the event or coverage on television.
Hannah had said the damn thing was televised. Not that they
watched all that much, but somehow, thanks to YouTube, everything
managed to find its way back home.

West looked back down at the pants and sighed. He had not exactly grown up in a fashion-forward family, and the outfit would no doubt provide enough comic material to last them all until next Christmas.

He preferred to dress himself from his vast collection of jeans and T-shirts. In the early days, that was fine, but once the movies started taking off, he was given a "team." That included his stylist, Tamara. West had reluctantly agreed to be "dressed" for talk shows and other publicity-related events. Not that he considered an environmental symposium publicity, but the press would be there, so Hannah and his publicist were given final say on the outfit.

West had to admit, when he first decided to commit to acting for a "finite period," as his dad had suggested, he'd never imagined going from blind auditions for bit parts to being followed into the grocery store and receiving public bathroom selfie requests overnight.

Things had died down a bit now that they were on the fourth film in the franchise, but the week the first *Full Throttle* opened, his world changed. The ride had been trippy. He wasn't going to pretend he didn't enjoy the money and the things it afforded him and those he loved, but he was getting older. How long could a guy wear leather pants and a tank top before people started laughing? Even if he stayed in shape, the work wasn't exactly stimulating.

"Your face is not what independent films are looking for, hon. Most moviegoers want to picture you naked, not spouting endless monologues on being misunderstood," Hannah had said a few years ago when he expressed an interest in working on a project outside of the *Full Throttle* franchise.

West used to pride himself on balking at authority. In fact, being the family rebel, the one McNaughton boy who wasn't going to settle for a small city, fueled everything he did up until recently. It was who he thought he was, although LA had a way of knocking a person around. He might have started out with a fire in his belly, but after years of trying to make his life, his career, into what he'd imagined, West had given up and made it big at the same time.

He'd worked hard and now made good money. The people in his hometown thought he was a genuine badass thanks to a few stunt men and excellent lighting. He'd even been able to use some of his success to help his brothers start a brewery. But along the way, he gave up on showing people what rested beneath his bravado. That was why he was drawn to acting, wasn't it?

Mr. Hernandez's Acting 101, and his first monologue made him feel completely exposed and protected behind a fictional character at the same time. By his senior year, the applause convinced him he could take people somewhere, give them a good cry or a laugh, and return them safely to their seats. It was the rush of feeling, wasn't it? Hell, West couldn't even remember anymore.

All he knew was that at some point, he realized he was successful in a world where most dreamers were destroyed or sent home. If that meant people defaulted to the face he was born with and his extra hours at the gym, he needed to accept that. The thirst for that first rush or the desire to transport people somewhere else through his acting rarely surfaced anymore. After the third *Throttle* film had topped the box office for three straight weeks, Hannah threw West a bone by getting him some more interesting press opportunities, and most of his endorsements now were things he cared about. In return, he agreed to stop "trying to be something you're not," as Hannah so bluntly put it, and to reprise the role of Nick Shot as many times as the franchise requested.

He was grateful and hardly wondered anymore if the only McNaughton brother to leave their town for "something worth doing"—as he'd said in a rage when his father told him it was time to come home and stop playing around—was reduced to expertly tousled hair and a smoldering gaze.

He was still the same kid who held the family record for school detentions. The guy who went to LA with nothing more than clothes and a cash deposit for an apartment. Somewhere underneath his glossy exterior, West still had a soul. The problem was no one ever asked to see it.

The car came to a sudden halt at a large metal door by the back of the convention center. Perfect timing, he thought, wondering what the hell had gotten into him today. Reflection time was over.

"Three minutes," the driver said as he opened the door.

West bounded up the metal stairs and was struck by the simple joy of getting out of a car without fanfare. Before he had a chance to enjoy the moment, he was plunged into darkness.

"Mr. Drake," a soft male voice behind a tiny blue light said, carefully closing the door and pulling the dark draping behind them.

West nodded, not sure if he was allowed to speak. With controlled urgency, he was taken by the arm and led to what looked like some kind of cage behind the set.

"Since you are on in less than five minutes, you missed the direction. You'll have to wing it. Ms. Jeffries is already in place. Between you and me, she appears to be struggling a bit. The platform over there will lift the two of you up over the audience and deposit you both center stage. Your job is to keep Ms. Jeffries calm, get her to the podium safely, and read the introduction."

"Easy enough," West said, his eyes now adjusting so he was at least able to make out the stage manager's goatee and the woman he was supposed to introduce. Instructions came over the stage manager's headset and West moved into place.

The woman next to him was shaking. Not exactly a seizure, but she was generating almost as much buzz as the backstage motor that jolted them a bit and then began moving. There was no time for introductions or chitchat, and West wasn't sure why there needed to be such a production to introduce a woman who clearly didn't enjoy the spectacle, but he wasn't in a position to argue. Instead, he held on to her surprisingly solid arm and worked out his own breathing so at least one of them would still be standing. Whoever Megara Jeffries was, she probably wasn't going to make it once they landed on the stage.

The weight of her body pressed up against his side as the platform shifted. She smelled like an umbrella drink, one with coconut, and West instantly wanted to be on an island somewhere, beer in hand and his feet in the—

"I'm not wearing any underwear," she said in a shaky voice, interrupting his mini-vacation and squeezing his arm tighter.

"One more time?" West leaned into her.

"My underwear, I left it at home by accident. I decided on my favorite skirt instead of the green one." She closed her eyes as if silencing some internal conversation. "It doesn't matter. In seconds, we are going to be dangling over that audience. Not good. Up and over is not good without underwear."

They were in virtual darkness now, suspended over the stage and poised to reach over the audience. There was no time to find the situation humorous. He'd do that later.

"Cross one leg in front of the other like you have to pee and then take a deep breath. There's no way from this distance, even with the lights, that anyone is going to see up your skirt. It's not possible and even though I'm sure you feel crazy exposed right now, trust me, you're all right."

She looked up at him as the deep breath left her lungs and nodded. The platform was now hovering over a large crowd as the announcer introduced them both. Her hand tightened, and despite being the youngest in a family of all boys, he had once talked Marcy Billings through four complete rotations of the Ferris wheel at the high school fair, so he knew it when he saw it: he recognized fear.

"First lecture?" he asked, hoping to calm her down before the music stopped. It sounded a bit ominous, like they were introducing the heavyweight champion of the world rather than a photographer who looked like she might pass out.

She nodded.

"Megara is an interesting name." He was trying anything at this point to get her to relax. If she didn't, by the time they finally landed back on the stage, he'd be doing this whole thing alone. He knew a bit about polar bears and loss of habitat, but no one wanted to hear from him in that capacity.

"Greek," she said and closed her eyes.

"Almost done," he said over the roar of applause. "Greek, huh?"

"Yes. My parents came home from a vacation in Greece, and my mom was pregnant with me. I was a surprise, so they named me after the city where I was conceived."

The platform lowered and West held on to the railing. Her grip on his arm loosened a little.

"That's cool. Are you ready to do this thing now?"

"Oh, wow. We're here. Done." She turned to him and now, with the stage lights shining, he noticed her eyes. Blue or gray with a dark brown circle. They were big, and West's gaze was locked on to her for longer than usual. She appeared to need something from him. Odd, he thought and stepped off the platform to help her down toward the podium.

"In case they didn't tell you, the prompter is off to the right if you forget anything you were going to say."

She nodded, now staring out into the darkness of the audience. He led her to the podium and read his fluffy introduction.

"And as if being on the cover of *National Geographic* for the second time this year was not enough, Ms. Jeffries is here this afternoon to share some of her adventures with us and explain how we can be nicer to the planet."

She had a death grip on his shirt and wasn't letting go. He leaned into her ear. "Don't lock out your knees. Keep them bent and remember, your body responds to your breathing. Steady. It gets easier. Besides, they love you." He gently placed a kiss on her cheek, and she appeared to gather herself and released his arm.

"Thank you," she whispered and faced the podium. West stepped back as the audience clapped, most of them on their feet. He pivoted to leave the stage and noticed she was bending and straightening her legs behind the podium.

West grinned, amazed that he'd spent less than fifteen minutes with her and was already grateful he'd woken up to Hannah yelling in his ear.

Chapter Three

Meg stood at the podium, her sweaty hands sliding along the smooth wooden surface as she tried not to grab hold like she had on that poor guy's arm. "At all costs, don't look scared and don't clutch the podium. You'll be fine," Amy advised the night before.

She wasn't feeling fine as the audience settled into their seats and she adjusted the microphone. Attempting to focus, she scanned the dark amphitheater and chose the banner that hung above the crowd as a focal point—Special Guest: Megara Jeffries. Was it possible that was the first time she'd seen her name in print like that, big and official? She was used to catching her first initial and last name in the lower-left-hand corner of photographs, but a banner was a hell of a lot more intimidating.

Looking down at her note cards and glancing at the space-age prompter that displayed the same information, Meg cleared her throat. She was glad she'd insisted on the cards. They were something tangible as she struggled to find her footing among thousands of eyes. It was as if the person on stage, the name on the banner, was inexplicably more important than her pictures. She'd slipped into a world where what she was wearing or her ability to deliver an amusing anecdote pulled focus. Meg had never been good at entertaining anyone. She captured nature's brilliance. Worked for it, framed it, and patiently waited. Who she was or what she did with her hair never factored into the equation. As she thanked the audience, the cards dug tighter into her palms.

Squinting to adjust to the spotlight, Meg wondered if the animals she turned her lens on felt something similar. She hoped not. Her entire career, she had worked hard to blend into their world and would certainly never lower them onto a stage in a cage-looking thing. But she had been an outsider, and maybe intrusion was intrusion. No sense candy coating things now, especially since she was the one being observed this time.

"Art in all its forms allows people to feel. It can move us to tears and laughter. It can teach us and make us think," she began. Her mouth was so dry that she thought she might cry when she looked up to find a glass of water on the podium. Meg took a sip and continued.

After stumbling only once during her prepared opening comments, the lights thankfully dimmed. Meg glanced at the screened wall beside her and clicked the silver wand on the podium. Her picture of Polar Three, or Phelps as Meg had named him, burst into the space. Most of her shots of him were in the water, hence his nickname. Suspended in a sharp blue sea and framed by ice, Phelps filled the screen. The audience cheered, but Meg kept her eyes on Phelps as if he were a long-lost friend she'd missed terribly. He needed her to get this right to communicate for him, so Meg let out her first slow, steady breath of the morning and let her memories lead.

She had shot feverishly over the last two days of the shoot because up until the day she captured Phelps, she'd had next to nothing to show for over a week of frigid temperatures and cumbersome gear, Meg told the audience.

"When I saw him, I desperately wanted to capture the sheer mass of him, the life force I was witnessing firsthand. I suppose I thought if I could somehow bring his world home, it would make a difference."

The audience was attentive but quiet. Meg could practically feel them. Looking up at the image that had been selected for the magazine, she explained that while she strived to capture these animals, she rarely succeeded.

"They're simply too alive, too vast to fit in my lens, but we as photographers give it our every effort. It's our life's passion," she said, clicking the remote again.

The darkness was comforting. Her shoulders eased, and Meg attempted to share without preaching. For the first time since she'd returned home, the focus was solidly where it belonged. She had to believe her images were connecting on some level. That they would eventually bring awareness and that the idea wasn't simply Amy blowing smoke up her ass. Because without that purpose—the animals—Meg was some out-of-work photographer in "desperate need of a manicure."

Her mother had pointed out the manicure over breakfast last week while she, Meg, and her sister Annabelle were sampling wedding cakes for her sister's upcoming wedding. Anna was her big sister, Middle Two, and she'd asked Meg to be her maid of honor in a text message while Meg was still in Canada. The idea of being something so mainstream had thrown her for a minute, but then she was honored. So far, with the help of a book and a few websites, she was finding her way through the bridal adventure too.

Weddings, like the dimly lit faces looking up at her as she neared the end of her slide show, were serious business. Meg wasn't expecting to feel so discombobulated on all fronts of her life, but there was no time to back out now. She'd made choices, and not unlike Phelps and so many other bears like him, Meg needed to work with what she had and find a way to survive.

The final image of Polar Four and Polar Seven on their hind legs fighting flashed on the screen, followed by Meg's name in twirling script. She swallowed the lump in her throat again that she now recognized as change and the lights came back up. People in the audience were on their feet with praise and attention Meg couldn't begin understand. She smiled, collected her cards, and wanted to be back doing something that made sense.

That's not true, she corrected herself as the bearded event host joined her on stage and instructed the audience it was time to open things up for Q & A.

If she wanted back on assignment, she could leave tomorrow. Something had called her home. Her sister wanted Meg beside her at her wedding, her father was coming over tomorrow to help install her new speakers, and then they were going to Carl's Deli for lunch. She'd missed things while she was away capturing other families. It was time to be with her people now. She owed them that. Every new experience was uncomfortable for a while, but she'd once hiked twelve miles with blisters. Another assignment left her with twenty stitches in her side with nothing to numb her but a bottle of tequila.

Meg had always been a woman in a man's world. She was tough and resilient. Only a few more questions and she'd survive her first presentation. It would only get easier, she thought. Next time she'd remember underwear.

"Most of the time I think of myself as a witness, being there with a camera in my hand. I try hard to know my equipment so when nature provides the moment, all I have to do is push the button. So, while it probably seems like a lot of work, I am so grateful to *National Geographic* for sending me to these incredible places and allowing me to bear witness," Megara said, sounding much more confident.

The moderator quipped at her clever use of "bear" and called an end to the Q&A. West was sitting on a black box, stage left, mesmerized until the clapping snapped him from the moment. He tried to recall the last time he had been mesmerized by anything. When he was a kid and his grandfather let him watch a foal being born, or the spring before when Aunt Margaret helped him start a beehive. Maybe he'd been mesmerized a couple of years ago when he took three months during a "dry spell," as Hannah had delicately put it, and hiked all 2,300 miles of the Pacific Trail. He'd lost himself then, forgotten everything and practically everyone. He was mesmerized then, but by solitude, life. Megara was simply another human being, but the places she'd been and the passion with which she spoke were so fascinating, West realized he was nervous as she made her way off the stage.

He stayed put as she pulled in a shaky breath, her eyes closed. When she opened them and seemed to scramble for where she was supposed to go in the darkness of the production, West stood, and their eyes met under the faint blue backstage light. He would never be able to explain it, but he felt awkward. As if the culmination of his life experiences so far left him ill-equipped to even help her find the exit. He hesitated and then remembered who he was, who everyone around him told him he was, and smiled.

"How'd it go?" He stepped toward her.

"I... I have no idea. It was terrifying, but then it got better. I'm sure it wasn't as bad as my eighth-grade science fair, so that's something."

"Looked like you had them in your palm from where I was sitting." He gestured toward the box. "What happened at the science fair?"

"Huh?" She was looking around, as if still shocked she'd survived. "Oh, sorry. I don't know why I brought that up. My hamster got loose and the math teacher, who was a judge, was terrified of rodents. She started screaming but I eventually got Triscuit back in his cage," she said softly as if they were in a quiet restaurant.

West became aware of his heart thumping in his chest. "Triscuit?"

"Favorite snack growing up. Obvious pet name, right? You watched from there? Why aren't you out in the audience by now? Thank you so much, by the way. I'm not sure I could have made it through this without your help." She finally took a breath and extended her hand.

West shook and instinctively laid his other hand on top of hers. They were cold and she was still a little unsteady. He was beginning to wonder if the energy spilling off her was her natural state. Was that possible? Surely she'd run out of steam at some point and collapse to the ground at that rate. Holding on to her hand a moment too long, he met her eyes again, but she didn't pull away. This was a woman comfortable with contact and men. Somehow that threw him.

"No problem at all. I'm glad I could help. Are you finished?"

They both glanced toward the stage now lit with music and dancers.

"I'm not much of a dancer, so yes. My part is over. I think I'm supposed to stick around after to 'schmooze and drink champagne.' Those were my instructions anyway. What is your role here? I'm sure they didn't bring you in to get me on the stage."

She had no clue who he was. Her nerves must have drowned out the introductions shortly before they descended onto the stage. West had a feeling even if she had heard his name, she still wouldn't have a clue. Disappointment and joy filled his chest in equal measure. Both caused him to stumble over his response.

"Oh God. I'm sorry. I haven't been paying attention. Are you speaking today too?" She winced, and her eyes drifted to the ceiling. "I am so not in my element now. You're probably a microbiology specialist or something, and I've just stepped in it. I'm Meg." She extended her hand again, scoffed, and pulled it back. "You know that already. Sorry. What was your name again?"

"West, and you're fine. I failed biology."

She smiled, and it was so open and authentic that he almost wanted-ed to tell her to cut it out. That no one in the real world let out that kind of sunshine. It was dangerous. Instead, he returned to the job he was sent to do and attempted to put her at ease.

"If you go through this door and turn left, there's a patio. You'll find some fresh air. I'm guessing you need a few deep breaths. There's seating out there too."

Meg nodded. "Perfect. Thank you. Enjoy the rest of the show, and again, I appreciate your help." She walked toward the hazy exit light and ducked behind the dark wall of masking. West watched as the door eased closed.

Who the hell are you, Meg Jeffries?

The energy fell at least by half in her absence, and he was unexpectedly tired. Bone deep, as if he'd spent hours with the stunt director.

West could join her outside and ask some of the dozens of questions swimming through his mind, or as he had back in high school, he could heed the advice of his acting teacher when he wanted to do a monologue from *Death of a Salesman*. "Recognize your limitations at any given point in your study and while risk-taking is encouraged, proceed with caution." He had respected Mr. Hernandez and while West thought he had what it took at fifteen to tackle a middle-aged man in a crumbling-life monologue, he settled for something from the more age-appropriate *Picnic* and received an A.

Recognizing he was in over his head again with Meg and her alluring sunshine and remembering he had a massage scheduled at five, West checked in with the stage manager and left out the door he had entered only a few hours before, sunglasses firmly in place.

Chapter Four

*S*he should have taken her makeup off last night, but she'd been so drained by the time she finished shaking hands and pretending to have her act together that she grabbed a falafel on the way home and collapsed into the quiet isolation of her apartment. Now Meg was paying the price as she stood in front of the bathroom mirror with her third makeup remover wipe and Anna on speakerphone.

"And Mom will not let it go that her friend Frida is allergic to nuts. She's brought it up at least a dozen times. I told her the restaurant could not guarantee a nut-free environment."

"Especially since you're serving almond-crusted salmon. Wild caught in the US, by the way, I did check."

"No. I changed it. It's salmon and a dill sauce now."

"Why?"

"Mom would not let it go. Are you on Twenty-Fourth or Twenty-Third?"

"Twenty-Third." Meg pulled her toothbrush from her mouth to respond and rinsed. "I can't believe you changed your menu for Frida. Who the hell is she? I've never even heard of Frida." It occurred to Meg that there were probably a lot of her mother's friends she'd never met.

"Naughty Book Club. They've known each other for a few years."

Meg took her phone into the bedroom and pulled the covers up on her bed. Sage, Middle One, had e-mailed her an article that outlined the habits of highly successful people. Most of it had given Meg a headache, but she did remember the part about always making the bed.

"Did you say naughty?" she asked.

"Yes. They read steamy romance and then meet over drinks to discuss."

"Are you kidding me? Our mom?"

"Let's say she and her lady friends have an extensive knowledge of firefighters and all of their... equipment." Anna chuckled.

"Wow. That is a surprisingly clear visual, so thank you for that. Back to Frida, you need to tell Mom her friend needs an EpiPen just in case. You've already rearranged your menu, which is more than I would have done."

"I was hoping you could help me with that and the florist. I somehow ended up agreeing that if the color of the snapdragons isn't right, she could use something else, but I need snapdragons." Anna sighed. "I foolishly thought getting married was going to be enjoyable, but things keep coming up and..."

"I will take care of Mom and the snapdragons. You're too agreeable. This is your wedding. You need to make it know who's boss."

"Not my strong suit. I'm here, parking now." Anna disconnected and Meg wondered how her sister could so confidently guide her classes through Shakespeare and yet allergies and flowers threw her.

Meg pulled on a T-shirt and, catching her reflection in the mirror, stepped closer. "What the hell?" she said to the specks of black still clinging to the skin under her eyes. Was there a reason mascara had to hold on for dear life? NASA could put something this sturdy to good use.

After picking the last of the bits off her cheeks, Meg slathered her face with coconut oil. No matter how many spas or facials Amy tried to lure her to, Meg knew all about keeping things soft and moisturized. She had spent years in the elements. She'd found coconut oil on one of her first assignments in the Philippines. Jessa, a woman at the local fruit stand, warned that if Meg didn't start putting something on her skin, she was going to look like an "old ox." From that day forward, Jessa was the only beauty expert Meg had ever needed.

Nothing worked better than an eight-dollar jar of coconut oil, and the smell was a bonus. The guys on assignment used to tell her she smelled like an Almond Joy. Toby, who carried all their gear in the Arctic, still addressed his emails to Almond Joy. Now that she was back in the city and things were a different kind of harsh, Meg had a feeling she might need something more than coconut oil.

In addition to her professional photographs, Meg had taken pictures of the people she'd met on her travels and thought about framing a few for her apartment. They too were a collection of her experiences and might add perspective to her current state of disarray.

Deciding she should ask her mom for a good frame shop once they went over Frida's EpiPen, Meg pulled her hair off her face with the elastic around her wrist and heard the knock.

"You're early," she said, opening the door to find her sister Anna looking more like a future bride every day. She deserved happy, and while most of their family was still a bit shocked she'd found it with a football coach, their father was thrilled. Said he knew all along his "Anna Banana" was a closet football fan. Anna humored him, but they all knew by now that Dane, her fiancé, was so much more than his job. He was a welcome addition to their family, joining Garrett and Matt as the men who loved the Jeffries sisters.

That left Meg, which was fine. She was used to being last and was starting to think her happiness required a kind of wild rarely found indoors. Besides, she was focused on planting roots of her own and was in no hurry to take on anything or anyone more than she already had at this point.

"I am right on time." Anna closed the front door and glanced at her watch.

"Why are you wearing work clothes?"

Her sister looked down at her skirt and blouse. "I'm not. We are going to try on the dress. I needed to wear the undergarments I'm wearing for the wedding. I can't do that with jeans."

"Why not? What's under there?"

"Lace and silk."

Meg opted for her jacket instead of the sweatshirt she was planning to wear. She didn't want her outfit to scream, "Hey, I'm the unpolished one," through the bridal boutique. She pulled out her phone.

"Okay, so I've added naughty mom and the snapdragons to my to-do list," Meg said.

"You can't call her naughty mom."

"Oh, but I can." Meg turned her phone to show Anna that their mother was now in her contacts as Naughty Mom.

Her sister tried to register her disapproval but ended up laughing. "How have I gotten by all these years without you?"

Meg felt an apology swell in her chest, but there was no reason to apologize. They'd all left her first. She needed to remember that and not completely dismantle the choices she'd made in return. Her sister hadn't meant to make her feel guilty, and there was no reason to be.

"So, last fitting and then you need to decide on the shoes." Meg's thumbs tapped. "Vivian"—she looked up, her face scrunched—"is that honestly the shoe lady's name?"

Anna nodded and put a mint in her mouth. Meg had mints somewhere.

"Right. Well, Vivian has your final three choices, and she's meeting us at the boutique. You didn't go with the dress that makes you look like a pilgrim, did you? I can't remember which one you finally picked. God, it's like a sea of white and cream when I try to focus on the dress."

Her sister laughed, took her by her shoulders, and kissed her on the cheek.

"What was that for? You did choose the pilgrim one, didn't you?"

"No pilgrim. I love you."

"Your breath is so minty. Give me one of those."

Anna held out the tin and Meg placed two little disks on her tongue.

"I love you too. Now let's get going. You promised pizza for lunch and since I am going to join a gym soon, I need pizza."

Meg grabbed her bag and locked the door. "So glad you didn't go with the pilgrim. I'm not sure I could have kept quiet about that."

"I did not look like a pilgrim." Anna pulled her coat closed as they flagged down a taxi.

Meg opened the door for her, wanting to be a full-service maid of honor. "Oh, but you did. That collar was screaming for a pumpkin pie."

Anna smacked her shoulder as Meg scooted in next to her sister while giving the driver an address. This was why she was home, Meg thought as they pulled into traffic. If she'd come back solely to stand next to Middle Two, that would be enough.

The Jeffries girls were born Hollis, Sage, Annabelle, and Meg. Their mother was an only child and used to stare in transparent fascination that despite the same parents, her daughters had each turned out differently. Hollis was "a textbook firstborn," their mother used to say, and she often bellowed down the hall, "Why can't you be nice like Sage." Hollis and Sage, almost opposites, were close growing up. Hollis was the popular yin to Sage's good-girl yang. That left Annabelle, the second middle child with her head "always in a book," and Meg. She was the baby and the sister most likely being lectured when their mother assessed all four of them and scrunched her face. "Meg, honestly, did you even try brushing that rat's nest?"

Anna and Meg were the two daughters least understood, and that somehow bonded them growing up. Meg allowed and appreciated the silence when her sister read most days they spent together. Anna had a subtle way of sticking up for Meg and her efforts to protect creatures large and small. She taught Meg how to braid her hair so she could be outside until the last minute and pull herself together quickly. She ran interference, often stepping out from the shadows to protect Meg. When Anna left for college, Meg was devastated. At the time, she turned the loss into anger and rebellion, but years later, she recognized that losing Middle Two to reality had left a mark on her heart forever.

Such a strange thing to grow up one, two, three doors down the hall from one another and then be sprinkled into the world to fend for oneself, Meg thought, glancing at Anna, who grasped the bench seat between them as the taxi swerved to avoid a double-parked delivery truck.

"Mr. Westin Drake." Artie, the maître d' of Deluxe, approached, arms outstretched, causing the smooth white linen of his tailored jacket to inch up past his belt. "A pleasure, my friend." He hugged West and gently guided him toward the dining area. "Hannah has already been seated, and I will order your Tanqueray and tonic now that you have arrived."

"Club soda with a lime today. Thank you," West said as he sat in the chair pulled out for him and took the white cloth napkin presented to him with more flair than he ever understood. It was a napkin for crying out loud. But, Deluxe was the best, or so everyone said. And it wasn't like West wanted to go back to eating the economy bag of hot dogs from Costco.

"Absolutely," Artie said, leaving West to his agent and her iPhone.

Hannah glanced up quickly and focused back on her screen. After a moment, she held up her finger to indicate she was almost ready for human contact, her thumbs flying feverishly about. West took a sip of his water and enjoyed the bubbles as they danced across his nose. Looking out the enormous bay windows as other diners began filling tables for what would soon be the see-and-be-seen lunch crowd Hannah loved so much, West realized he didn't look around much anymore. His head was often down or hidden. What did that do to a person? he wondered as two women pointed and reminded him why he rarely looked up. Closing his eyes for a beat, he picked up his menu and prepared to smile as the taller of the two approached.

"Here," Hannah said, not the least bit startled by the interruption or finally being torn away from her phone, "the life source" as West liked to call it. She stood. "Let me get a shot with you and West. Did you want to include your friend?"

The woman extended a frenzied gesture to the other woman, and by the count of three they were all huddled together and smiling as if it was the most natural thing in the world to stand up in a restaurant and take a picture. Not like there were people paying to eat or discussing their lives. He was Westin Drake, and that meant something, or so Hannah would say if he ever hesitated to stand up anywhere in the name of pleasing a fan.

After signing one of the menus, West returned to his seat.

"So, the press loves you with the photographer." Hannah shifted gears flawlessly and downed the last sip of her martini.

His brow furrowed. "Sorry?"

Her ice-blue eyes peered through the delicate tortoiseshell frames perched across her pointy nose. "The woman, at the thing. The one in the thrift shop skirt."

"That's her favorite skirt."

"Okay. The woman in her favorite thrift shop skirt. The press saw you kiss her and rumors are flying. People are loving it. National Geographic is trending. That never happens."

"I'm sure there are several reasons an institution like National Geographic would be trending. It has nothing to do with me." He took another sip, somehow enjoying the bubbles less.

Hannah shook her head. "It has everything to do with you, well, that kiss. People want to know who she is and more importantly, what she means to you. Which, I'm sure I don't need to tell you, is good PR for you."

"I didn't kiss her. I mean, I did, but it was a peck on the cheek."

"They saw a kiss."

"Neat."

"Don't 'neat' me. I know what that means." She pointed at him. "You say neat when you're on your 'this is so trivial and superficial' trip. I sat next to a crying baby on the plane this morning. In first class, mind you, so I'm cranky. Please don't be an asshole."

"Her name is Meg." West signed two photographs their waiter slid in front of him. He'd gotten to the point that he signed practically anything, except for skin. A guy had to draw the line somewhere.

"Good. Well, Regis called me this morning and Next Generation, who chose you last year as their spokesperson mostly due to the fact that I spent three conference calls pretending to be fascinated by their new workout pants made from recycled bottles, just saying, is interested in the two of you for some of their upcoming promotions."

"The company that does the solar panels?" he asked and tried to remember the tagline from the commercial he'd done. "Reinventing what's green?"

"What's right, it's reinventing what's right."

"That's bad. I said that?"

"Yes, you did. Several times, and they paid you incredibly well. Based on the call yesterday, they would like you and the photographer to participate in some of their community events. She has a gallery show coming up or something like that. We, that is Regis and I, think she's hot right now and you two both care about... fish or birds. That part is irrelevant. Next Generation is global and they appeal to your earthy, introspective side. It's a win-win, so why not?"

Hannah had been West's agent for most of his career and sometimes, he wondered why. He wasn't sure he liked her and he was positive her percentage was inflated, but he'd never bothered to shop around. Hannah brought him *Full Throttle* and had been in his ear or up his ass ever since. His dad liked to say, "If it ain't broke, don't fix it," but it was safe to say if he and Hannah were married, West would be looking for a good lawyer.

"We start filming in four months," he said.

Hannah nodded with her wide-eyed "you're a moron" face. West hated that face. They ordered salads, and she removed her glasses and proceeded to fold them with a dramatic pause.

"I know when you start filming, Westin. I want you to do the feel-good shit before filming. I've done all the hard work here. You simply need to show up and smile." She leaned in as if she were a mother scolding her son in the middle of Sunday service.

"And if I don't want to do this? If I want to continue having some down time before I slip behind the wheel again?"

"It is certainly your prerogative to decline."

That was too easy.

"Of course, Regis thinks these events and hanging around Bad Skirt could give you some depth, especially since you mentioned wanting the lead in that sappy independent film. The one about the guy with a bicycle or something else utterly ordinary. Christ, when did real life make a comeback?"

"*The Messenger?*"

"Yes, that's the one. Word is they're going to start looking for the principals in a few weeks." She popped a tomato into her mouth, and her expression was downright fairy-tale evil. "Might help if you were seen schmoozing with the patchouli and essential oils crowd, huh?"

West rubbed his eyes. Why did everything feel like a compromise? Wasn't success supposed to bring with it a certain amount of pull?

"Fine. What do I need to do?"

Hannah patted her mouth with the white linen napkin. She picked up her phone, and West felt the puppet strings snap taut into place.

Chapter Five

Meg had never seen tinier water bottles than the ones clustered on the metal conference room table at the Regis Agency. What was that? Two sips of water and a bottle that would take one thousand years to decompose? Stupid, and the older Meg got, the less patience she had with stupid.

Clearly the first one to arrive, she politely asked the receptionist for some tea and set her bag down on one of the conference room chairs. Meg smoothed her hands along her new black pants and willed her nerves away. She needed to start getting a handle on these types of meetings if she was going to make a business out of photography. That's what she was trying to do, wasn't it?

The truth was she didn't know what she was doing, but instead of continuing to question her decision, she woke this morning determined to take back control. That started from within. She didn't need one of Sage's motivational Instagram posts to remind her. Meg knew who she was. She simply needed to figure out how that person fit into her new picture.

Tossing her tea bag in the small trash can, Meg walked slowly around the conference room, which was larger than her entire apartment. There were movie posters and glossy pictures of beautiful people, some of whom she recognized and others she wasn't sure were real. On the other side of the room were windows, floor to ceiling and framing an almost omnipotent view of the familiar skyline. The fog, which Meg knew from her father wasn't fog at all, but low-lying clouds, began to burn off as the morning sun continued its climb through a blue-gray sky. The Golden Gate Bridge came into focus right before her eyes through a cloud that caressed the crimson metal into view.

Meg was used to being surprised by the natural world. Her job had practically been a model for the unexpected, but she felt unprepared for beauty in the middle of the city. Stepping closer, she touched the window as the receptionist in all white informed her the others "would be along shortly."

How did she keep all that clean? Meg thought, turning from the window to the portraits. They were twenty by thirty-eight maybe. Artificial light for effect, Meg guessed. The angle, while flattering to each model's features, made most of them look detached and intimidating. She supposed that was for effect too. She wondered if they held interviews for new employees in this room. Nothing like two dozen beautiful people looking down at some poor hopeful candidate in a callous, industrial-chic conference room. All of them subliminally asking—Are you sure you're gorgeous enough to be here?

Her eyes moved past a stunning woman. Dark hair slicked back, red lipstick smeared as if she'd just been kissed, and thigh-high boots. She must be six feet easy, Meg determined as her gaze fell on a black-and-white photo of the man who introduced her at the convention center. There was barely light the first time she met him, but that face was memorable all the same. Staring at his picture now, it was hard to believe she didn't know who he was until Amy told her over lunch yesterday.

"Westin Drake is big-time, Meg. *Full Throttle*. Please tell me you've seen at least one of them?"

Meg had shaken her head, all the while wondering why Amy was surprised Meg would have no interest in a movie titled *Full Throttle*. True, she was a new client, but an agent should have a basic understanding of the people she was representing, right? Did Meg seem like a *Full Throttle* kind of person?

"Well, he's a massive deal, hot as all hell, and he's into the environment too."

"What does that mean?"

"He speaks at functions, owns an electric car, you know. He cares."

Meg hoped her face didn't disclose how absurd she thought Amy's comment was, but it must have. Her expression grew impatient.

"Fine. He's not you, but he has made millions and has millions of social media followers. He's a bright light to shine on your message."

"I'm not ready to share a message. Honestly, I'm hoping my first gallery show pays for itself. I don't even own a toaster yet. I'm not looking to get on someone's bandwagon, especially not a celebrity. And I'm an awful candidate for preaching. That never works."

"Well, the press loved you guys at the symposium, and his agent called me this morning. They would like to meet and discuss co-branding for a few of Next Generation's community events. He's been their face for a couple of years."

"English please, Amy."

"Sorry. Westin Drake is their spokesperson. They are pushing their latest project, which is a smart house. The thinking is that since the public went a little nuts for the two of you on social media, as a couple, you would bring even more attention to their causes and products. In fact, Next Generation contacted his agency, Regis, and asked for you. Can you believe that?"

"No, I can't. What does any of this have to do with my photographs? And why would I put my name behind a big corporation? Is that wise?"

"They are a well-respected green company and would like to use some of your images for promotion. There are worse things than hanging out with Westin Drake, and you don't have anything more... lucrative at the moment."

"I thought I was 'hot, hot, hot.' Did I cool off already?"

"You're still hot, but the foundations and functions requesting you as a speaker don't pay all that well. When we first talked, you needed to make a living, correct?"

Meg nodded.

"Good. Seeing as I make my living off a percentage of yours, I think this is an excellent opportunity."

"I have the gallery show. And, I need to put some time into my sister's wedding, or I'll go down in history as the worst maid of honor. I was hoping for some freelance work or speaking engagements for conservation groups like the one at the convention center. As you said, Westin Drake is huge, and I'm not sure I'm equipped to run around with the Hollywood set."

"It's a lot of money, Meg."

"I don't need *a lot* of money, Amy."

"And, we have to iron out all the details, but they'd like to sponsor your gallery show, as well as make a sizable contribution to a wildlife initiative of your choosing."

"They said that? How sizable?"

"They want this, so I'm guessing it's a lot. Let's meet with them and listen to the plan. Then you can decide. Okey?"

Meg had acquiesced after the "okey," which she assumed was some urban or corporate version of "okay," and that's why she was now standing in an empty conference room considering a close-up image of a man she hardly knew. One thing was clear: the camera liked his face and his eyes were exceptional; they reached out and strangely put her at ease. Meg rarely photographed humans because it was difficult to find the truth, but in a room full of faces, his had her reconsidering that stance. He was wilder than the rest of the gloss, and she wondered if that was a character or the camera capturing his essence through all the bullshit.

Pictures, good pictures, rarely lied. She was drawn to the disarray of him and at the same time understood why he was successful. Meg was certain Amy would call it star power. Whatever the catchphrase, the photograph drew Meg in as if the man in the picture somehow understood. Well done, photographer, she thought, turning back to the window as she heard an approaching rumble of people outside the conference room.

She gazed out past the foreground of man-made and steel to the vital green of the rolling hills she'd grown up exploring. Both coexisting in the same space. One making way for the other. When Meg was out on assignment, it was easy to pretend that money didn't matter. But she'd been capturing animals and living among the community of people that protected them for a long time now. It would be juvenile to say that money didn't matter. It did, and teaming up with Westin Drake might put some of that star-power cash to good use.

But oh, the irony of meeting about green initiatives over tiny disposable water bottles.

West had five minutes to spare as he squeezed into the closing elevator at Regis. He was hoping to get up to Petaluma by sunset. It was his dad's birthday and West had been put in charge of the cake. He knew it was his oldest brother's way of busting his ass. West had missed their dad's last three birthdays, but asking him to find a cake their mother wouldn't roll her eyes at was a setup. Boyd was no doubt waiting to watch West fall flat on his face, but that wasn't going to happen. He had Towner, and it was becoming clear to him that the woman knew everything.

"Nothing too fancy, but fresh and incredible," that's what he'd said, and that was exactly what she'd delivered. A triple chocolate cake from some neighborhood bakery on Twenty-Fourth Street at Castro. Towner had brought him a sample and when he told her he'd never tasted a cake like it, she ordered one for him. The damn thing was better than homemade and his brothers, all of them, were going to line up to kiss his youngest brother ass.

But now, he thought, stepping from the elevator, he needed to survive this meeting so he could get on the road. He'd opted for his own clothes and drove himself so he could leave once everything wrapped. *Like a big boy*, he could hear his brothers mocking already.

"Okay, well let's take our seats..." Hannah's practiced words brought the conference room to order as she noticed West enter through the glass doors. She surveyed him from head to toe and was inches from his face before West had a chance to take a seat.

"What's with the beard?" she quietly asked, tugging his barely-longer-than-stubble facial hair.

"Ow! It's Friday, who the hell calls a meeting on Friday?" he asked, attempting to duck past her.

"You realize these people pay you to represent their products, right?" she added under her breath as the men West recognized from Next Generation began jockeying for one of the incredibly uncomfortable seats around the massive conference room table.

"I do, and they should appreciate the natural look."

"What's going on, West? Is this another 'poor you' party? I'm all out of small bottles of vodka, and I need to catch a flight back to my beautiful city of angels by three," she said between her teeth so she could keep smiling as attention began to shift toward them.

West kept his voice low. "I didn't shave. I'm here. Deep breath, Hannah. The suits are waiting for you."

"Okay. You want to play? I've mastered this game."

"I do not want to play. I simply want to get this over with so I can start the weekend." West took a seat and as he began to wonder how much they paid for these pretentious chairs, he saw her. Eyes darting, taking in everything as if her mind had been left on since the last time he saw her backstage a few days ago. The woman sitting next to her whispered something in Meg's ear and when she looked up, their eyes met. Hers were blue now that she was bathed in the filtered light of the conference room windows. West nodded a greeting and she did the same. He liked Meg Jeffries even more with the lights on. She was a refreshing contrast to the moneymakers—or, he should say, money collectors—who filled the other seats around the table.

When West decided to move to San Francisco, Hannah had used everything in her bag of tricks to get him to stay, but he was, fortunately, able to pull his I'm-the-star card. It wasn't something he did often, but he wanted to live somewhere other than LA, and pushing around his weight had worked. As part of the deal, he agreed to Skype meetings and Hannah, in turn, flew up to the Regis Agency's San Francisco offices twice a month. West swore the inconvenience made her less tolerant and pricklier if that was possible. It was never wise to poke at her, but sometimes, he couldn't help it.

Rubbing her lips together, most likely making sure her lipstick was firmly in place, Hannah swirled away from him and back to her audience, but not before flashing him a sadistic grin that let him know she was going to win. This power play shit was getting old.

"Okay, so thank you all for making it here on a Friday. As West pointed out, Fridays are not easy. So, I wholeheartedly appreciate the effort and that most of you managed to shave."

She glanced at him and the table laughed. West ran a hand over his growth and laughed along with them. *No way that's her best move.*

"Before we get started discussing the sensational project Next Generation has put forth, I wanted to give a quick mention and congratulations. This morning I was informed that West will be in *People*'s Sexiest Men Alive issue. He wasn't named *the* sexiest man alive. Not this year anyway. But he will be in the issue."

There was the ruthless warrior he paid to torture him. *Well played, Hannah.* West kept his expression neutral. Lately he used all those acting classes he took when he first moved to LA more off set than in front of the camera. Hannah was good, there was no question. Those around the table nodded and clapped, including a few hoots from the suits, which was plain odd. The entire scene was reminiscent of the time his mother told his homecoming date that he'd wet the bed until he was six.

West shook his head as the cheering continued. The receptionists were into it now. Every person in the room was clapping. Except for her. He was drawn to Meg Jeffries like a school kid hoping to be teacher's pet. The woman he now assumed was her agent looked at her, bumped her gently, and raised her clapping hands. West recognized the gesture and had had enough.

"Thank you for that, Hannah. Now, can we please get down to why we're all here? I'm sure no one drove in here on a Friday to hear about my prestigious accomplishments."

"This is tremendous exposure, West," she said, walking behind the conference room chairs until she was two down from Meg.

West felt a sudden need to protect Meg, which was ridiculous. He barely knew her.

"I'm sorry your new friend here doesn't see that this is exciting news, but—"

"Meg. My name is Meg." She craned her head to meet Hannah's eyes.

West settled in. Meg Jeffries could obviously take care of herself.

"And while I am incredibly grateful to Mr. Drake for keeping me upright during my first presentation, it's a bit of a stretch to call us friends." She looked at him, expression solid and fearless. "I'm sorry for not clapping. You are, in fact, sexy."

West raised his eyebrows and realized he was searching her expression for genuine interest, which was again ridiculous. She didn't seem like the kind of woman who ranked sexy as an accomplishment.

"But honestly, Sexiest Man Alive is absurd. Does this magazine know every man alive? There are some incredible faces in South America and Kenya for that matter. It should be Sexiest Man in California, if they're going to do it at all." She looked around as a few jaws opened and the rest of the conference room sat poised for a train wreck. To everyone's surprise, Hannah ignored Meg's comment and walked to the other side of the table.

"Sorry. I'm working on the selective speaking thing, but you don't look too thrilled, so I simply abstained. Should I clap?" she asked West as if they were sitting at a table for two.

He tried not to laugh, but it was no use. He shook his head, held her eyes for a few beats more because he wanted to, and then the meeting was underway.

Everything went as expected with both Meg's agent and his crew as they sorted through the details of three events he and Meg would attend together for Next Generation. The CEO, always the one in the most expensive suit, seemed particularly motivated. He asked about press coverage and if West and Meg were truly dating. Meg almost toppled her tiny water bottle at the question, so West fielded the personal inquiries and assured the table full of agents, executives, and marketing staff that he and Meg barely knew one another.

"We met for the first time backstage at the convention center. It was an interesting first meet." West smiled and Meg's expression wasn't one of embarrassment; it was more like a challenge. Yeah, he liked her.

"I am looking forward to working with Meg again, but my kiss to her cheek was a gesture put forth to calm her nerves and nothing more. If the 'buzz' can bring attention to something worthwhile, then that's productive. But let's try to return Ms. Jeffries back to her normal life as unscathed as possible."

Hannah seemed pleased with his response and the others that followed as the discussions continued with a mixture of business and gossip. It was decided West and Meg would begin by introducing Next Generation's new smart house, visit and bring attention to their state-of-the-art composting facility, and finish up at Meg's gallery show in early August. Meg's agent thanked Next Generation for their added sponsorship of the exhibit and firmed up their $10,000 donation to Bear With Us, "a small wildlife relief agency close to Meg's heart," as the CEO announced.

Close to her heart. The words swam in West's head as he zoned out a bit during the details and instead wondered what else was close to her heart. He glanced across the table and found Meg looking out the window. The longing in her eyes was apparent to anyone who bothered to notice, not that anyone, other than him, was looking. She'd become a product to them, an opportunity to push their agenda. West knew the drill all too well and felt a bit of guilt that he'd kissed her cheek at all. That was nuts. He had no way of knowing something as simple as being kind would propel her onto a treadmill that was often cruel.

He should have known better, but at the time he wasn't thinking about himself or his celebrity. He'd wanted to put her at ease. It was simple, yet thanks to social media and some other crap, it wasn't.

"Fantastic. Well, I think that covers it. Our people will draft up the agreement and get that sent out to everyone by the end of the day," Hannah said, shaking hands around the table.

West broke free of his thoughts, of her face, and stood to shake the hands he knew Hannah expected. All three events would be wrapped up before he started shooting mid-September.

The world was such that any cause in want of a spotlight needed a celebrity. There were scientists, activists, and photographers like the one sitting across from him who did the work, but the public wasn't interested unless something pretty and shiny was attached. Meg probably wouldn't be at this table if he had not kissed her on the cheek. The thought sounded arrogant even in his head, but it was true. She had been places and seen things he'd only dreamed about, and she was better than this. And for reasons he would not bother analyzing, he didn't want what he knew was pure and real to be ruined by all the ugly expensive shoes in the room.

But hell, he was in the Sexiest Man Alive issue, so he'd probably ruin her all by himself. West snickered at his thoughts and left the conference room the same way he'd arrived. Under the glaring eyes of his perpetually dissatisfied agent.

Chapter Six

The San Francisco General Hospital Foundation's offices were green glass and brick, representing the innovation the foundation strove to represent while remaining vastly different from the much older buildings surrounding it. After her morning meeting, Meg walked out into the unseasonably cool June morning and was reminded of the last time she was at SF General, which was less than a half mile from the foundation.

Her middle sister Sage had her tonsils removed when she was eleven, which meant Meg must have been seven. All she remembered was that Sage had to stay overnight in the hospital for observation. Tons of flowers were delivered and the six of them all sat around eating ice cream until the nurse kicked them out. A few years later, Meg was devastated to learn her own tonsils were fine and could stay put.

"Why is Sage so lucky?" she had exclaimed, stomping toward the car ahead of her mother's laughter.

Meg looked out over the park across the street as the memory faded and she pulled her jacket closed. She'd been reminiscing a lot lately. So few of those memories were filled with the angst and frustration she felt so prevalently when she left home for college.

Funny how time dulled the drama and things had changed on so many levels, she thought, or maybe she was the one who had changed.

Glancing both ways, Meg crossed the street and checked her phone for the directions to the café West had texted her last night. He'd asked if they could meet to discuss the details of their first appearance together. When she told him she was busy, he said they could get together somewhere close to her meeting. Meg was taken aback that he would accommodate her schedule. She wasn't sure why his seemed more important, but everything surrounding him screamed priority. And yet, the man himself appeared to defy the stereotypical celebrity, at least so far. He was straightforward, which Meg appreciated.

Time Off was less than a mile from the foundation, so she walked. She circled back twice before realizing that what looked like a storage room was the café. The name was punched into a small metal sign above the single red door. A brass bell tinkled as Meg entered and took in the aroma of coffee and cinnamon. The hostess with a long blonde braid and a necklace that read Happiness waited for Meg to hang her coat on the hooks by the door and then sat her at a table right off the entryway of the small café.

Westin Drake was now almost fifteen minutes late and Meg checked to make sure she had the right address. This certainly didn't seem like a place he would frequent, but she reminded herself he was practically a stranger, outside of a Google search that proved endless. Content to take in her surroundings, she ordered a tea and tried to make out the song playing faintly overhead. The place wasn't big and the tables around her were close, even by city standards.

Meg noticed the man and woman sitting directly to her left were speaking in sign language. She tried not to stare, but sign language was fascinating and somehow the silence among the clattering of dishes and the zip of the milk frother was comforting. It had taken Meg a few weeks to acclimate to the noise of the city when she returned. The televisions that seemed to be in every corner, the clicking of heels as she made her way through crowds and intersections, even the whistle of a tea kettle had all mixed together like a rock concert at first. The sounds had recently dulled into the new background of her life, but sometimes she missed absolute silence. Trying not to be obvious, she glanced over at the couple again and relished the peace of their conversation.

Meg barely noticed the front door open, but she was immediately aware that the buzz of conversation amplified and the energy in the room changed. She glanced up and wondered if Westin Drake ever had peace. He probably didn't want it, she thought. Some people thrived in noise.

Removing his sunglasses, West quickly found her and made a direct line for the table. He put his sunglasses back on. The hostess was close behind him with a luckiest-girl-in-the-world grin on her face.

"Do you mind if we move?" he asked in a low voice that felt as intimate as morning sheets.

Meg's pulse jumped and the harmony she'd been enjoying was gone, replaced by a feeling that something was coming and West was there to quietly warn her. Meg glanced at the couple next to her as she stood and grabbed her bag off the back of the chair. They were both staring at her now, the woman pointing at West. Meg turned to follow, something she rarely did and never without explanation, and dropped her phone.

"Is everything okay?" West circled back and bent to get her phone.

"I... yes, I'm fine." She took the phone from him and noticed the line of his arm, the corded muscles, and the deep rich gold of his skin. That was southern California skin, and Meg wondered why a Hollywood actor would be in San Francisco. Her eyes were fixed on his arm and West cleared his throat. She looked away quickly as they both quietly followed the blushing blonde around back to a table in the corner.

"You're late," Meg said, trying to balance the sense of power as they took their new seats.

West looked surprised, but before he had a chance to answer, they ordered. Meg wasn't sure if he was going to respond. He grinned. Was that an answer in his world? Downing a triple shot of espresso in a tiny ceramic cup, he quickly glanced at his phone and turned it face down on the table.

"Sorry I was late. Why were you at the hospital so damn early? Everything all right?"

"I was at the foundation offices, not the hospital. They asked me to do a heart for the city. Have you seen those?"

"The big painted heart sculptures? Yeah, I have. They're cool, but you take pictures. Do you paint too?"

Meg shook her head. "They requested a heart with Polaroid pictures. I'm sure the opportunity is due to the latest buzz, but it seems fun. They're letting me do anything I want."

"Do you have a Polaroid?"

"I have a printer that turns my digital images into Polaroids. My mom bought it for me last year. I used to have one when I was a kid, and she is forever trying to remind me that I am the youngest."

"Me too."

"You have a Polaroid camera?"

"No. I'm the youngest. Four boys."

"Huh. Four girls."

"Look at that, no wonder we are becoming BFFs."

Meg snorted but managed to swallow her sip of tea. "I don't think so."

West checked his phone again and nodded as he shoveled egg whites and salsa from his plate. He looked like a kid, which was a bit unnerving. He was the most put-together kid she'd ever seen. His wallet was placed on the table next to him, phone on top, keys next to those. The clothes on his body were characters all their own. A worn T-shirt that should have looked like something from Goodwill, but on him, it came across vintage, expensive, and as if he'd simply rolled off the couch to meet her. His belt was dark and worn too. Meg wondered if he bought this stuff "distressed," as she'd seen on a website last night when she was looking for some new clothes.

She loved distressed and worn in when it meant something had been put to the test and worked into worn out. She wasn't sure how she felt about buying experience and texture in a store. It seemed fake, which led her to wonder if West's jeans were that kind of fake. This thought, in turn, caused what often happened to Meg: her mouth engaged.

"When did you buy those jeans?"

West, fork still in hand and eyebrow cocked, looked down at his lap as if he needed to be reminded what he was wearing.

"Not sure. I've had them for a while. They're part of my pre-stylist collection."

Meg moved the melting glob of butter around her French toast and realized he never seemed bothered by her questions. It was a refreshing change.

"So you wore them in yourself?"

"I... no. I bought them kind of lived in. Aren't all jeans that way now? No one wants to rub around on rocks or wash them in a stream."

Meg met his eyes over her tea.

"I mean most people. Have you honestly washed your jeans in a stream?"

"Not jeans. I think that's only for commercials. It would take forever for a pair of jeans to dry out on assignment. I wear fast-drying material."

"See, so not even you, Ms. Adventure, can create what clothing companies make in a factory somewhere. Ironic, isn't it? We are probably polluting all sorts of things so we can look natural and rugged."

Meg nodded. "Is that the look you're going for today?"

"Is there a problem with my outfit? The day we met, I was wearing red pants. Believe me, jeans are a vast improvement."

He wiped his mouth, leaning his forearms on either side of his plate as if he was about to relay some important news. "Enough about my clothes. We are supposed to sound like we know what we're talking about at this model smart house by the end of the week. I've been through it and the damn thing freaks me out. I'm hoping you have something intelligent to add because I doubt Next Generation is looking for my kind of feedback," he said as four young girls walked by their table on the way to the bathroom. The realization of who West was spread a blush across their faces, and it occurred to Meg she'd never been a fan growing up. It must be so odd being on the receiving end of such surface adoration, she thought.

"I Googled you last night," she said, taking a bite of her French toast. She had not meant to, but curiosity got the better of her and before she knew it, she had to shut down her laptop before she allowed herself to read "Westin Drake's Favorite Date Spots." That was a real article in the *Los Angeles Times*. He was certainly well known. By "millions on several continents," per her sister Annabelle during their phone call last night. Meg had telephoned to ask her what the rules were again for skirt length and heel height. She was still trying to shop online and hated the idea of heels. Millions of people knew him, but for what? Meg wondered and then opened her Internet browser.

"Yeah? How'd that go?" he asked as another espresso was delivered. Had he even ordered another one? Did they know his order everywhere he went? There was probably an article on Westin Drake's breakfast routine.

"Almost crashed my computer," she said.

He looked up, and Meg couldn't help but grin.

"Just kidding. Turns out you've done some movies that a few people have seen."

The corner of his mouth turned up a little, and somehow that eased what appeared to be tired eyes. That little bit, that tiny tilt of a grin was rich and warm. The man was definitely a professional.

"I did notice some inconsistencies," she said after a few moments of silent eating.

"I'll bet."

West asked for some hot water and lemon as the waitress took his plate. Meg automatically sucked her stomach in but snagged the last bite of toast anyway before her plate was whisked off the table too.

"Your eyes are brown, but in the advertisements for your movies, they are green."

"I wear contacts when I'm Nick Shot."

She almost spit water across the table. "That's your name, I mean your character's name?"

"Can't make that stuff up, and Nick has green eyes. The producers wanted them green."

"Interesting. I wonder why they made that choice. Is there symbolism in the green? Does it say something about your character?"

"It does. It says women love green eyes and most men want green eyes. It's incredibly scientific."

Meg tried to hide her confusion. Where did moviemakers get this information? It made people sound so predictable, and Meg was again glad she didn't own a television.

"You were on the cover of *Outside*," she said, changing the subject to something she understood.

"A couple of times." West discreetly checked his phone again and blew on his mug of water. Meg could smell the lemon.

"This one was titled 'The Earth Issue' and they photoshopped a young polar bear next to you."

He nodded, still blowing over the mug.

"Does that bother you?" she asked.

"Is that the one where I'm in that jacket with the huge hood?"

"Yes."

"That was a great cover and the interview was pretty legit. The guy did ask me my favorite color, but other than that, there were some valid questions about some of the organizations I endorse." He sipped his lemon water. "No, it doesn't bother me. The bear worked for what they were going for with the cover."

Meg looked down at her hands. What was there to say? They lived in different worlds, and his was a place where it was acceptable to not only alter images but also alter reality. She supposed that's what the movies and entertainment were about, but it still jolted her when fiction was passed off as a real world she knew all too much about.

"You think that's wrong?" he asked.

Meg shrugged and took a sip of her tea, which was bitter from too much steeping.

"It's a magazine cover and it brought awareness," he insisted when she said nothing.

"To whom?"

"Readers, people, citizens of the world." He spread his arms wide and dropped them when Meg made it clear his dazzling smile wasn't working on her. He was messing with her bears, so even though his teeth were mesmerizingly straight, it didn't matter to her.

"Is that what you tell yourself? That a cover of a magazine where someone clearly blow-dried your hair and you are standing next to a polar bear who would never stand next to you in that way, nor would he look up at you like some animated critter, brings about change? Do you think that restores some of their sea ice? Helps them make it through another summer? Your pretty face gets people to understand that as a community, we need to want better and stop expecting more?"

"Well, when you put it that way..."

"What other way is there to put it? A person could call it manipulation, false representation. You've never been to the Arctic."

"How do you know?"

She tilted her head in a gesture that communicated "come on" without a word.

"Fine, but I have been to Canada and I filmed a watch commercial in Alaska last year, so I was pretty damn close. I've hiked the entire West Coast, Machu Picchu, Kilimanjaro. Holy shit, I'm giving you my hiking resume. Now that's a first."

"True, and points for even knowing where the Arctic is—most people don't."

"I'm not most people."

"I can see that," she said, looking around as almost every patron in the café, save the elderly man reading a newspaper in the corner, watched them and strained to hear their conversation.

"Not what I meant. I'm not an idiot."

"I never said you were."

"But you're thinking it. Can't blame you, especially now that you've Googled."

Meg somehow felt she'd put her foot in her mouth, but she wasn't sure how. She'd never met anyone so at odds with himself. One minute he was defending some side she didn't find on the Internet and the next he was knocking down a larger-than-life persona most men would kill for. Westin Drake didn't make any sense, but she found that similar to her fascination with other species, and despite the bright lights surrounding him, she wanted a closer look.

"I wasn't insinuating you didn't know the Arctic was up by Alaska."

"Sure you were. It's part of the chip you have on your shoulder."

"Excuse me?"

"Yeah, most people could give two shits about the animals and causes you spend your life trying to capture and protect. It's your defense."

Meg normally loved honesty, but the guy barely knew her.

"Am I close?" he asked.

"I have a lot of patience, but rarely with people."

"I get it."

And he did, there was no doubt in her mind.

"You probably get the dumb beautiful guy thing all the time and while I'm sure that's annoying, it only seems fair if you're a little dense. I'm not sure how I feel about you knowing your geography too." Meg tried for light and funny. This was their first breakfast, and things felt a touch more personal than even leaving her underwear at home.

West took pills or vitamins from his pocket. "I'm all ears for this rationale."

"It would simply be too much if you look the way you do, were given fame and fortune, *and* you went to Yale."

"Stanford." He swallowed the whole handful of colorful capsules, and Meg hoped they were vitamins or she would need to call the paramedics in a few minutes.

"Seriously?"

"No." West was going to say something else, but their conversation was interrupted by a young couple. The guy already had his iPhone out and his girlfriend or wife looked to be hyperventilating.

West closed his eyes for less than an instant as if he were slipping on a mask. Then he turned to the couple, smile bright.

"We're so sorry to bother you, but you're Westin Drake," the man said.

"Guilty." West put his napkin down and stood as if he knew the next question.

"Would you mind if we—"

"Not at all. Hey, thanks for asking instead of creeping around." West stood in the middle of the couple, who were in matching flannel shirts. After offering to hold the phone since his arm was longer, they took a few shots and West handed the phone back. The woman with the ombre hair then asked if he would sign her neck. West declined, but grabbed his cloth napkin and producing a Sharpie from his back pocket, signed the napkin instead. Husband and wife, from Reno they told West, left the restaurant as giddy as two kids on a field trip.

He sat and when the waitress came by to apologize for the intrusion, he was gracious and asked if he could have more hot water.

"Sorry," he said after things had settled back down at their small table in the back. He didn't meet her eyes and it seemed he was embarrassed. Was that possible?

"No need to be sorry. Do you always carry one of those?" Meg, still a little dumbstruck by the whole experience, gestured to his jeans.

"Sharpies, yeah. I should own stock."

"Do you ever say 'no'?"

He shook his head and squeezed more lemon.

"Never?" She tried to imagine what a life of constant interruption must be like.

"It's part of the job. There are two kinds of actors—serious and awarded actors, who are entitled to grumpy or introvert tendencies, and what Hannah calls 'pretty and polite.' Have you seen any of my movies?"

She shook her head.

"Huh, well we'll have to remedy that if we are going to be friends."

Meg wondered how it was possible to be friends with a force like Westin Drake. Did he have a lot of friends? If he did, were they intimidated by being completely eclipsed in the presence of his celebrity? She thought the whole business sounded lonely. She loved being alone, preferably outside where it was quiet. It must be a special kind of torture to be isolated in noise, she thought.

"When you do see one, or all of them for that matter, you'll understand that I'm part of the latter group of actors," West said. "It's a lot like being one of those Disney characters that walk around the park."

Meg didn't know what to say. She wasn't familiar with the celebrity lifestyle, but it hardly seemed the plight of the aboriginals.

"I know, boohoo, right?" West continued as if now reading her thoughts. "I'm not complaining. You asked and for some reason, I tend to share when I'm around you. That will need to stop too before we can be BFFs. I prefer to stick with surface small talk."

"Somehow, I don't think that's true."

Their eyes met and Meg was intrigued, which was annoyingly predictable, but there was something alive behind that perfect chin.

"And you determined this in the what? Week you've known me?"

She was trapped between what she thought she saw and what he was willing to share.

Meg changed directions. "What organizations do you work with? I honestly didn't keep reading the *Outside* article when the reporter asked you your favorite color."

His shoulders relaxed in laughter. Full and hearty without regard for the onlookers surrounding him. There he was, the guy who'd helped her fumble through the dark in complete discomfort.

Meg had photographed hundreds of animals, many of them closed off and protected for good reason, but she'd never encountered a man quite like the one now paying the bill across from her. Pissed when she insinuated he was less than brilliant and insistent that he was no more than a Disney character at the same time. She had spent her entire life being curious despite the bite or the scratch. Her father used to say she was a deadly combination of "daring and patient." As West stood and pulled her chair out for her as if he'd been raised that way, Meg wondered if he had any idea what he was getting himself into being her best friend forever.

"UCLA. I majored in geography, but don't tell anyone," he said softly.

She walked past him as he held the door for her and did her best not to notice he smelled like green grass.

Best friends forever. Meg had never counted on anything forever.

Chapter Seven

The chocolate birthday cake was a hit and shut his brothers up, at least for the weekend, but that hadn't kept them from putting West to work moving equipment and painting the new Tap House. Cade, the second youngest brother, would oversee the new addition to Foghorn Brewery once things were up and running next year. Although West had been happy to help, even happier to spend time at home, he'd returned to the hotel after midnight and was dead tired when his alarm went off for his first breakfast meeting with Meg Jeffries. And yet now, walking out behind her, he felt a second wind coming on.

He signaled for the car waiting across from the café and turned to find Meg already walking down the street.

"Where are you going?"

"Oh, I thought you walked here too. I need to get going, so thank you for breakfast."

Unbelievable. She was some sort of otherworldly being. "You walked here?"

"I did. It's a gorgeous day."

West looked up and felt the warmth on his face. He needed to do that more, he thought. As if on cue, his driver, Vince, opened the door. Meg's expression could have been the lead-in to a romantic comedy.

"We spent more time talking about your Google search than our smart house gig, so I can drop you somewhere and we can talk in the car."

"I... prefer open space. You could walk with me."

"That's not a good idea. Where do you need to be?"

She adjusted the bag across her chest and stepped closer. "Nowhere, sadly. I mean, I should go to the grocery store. I'm out of almond milk, but it can wait."

West laughed and hoped like hell she was going to get in the car. He wasn't ready to let her walk away yet.

A lively group left the café. He put his head down, resigned to disappear and let Meg leave, but to his surprise, she slipped past him and into the car. He followed and the door closed right as he heard, "Excuse me, do you mind—"

Vince waited patiently in the front of the car until West finally told him to drive the street art route.

"You seemed anxious to leave the café. If we still need to discuss things and we can't walk, why didn't we stay at our table?"

"I know the owners. It's usually busy and seems only polite to let them turn over the tables as quickly as possible. I tend to eat and run when I'm there." The explanation sounded lame to his own ears, and Meg appeared equally confused. Why *hadn't* he recommended a place they could sit at for a while? Truth was, he didn't know many of those places. He was so used to getting in and out unless he was behind the walls of his suite or in some secure conference room. She'd casually asked if they could meet somewhere near the foundation, and West relished the normalcy of the request so he picked the only place he knew in the area. How was he supposed to explain that to her?

"I realize this is a bit unconventional for a meeting, but it's a pretty cool driving tour. I take it at least once a week. Have you seen all the street art in this city?"

"I have not." She looked out the window as they pulled into traffic.

"Well, there you go. I'm going to take you some places you've never been. Tough to do, right?"

Meg smiled. The plush interior of the backseat stood in stark and stifling contrast to her. West caught himself wondering how long Next Generation would need the two of them. Sitting beside her, he was sure he could spend a good deal of time with Meg Jeffries.

"When are you heading out again?" he asked, needing to remind himself this was a job for both of them.

She seemed surprised by the question, as if she wasn't used to talking about herself. "I don't know if... I'm not sure. I might leave in a few months. Maybe back to Uganda."

West tried to look unfazed and failed miserably. She returned to looking out the window.

"What's in Uganda?"

"I think there is interest in doing another update on... mountain gorillas." She was twisting her hands again like she had before they clasped her index cards at the convention center. It was entirely possible she had no idea how extraordinary she was compared to the general population. West was filled with an urge to help her see herself.

"Incredible. I know you've photographed them before. Are you thinking of doing anything different if you go back?"

She glanced at him as the car stopped at a light.

"What? I have Google too."

She blushed, full bloom and completely unassuming. Something warm and foreign rushed through his body. On paper, she was one of the more accomplished people he'd met in a long time. In person, she was... it was hard to explain. She was an early-morning campsite right after zipping open the tent. She was fresh and full of a kind of life West had to keep reminding himself existed.

"Incredible shots," he said after a minute of silence.

"Thank you."

"What's it like in Uganda?"

"There are no words. That's why I take pictures."

The driver honked, changed lanes, and pulled over for their first stop. This one was famous. An entire wall of daisies with a rhinoceros sitting in the center.

"Green and moist, quiet. It's real on a level that is both sadness and elation," Meg answered before he could push the button to roll down the window. She appeared to swallow back emotion and West recognized the longing.

He touched her hand, not surprised by the warmth.

"I was raised in Petaluma. Do you know where that is?"

Meg nodded, still looking out the window as if collecting herself. Vince would stay parked in front of the rhino until West was ready to move on. That's how it worked every week.

"It is probably the only place where I get to be myself. The place, my family, practically demands it," he said.

Meg finally faced him and let out a slow breath.

"I looked at a lot of your photographs last night. I would miss being out there too." He took his hand back and was glad his eyes were hidden behind his sunglasses. When he was around her, he found it difficult to keep his usual distance. The feeling that she saw right through him and that he, in turn, understood her discomfort was strong.

West needed to keep himself together. Women like Meg did not date men like him. Holy hell, where had that thought even come from? *Please try to remember you are a movie star.* He could hear Hannah now, but West had never figured out how to do that.

He hit the button that rolled Meg's window down. "Well, we are still in San Francisco, so this will have to do for now. I give you our first stop. I call this one Rhino."

She leaned out the window, taking in the entire painting, and chuckled. "I can see why you chose that title."

"Right? This one was painted by two brothers. One of them does the outlines and the other splashes in the color."

"Amazing. Any idea what they were trying to say? The likeness of the rhino is spot on, but the daisies must mean something."

West shrugged. "I guess we are supposed to come up with our own meaning. I have looked at it dozens of times, and all I come up with is rhino."

"Some things are that simple, I suppose."

She turned to him, the joy of the unexpected still dancing across her face, and West held his breath. Where had she come from, and why did being with her somehow accentuate how lonely he'd been?

Shit, he needed to drop her off. They could discuss things over the phone from now on because he was losing his mind. Scrambling for something, anything that took his mind off the way freckles bridged her nose, he said, "Is that a poncho?" He touched the fringe.

"I guess. It's a sweater without arms, so yes. It's a poncho."

"Where would someone find one of those?"

"Peru." She ran a hand across the knit.

"Christ."

"What's wrong with Peru?"

"Nothing at all. I've been there. I didn't want to leave. You're a walking United Nations."

"It's my job, or it was my job."

"What does that mean?"

"Nothing. I'm doing this stuff right now."

"I'm sure you'll be running back to your job after a few weeks with me."

There it was again. The air seemed to leave the car when their eyes met.

"Why is there such an interest in my clothes?"

"Hey, you started it. You were obsessed with my jeans." West couldn't remember the last time he'd teased anyone other than his brothers.

Meg shook her head in annoyance and looked back at the rhino. He reined in any further thoughts about her clothes or her body. The only saving grace so far was that he'd barely seen her figure under all those layers. Best to keep it that way, he thought, at least until he got his head together.

"Next stop," he said to Vince, and they thankfully were moving again.

By the fourth stop, the one with a row of brown paper bags on fire, they had managed to discuss who was going to do what on Friday.

West had already been inside of the smart house, so when he suggested that he could talk about the ease of using a smart house and Meg could touch on how reducing energy trickled all the way up to the Arctic and allowed other countries, some without electricity, to share in the consumption, she agreed. When Vince opened the door in front of her apartment, West was back to being a professional, sort of.

You are going to liar's hell, Meg's conscience chastised all night as she tossed and turned, trying to get him and the way he made her feel, both good and bad, out of her mind. *There are not enough hours of meditation to undo using Africa or the precious endangered gorillas for your sick ego-balancing act,* her conscience had continued while she dressed.

He was a fascinating combination of interested and aloof, but the world he lived in made her uncomfortable. She didn't know how to compete with fame and adoration, so she found herself pumping herself up with her work and the places she had been. None of that ever mattered before and she certainly wasn't one to brag, but all this hype and being paired with him was making her crazy.

I lied, Meg thought as she poured herself some orange juice. Feeling backed into that car and his life, she bolstered the one thing she felt she had going for her—adventure. It was the right decision stepping back from fieldwork, but since that first night when he'd guided her on stage, she felt nothing but awkward.

She didn't belong, proof being the moment West asked when she was returning, despite her steadfast life rule of honesty for the people in her life, she had lied.

Westin Drake wasn't technically in her life, she rationalized as she rinsed the dishes in her sink. She had done nothing wrong, and yet she felt off balance, as if all the insecure parts of her were ruling her present. That pissed her off. She didn't need to be guided anywhere, so why was she driving around in town cars and sitting patiently while he appeased people who didn't even know him? Why had she allowed herself to be talked into this PR stunt anyway?

Meg was a professional and her intent in coming home was to find another outlet for her creativity, one that allowed her to spend more time with her family. It was never her intention to be a movie star's sidekick. She needed to talk with Amy—this wasn't going to work. She wasn't interested in some glammed-up campaign based on public opinion. She would not be able to create that way and after one car ride with West, she couldn't seem to stay true to herself either.

If this was the only avenue to pay her bills, she would have to re-think things. The easy answer was to leave. It had worked for her in the past, but she had a niece and a nephew now. Anna was getting married and their parents weren't getting any younger. Meg wanted to be in their lives, but she'd been away for so long she wasn't sure how to do that anymore.

Not feeling any better, no matter how much she talked to herself, Meg turned on Vivaldi's Four Seasons and sank onto her couch with her laptop and a bag of popcorn. She used to buy the caramel-and-cheese mixture, but in the interest of less anxious clothes shopping, she'd downgraded to plain.

It was unfortunate, she thought, typing in her laptop password and grabbing a handful of boring.

Her top e-mail was from Hollis, her oldest and often impossible to deal with sister. Meg clicked on the link and felt the deep bond of family that she could never explain, nor could she shake it. Her screen filled with images of her nephew Ansel. He was a little over a year old now and was the image of his dad, Matt, the only man brave enough to melt Hollis's heart. Ansel did have the Jeffries gray-blue eyes, though. Dressed in jeans and a sweater, he was beautiful and confident, much like his mom.

There were seven years between oldest and youngest, but Meg always felt there were more. As far back as she could remember, Hollis had been an adult. When Meg forgot to brush her teeth, Hollis flossed twice a day. She was the ultimate untouchable big sister, which explained why she was forever lecturing and pointing out Meg's shortcomings. Meg supposed she could thank her sister for planting the seed of home deep in her heart, which meant she could also blame her if she fell on her face trying to live a different life.

Meg had never set out to be a "runner" or a "wanderer" as so many had called her over the years. She simply grew tired of being left behind and decided the best way to remedy that was to be the first to leave. She knew it sounded ripe for some therapy couch, but it was the truth.

When she told David she couldn't—wouldn't—marry him almost two years prior, that was a clear decision. She regretted hurting him, but there was no way she was going to leave her job at that point, and certainly not to become his wife. She cared about David, but that wasn't enough to turn her life upside down.

Family was another story entirely. She loved them with a force that was at times unexpected and painful. When she was eighteen, she left for college and never looked back, never thought anyone cared honestly. By the time she moved up to Berkeley, her sisters were all gone and her parents had a renewed interest in their small architecture firm. Meg was the last remaining "have to" in her parents' lives, at least that's how she saw it at the time.

The month following her early-morning epiphany, Meg told her boss she would be taking an indefinite leave from assignments. He'd been so shocked he'd blurted out, "What? I didn't even realize you *had* a family."

Ouch, Meg had thought, but it only served as further confirmation that she needed to find some balance. Which explained why less than six months after her little face-to-face with Hollis, she was now sitting in her apartment, tearing up again. This time over her sweet baby nephew and the hope that she had what it took to stay put for all of them.

Chapter Eight

*W*est received the latest script for *Full Throttle 5: Floor It* via courier, at around nine that morning. Fifty pages in, he stopped after reading his line—"More money than you've got, cuz."

Is it too early to start drinking?

He flipped the remaining pages closed and tossed the packet on the table. Needing to get away from his suite before the walls closed in, he went down to the lobby.

"Does that deli deliver?" he asked Towner once she finished handing a young couple one of her famous black envelopes and they'd left. Lucky bastards had tickets to something.

She nodded in response and produced a one-page menu from somewhere behind her orderly desk.

"Are those two on their honeymoon?"

"Good eye. Yes, they were married on Saturday."

"What completely sold-out entertainment did you procure for them?"

"*Hamilton* at the Orpheum," she said with a nonchalance only she could manage considering the accomplishment.

"Nice. Were they appreciative?"

She shrugged. "The husband mentioned naming their first child after me."

West laughed.

"Would you like me to order you some lunch?" Towner asked.

"Only if you order something for yourself too."

"I already—"

"Yeah, whatever you already have will keep in the fridge for tomorrow. I'm buying you lunch."

She pursed her lips, narrowed her eyes for no more than a beat, and then she gave in. "Very well, but I'm not having the chopped liver. It is too rich for every day and I have the Lithograph Society's monthly meeting later today. Onion breath is simply not acceptable for them."

"I'm surprised onion breath is ever acceptable."

Her nose scrunched in a way that West thought made her look like a genie. There were definite superpowers present.

"So, what are you having then?" he asked.

"I'll have a half of a turkey on marble rye and a cup of their minestrone soup. It's delicious and"—she looked toward the massive revolving glass door—"I think the weatherman is finally right. It should rain by sunset. Soup takes the chill off."

"I'll have the same. Throw in some potato chips with mine." He handed back the menu. "Meet you in the bar?"

Towner nodded and picked up the phone.

West ordered a beer and Towner stuck with water. This was the first time they had spent together sitting instead of shuffling through some secret corridor. West had a million questions stirring in his mind about his orderly and unflappable friend, but seeing as he wasn't a fan of intrusion, he never wanted to bother her. Towner was a bit of a celebrity in his eyes, which was such an obnoxious word to him until he'd looked it up one night when he couldn't sleep. Celebrity, according to the dictionary, was all the things he'd known it to mean, but it also referred to "an important person," and "someone looked up to by a group with similar interests."

West realized that night that he followed celebrities too. His parents, his family, were all important people. He cared about what they were doing, whether they were happy, and often pushed his way into their business. His acting coach wasn't exactly a celebrity. That was more of a hero worship thing—the man was insanely talented. But Towner, she was a celebrity in West's eyes. She was his friend in a life that rarely allowed for such luxuries. She had his back and never asked for anything in return, but he rarely peered into her life. Out of sight among the soft music in the bar, West decided he wanted to be Towner's fan. That started with gathering more information, so he dove right in.

"How long have you worked here?"

She glanced at him through her small reading glasses. "Why?"

West grinned. "Making conversation."

"We don't normally talk about me."

"That's not true. I know you have four grandchildren and that you bring your lunch every day. I know you do not approve of my overnight guests by the way your smile is a little pinched, that you don't drink coffee, and you collect owls."

Her hand went to the long dangling gold necklace around her neck. It was one of three or four with different owl charms. They had ceramic eyes and appeared to come from the same designer.

"I do like owls."

They returned to quiet.

"Two years." She removed the lettuce from her sandwich and cut the half in half again.

West was surprised at the answer but had more questions so he didn't hesitate.

"Were you born and raised in San Francisco?"

After taking a small bite, she ran her tongue under her upper lip, presumably to make sure she had nothing on her teeth. He recognized the gesture. His own mother did it often.

"No. My husband and I moved to San Francisco from New York thirty years ago."

"For?"

"We owned a boutique hotel in Sausalito."

"Owned?"

"He passed away."

"I'm sorry."

"Me too." She wiped her mouth and pushed her half-eaten sandwich on white paper away from her, as if the mention of her late husband made her lose her appetite. He must have been young, West thought but didn't say. Unless she married an older man. It was clear from the hint of pain that surfaced in her eyes that whatever the case, she had lost him too soon.

"How long ago?" West couldn't help asking, but then changed his mind. "I'm sorry, did you want to talk about something else?"

"Seven years ago this May, and yes."

"Okay. Let's see... I am almost finished reading the script for yet another *Full Throttle*. I'm feeling an Oscar nod for this one." West took a pull of his beer.

"That's how it is with sequels and the like. Although I enjoyed the third one. The car chase in Mexico where the gentleman with that horrid gold tooth loses his arm. I was a bit glued to my seat with that one. Oh, what was the name of that one? *Downshift*, that was it. Right?"

Had West not been sitting down already, he would have fallen over.

"You watch the *Full Throttle* movies?"

"I do. Your costar, the older guy, what's his name again..."

"The Hammer."

"That's his nickname, I'm sure, but yes. The body on that man is..." She fanned herself. "I'm pretty sure my cheeks are flushed every time I leave the theater." She stood from her seat and balled up their sandwich remains. "I need to get back to my work."

West held out his hands and took the trash Towner reluctantly handed over with a controlled smile.

"And you enjoy the movies?" West was stunned. It was as if Mary Poppins was casually mentioning that she enjoyed Eminem's lyrics.

"Some of them. They're not Harry Potter, but as I said, I appreciate The Hammer, and you of course, although my response to you, even in that fairly racy backseat scene, is more..."

"Motherly?"

"Oh, let's not get crazy. You already have a mother. I'm more like your crazy aunt."

West felt his expression fall at the reference and even though he tried to mask it, Towner noticed everything.

"What? Did I say something? Do you already have a crazy aunt?"

"Had one," he said without even thinking. His mind was preoccupied with images of his childhood.

Towner touched his hand and West pulled himself away from the past.

"I'm sorry," she said. "Sometimes I say things without thinking. Do you want to tell me about her? I don't need to go back right this minute."

West smiled. As sweet as the gesture was, Towner already knew enough about him. Aunt Margaret was not someone he shared with people. She was his ultimate celebrity.

"Maybe some other time." West stood and walked her back to the lobby. "You've shocked me with your knowledge of Snapchat, Towner, but you liking *Full Throttle* tops even that." West was happy when the concern left her face and they were back to their comfortable distance.

"The exotic places your movies take place in and the cars. They're fun. Do you like them?"

"I... don't know." She caught him off guard again.

"Well, you should ponder. I imagine it takes a lot of hours to make one of your films." She nodded to the small woman who had been handling the concierge desk in her absence.

"Four to five months," West said, still trying to figure out if there were any of his movies he liked.

"That is a long time. Well, thank you for lunch, Westin. It was fun spending time without you attempting to pay me. I enjoyed your company."

"And I yours." West found himself standing taller and using his big boy words around Towner. As hip as he knew she was, her presence and experience almost commanded a taller spine.

Her lips pursed in a way that he recognized as "if that's all." West turned to leave, but she called his name so he glanced back.

"If you don't appreciate your films, perhaps you should be doing something else. Money never made any man happy."

"Are you sure about that? I don't know a lot of happy poor guys, do you?"

She seemed to think about her response for a beat. "There are all sorts of stops between rich and poor. Don't be so all or nothing. You're too young for that."

"My aunt used to tell me black and white was boring," West said, seeing no harm in sharing a little.

Towner nodded. "Smart lady." The phone rang and she was gone in a dance of manners and hospitality.

West wasn't sure celebrity was the right word. Towner was a genie, or Yoda.

Meg had been selected to give a TED Talk in October, which was a huge honor, but she found it ironic people kept asking her to speak when her passion was being quiet enough to capture images. There probably wasn't money in silence and since Meg had arrived home, money seemed to be at the forefront of everything. Price lists for her pieces going up in the exhibit, speaking fees, and of course the "jumbo paycheck" tied to the three engagements with Westin Drake. The first of which started in less than four hours.

Examining herself in the full-length mirror recently installed on the back of her bathroom door, Meg wasn't sure how she was supposed to look anymore. She swore if she had not babysat her niece Olive two nights ago, she would be back in her North Face parka and on the next plane to anywhere.

Should she wear her hair up or down? *Who gives a shit?* a distant part of her brain exclaimed. She pulled the sides of her hair up, wondering if a half and half was the answer.

For crying out loud, she needed to calm down. It was clothes and makeup, not open-heart surgery. She turned her face from side to side and wondered if blush was supposed to look that way. Grabbing a tissue, she wiped both of her cheeks and instantly felt better. After a few more stops in front of the mirror, she decided to wash her face again, put on the heaven of her coconut oil, and pull her hair back in a ponytail. She wore the plain black skirt she and Anna had found at a shop near Berkeley. It flowed like Meg's favorite skirt but was more professional. "Professional flow," Anna had joked.

Meg pinched her cheeks, a trick her mother employed right before their Christmas picture when they were younger. Her mind wandered off as she put on her earrings. She needed to find hand-poured candles for the wedding favors. Anna wanted to order them online, but Meg was trying to inject recycled materials and small businesses where she could. She had lost count of how many times the wedding planner rolled her eyes at each suggestion, but the candles were a win for Meg, so she needed to deliver.

Finally satisfied that she had found a balance between comfort and presentable, she put a tamale in the microwave and reviewed her remarks on energy conservation and four simple ways to reduce energy consumption that could directly benefit wildlife. She'd thought about e-mailing it to West last night but decided if she couldn't get this right on her own, she shouldn't be getting paid. Besides, they weren't at the late-night e-mailing stage of the relationship. Relationship? Like that was going to happen. What, was she going to get all mushy now that he'd mentioned he grew up in a small town?

That was ridiculous, she thought as the microwave dinged and she tossed the tamale from one hand to the other before it landed on the plate. Westin Drake was an actor, a celebrity. It was his job to reach out and touch people, so to speak. Meg needed to remember that, although she was curious about his life. Not the celebrity part—that seemed next to unbearable—but the way he navigated it. He was like an animal in the wild, constantly on the move for a kind of protection—car rides, corner tables—she thought, looking out the small living room window as she stood eating.

Meg shook her head and decided she'd spent enough time thinking about Westin Drake even though she did like the beard he was sporting in the meeting. It made him look less pretty and a whole lot more... attainable. There she went again. She refocused and rinsed off her plate. Looking down at her hands, she wondered again if she looked, in the words of Amy, "a bit more polished up."

Her nails were clean and trimmed short since she was used to spending her work days on her stomach or up a tree. She wasn't scouring a muffin basket or sipping on a pumpkin spice latte, although she'd recently tried one of those and they were good. But Meg was getting a little sick of the veiled comments about her appearance. Amy had sent her a few pictures from her first engagement, and it was true after objectively looking at her image that the new skirt was a good idea. That didn't make any of this less confusing or irritating.

She'd hoped to find a job where her past work and even future projects closer to home spoke for themselves. She had recently spent money she didn't have on sheets for her new bed, which brought home the need to earn more, but so far, it seemed her hairstyle was more important than her pictures or even what she had to say about them.

Chapter Nine

West lightly bumped her shoulder when the guy responsible for the electrical system in the Next Generation smart house droned on in way too much detail about the design. She gave him a sideways glance and a smile teased her lips. He honestly needed to get his shit together. He'd been thinking about her on and off, mostly on, since dropping her at her apartment. Last night he'd figured out the attraction. Being around Meg was like slipping out the back door of a smoky bar and into the refreshing air of an endless night sky. Damn poetic if he did say so himself. Turned out he was full of flowery thoughts when he couldn't sleep.

"We're done," West said as the guy finally finished up and the tour group of movers and shakers, as well as deep pockets, began clapping and filing toward the refreshments on the patio.

"Don't we have to talk with people?" She looked around.

"Nope. It's four and we are off the clock. So says the contract." West guided her through the crowd, careful to avoid too much contact. There were cameras everywhere. Christ, he sounded like some paranoid recluse. She halted quickly to allow a server with a tray full of food to pass, and his body was flush up against her back.

West ignored the jolt and the coconut. They were friends, colleagues on assignment, he clarified, if only to himself.

West waved to the CEO and some other guy in a Next Generation polo who screamed marketing. They were mingling in the crowd and when the guy nodded in a way that suggested it was either his signature move or he was running for political office, marketing and sales was all but confirmed. West pulled Meg out into the early evening.

The car was waiting, and as he'd said, the job was done. He should have dropped her off and gone home. The default idea that he should call someone and go out for the night entered and left his mind in a flash as they made their way toward Vince. A club or dinner sounded boring, and Meg was anything but. He was having a hard time reading her, though, so they drove in silence for a few minutes before he asked.

"Do you want to go to the top of Sixteenth Avenue? There's a Mosaic Tile Project near Moraga and if you haven't seen it, you should." Holy shit, his heart was racing while she appeared to calmly consider him. She seemed to struggle for a response and West felt foolish, which was something that never happened to him anymore. People, especially women, wanted to be around him, jumped at the chance. Certain people anyway.

He wasn't sure why his ego was front and center or why the hell with everything at his disposal he was inviting her to look at stairs. Dinner, a tour around the bay on his yacht. Those were dream dates, the kinds of things women wanted. He didn't have a yacht, but shit, he'd get one if that would work. Still waiting for an answer, he realized Meg didn't want any of those things. He didn't know what she wanted.

"I have never seen the steps," she finally said. "But I thought you stayed off the streets."

West started breathing again in relief. "It's not a busy area and I'll keep a low profile."

"Do you know how to do that?" she asked with a humor and confidence she rarely displayed in public. Maybe they had more in common than he knew.

"I'm an expert."

"Honestly? You're not going to wear some rubber mask, are you? Those things freak me out even on Halloween."

"No mask. Are you up for it?"

She nodded, and West leaned forward to tell Vince the change in plans. The car was quiet, nothing but the muffled street noise mixed with the jazz Vince always had on low. West glanced over and saw a smile barely there on the edges of Meg's lips. He'd take that as excitement, and his ego sat tall and reminded him he could be fascinating too with a little effort.

"Do I look polished?" Meg asked as they watched the sunset atop 163 steps tiled in swirling blues and greens and smack dab in the middle of the city. West had put on a baseball cap and pulled the collar of his jacket high. They even found one of his sweatshirts in the trunk of Vince's car to go over her blouse. It was cold for a summer evening and when she scooted closer to him, West forgot she'd asked a question.

"Well, do I?" she said as their legs touched.

They were both entranced by the setting sun and trying to stay warm without crossing a line neither of them had set but they both understood.

"No."

She laughed.

"You asked."

"Well, what image do I project then?"

Spring, he thought, or the rich colors of the hills after a deep all-day rain. She looked alive and somehow despite her work, she didn't appear to notice the world could be a dreary place. Probably best to keep that to himself. The last time he waxed poetic to a girl, he was in the second grade. Trudy Chapman dumped her carton of milk in his lap and ran to tell the teacher. West learned that night at dinner with his family that navigating women was confusing business for all guys.

He had more experience now and knew humor was the escape route for most female situations. It was harder to throw things if they were laughing. Taking a slow breath, he turned to Meg.

"Right now, you seem comfortable. You are having a good time thanks to an incredibly charismatic guy who showed you yet another cool place you haven't been to."

"I am having a good time, and this is a supremely comfortable sweatshirt." Meg pulled her hands into the sleeves. "Since you are obviously avoiding my question, tell me who made these stairs. You know you're dying to."

"I am. I should have been a tour guide."

Meg grinned and ran her fingers along a section of tile. West resisted the urge to put his arm around her for at least the sixth time since they sat down.

"It was a project through the parks trust. Two women and then over two hundred neighbors joined in and added their touches. It has been around since 2003 or 2004, if I remember correctly. I stumbled upon it when I first moved here and was lost on a jog."

"What an awesome surprise."

"It was," he said, facing her again. He needed to see her cheeks pink with cold and her wide blue eyes one more time before the sun finally gave way to darkness. She stared ahead and he could see the puffs of air leaving her lips. He wanted to kiss her, and not on the cheek this time. Something else he kept to himself. They weren't on a date. They were... Yeah, he had no idea what they were doing, what he was doing. Standing up to create some distance, he put his hands in his pockets and Meg stood next to him.

"We should probably get going," he said.

"You didn't answer my question."

"Yes I did, you look comfortable."

"No. Comfortable and having a good time are states of being. They aren't descriptors."

"Wow, we're dealing in parts of speech now. I feel underqualified."

"I'm serious. You're in this visual business, and I'm asking you as a friend. If I don't look polished, then what do I look like?"

West ignored the thud in his gut at the friend label because it was stupid to think they were anything more. He toned down the imagery of how he saw her but still went with honesty.

"You appear to be a woman who has more important things on her mind than what she's wearing. Like you've spent your life on the other side of the camera. There's nothing wrong with that." Their eyes met. "Why do you ask?"

"Still no adjectives, but thank you. I've never given much thought to how people perceive me. I guess it's new and I'm curious. Amy keeps telling me I need to polish things up, so I put some effort in today and I was wondering if I'm any shinier."

"Well, I think you look great the way you are, but if it's polished you are going for, that's easy."

"Okay. Who polished you?"

He laughed as they walked toward the car in the dark. "Hannah would argue that I'm still not polished."

"The beard," she said as West held the door open for her this time.

"Yeah, she's a fan of shiny things too."

"Huh. I liked the beard."

West felt a juvenile jump in his pulse. It was the first time she'd even acknowledged that she noticed he had a body, apart from the sexy comment in the conference room. Yeah, he was still holding onto that one like a starved fan.

"It honestly wasn't intentional. Hannah made a big deal, but I didn't want to shave or be anything that day. I was heading to my parents' house after the meeting and saw no point in dressing up. Something about you being there made that okay for a moment, so thank you for that."

"You're welcome. Anytime you want to be unpolished with me, let me know." She caught herself, which was fun to watch.

"But in the meantime, any tips? Can someone polish me up to Amy and everyone else's standards so I can get back to occupying my time with things that matter?"

"I think I can help you."

The car pulled up in front of her apartment and West resisted the

urge to get out and walk her in. The woman was asking for a professional reference, not a nightcap.

"I will set up some appointments for you at R House and I'll text
you the address. Tomorrow?"

"You don't need to call a salon for me. I'm sure Amy has an entire
list."

"R House isn't a salon. They're a one-stop shop and it's private.
You can't call them yourself."

"That name is ominous. It sounds like some kind of underground
club."

"They specialize in polish, Meg. Tomorrow?"

"Are they going to make me look goofy? I saw this one place on
the Internet that waxes the inside of your nose." She flinched. "No,
thank you."

"Do I look goofy?"

She seemed to stumble over her words but recovered quickly. "Do
you wax the inside of your nose?"

He nodded.

"Really?" She tilted her head as if in the dim light of the car she
was going to be able to tell.

"Well, it's not waxed right now. I'm not filming, but when I'm
working, I get it waxed. If I have a crazy nose hair during a close-up,
someone on set will pluck it out, and that hurts more than having all
of them yanked out at once. Are we truly discussing this?"

The sound of her laughter filled the car. "I'm sorry. That's ridiculous."

"It is, but that's polish. Every hair in place. At least in my world.
Do you want me to make the appointments or not?" His face was
starting to hurt from smiling and the tiny space of the backseat
seemed to push her closer.

"Yes, please. Let's get this over with. How long will this take?"

"They'll probably want you for half the day."

"Good God."

West's fingers hovered over his phone.

"Fine, fine. How do you know they'll have time for me?"

He raised a brow in answer. Meg shook her head and grabbed the car door handle as Vince let her out.

"Oh, that's right, you're the sexiest man alive," she said as the door closed behind her. West rolled the window down.

"Not *the* sexiest. A runner-up. I guess that makes me sort of sexy."

"I guess it does." Her eyes were saying more, but West still couldn't figure out what. She crouched down and looked through his window. "Thank you for the stairs."

"You are more than welcome. That's what BFFs are for. Next week, we'll hit the pier."

"I've been to the pier, West. I have lived here my whole life." She seemed to mentally correct herself because she hadn't been in the city her whole life, but he didn't push.

"I'll bet you haven't been to my pier yet."

"Ooh, again with the mystery. Hey, they're not going to wax my butt, are they?"

He burst out laughing. "Not if you don't want them to."

"Do you..."

West began to interrupt, but she beat him to it.

"I know, I know, only when you're working. I honestly don't know why I can't control my curiosity." She turned toward her building.

"Still thinking about my butt?"

"No one wants that."

"Actually," he teased and was rewarded when she turned back to him.

"I know. I'm sure there are many women who—"

"Hundreds." This was fun, and her expression turned from silly to heated. Damn, the woman was a fatal combination.

She scrunched her face. "I think that's a bit of an exaggeration. They may want you, but your butt specifically? Do you have any real data on that?"

"I'm sure we could find some."

She laughed again and his hand went to the car handle of its own free will.

She put her hands in the pockets of his sweatshirt, and he imagined her in her apartment in his sweatshirt and nothing—

Yeah, that's enough of that. Back to BFFs, you idiot.

"I'll text you the appointment time and the address."

"Thank you." She raised her hand in a good-bye and was gone behind the door.

West finally stopped smiling when the car pulled onto Market Street. It was the best night he'd had in a long time. Hannah was going to be pissed—the beard was definitely making a comeback now.

Meg closed her apartment door and stood in the darkness replaying the evening. Had he been any other man, some blind date or a guy she met at work, she would have allowed the butterflies dancing right under her skin to continue, but he wasn't merely some guy.

No matter how easy he made it for her to forget, he was famous. Crazy famous and while they'd spent uninterrupted time together, she wasn't sure what was going on. Was he simply lonely in his self-imposed isolation and their agents had secured him a playmate for a while?

That sounded harsh, but it was insane to think that some Hollywood A-lister enjoyed hanging out in backseats and on city steps discussing her need for an image makeover. Meg dropped her purse and hit the light switch near the door.

Did she just ask him if she looked polished? More than once? When the hell was she going to find the off button for her mouth, or at least the pause until her brain engaged?

He'd given her a straight answer eventually and while "comfortable" and "the other side of the camera" were not exactly key words splashed all over fashion magazines, they were truthful. She was comfortable with him, which was crazy considering the situation. But despite the spotlight turned on them now, West had a way of distracting her as if they were sneaking under a blanket. Probably not the best visual considering she could see the vulnerability in his eyes when he asked her to go to the steps and still feel the warmth of his body when he sat next to her in the pink and orange of the setting sun.

Vulnerable *and* heat—a difficult combination to resist indeed. Not that he was offering her anything. He was a nice guy. A friend helping her navigate a different world. That was all. He probably looked at all women like they were fascinating. She would admit that particular look was a drug for Meg. She'd always preferred fascinating over sexy. He probably knew that, could sense it. After all, giving people what they wanted was his job, and he was good at it.

Too good, was the last thought Meg had before she drifted off to sleep hoping for dreams about orangutans or spiders even, something she understood.

Chapter Ten

*W*as it an unspoken rule that wedding planners had to be snotty bitches? Weren't weddings supposed to be rainbows and happiness? Meg was simply checking on the snapdragons. She'd promised Anna she'd take care of the vague florist and after two voicemails without a return call, Meg was getting pissed.

Dane sent Anna snapdragons after their first date. Anna wanted them in all the bouquets and "come hell or high water," as their Uncle Mitch would say, Meg was going to make this happen for her sister. Which explained why she was taking a deep breath as the wedding planner meanie transferred her to their "master florist." Christ, did everyone have a title?

Following some obnoxious music, the master florist informed Meg that creativity took time and "she was still inviting all of the colors onto her palette to create something truly unique for the couple."

Meg thunked her head on the kitchen counter and guessed she was now privy to what Anna meant by vague.

"Right. So, will there be snapdragons?" Meg asked again.

An exacerbated huff came through the phone before the florist said, "Most likely. If I say yes, will you promise me that you won't encroach on my creative space again?"

"You've got it." Meg felt encouraged for the first time since picking up the phone.

"Then yes. We were able to procure blush and ivory with rosy tips. I will include them in my creations. Good-bye, Maid of Honor."

Hanging up the phone, she texted Anna with a thumbs-up and that she would have snapdragons. She also mentioned that Frida would be bringing her EpiPen and their mother almost apologized for being "troublesome." Meg followed all of that with an eye-rolling emoticon and tapped the send arrow.

She rolled her head from shoulder to shoulder as if she'd managed to win an arm wrestle. Sometimes it felt like a cruel joke that Annabelle chose the sister least likely to own a lacy bra as her maid of honor, but when she teared up and told Meg she had missed her so much, there was the guilt again.

Guilt and love. She wanted to help, needed her sister to be as happy as the other two, but Meg was barely getting used to wearing heels. A wedding was akin to wearing high heels while gardening. But over the past couple of months, she'd realized that Anna didn't actually need her for dress fittings and cake tastings. She'd chosen Meg because she wanted someone at her back. A sister to fight some of her fights and keep her standing even at the "classy, but a little crazy" bridal shower Meg had put together with Cindi and some of Anna's other colleagues. Meg excelled in all those areas and discovered she fit in just fine as a maid of honor.

The wedding was five short weeks away and now that the florist had figured out her damn palette, the only things left were confirming things for what felt like the hundredth time and finding a dress.

Annabelle gave her some leeway in that area, as long as it went with the blush-and-ivory color scheme. Meg had put off shopping for a dress, but now that she was silky smooth and polished within an inch of her life, she was feeling equipped to head into some of the boutiques and check the dress off her list too.

Meg thought of West and wondered if her new BFF might help her find a dress. Why was she picturing an incredibly uncomfortable slit somewhere if Westin Drake oversaw the maid of honor dress?

Besides, he hadn't even seen the results of her day at the R House, which was an unnerving name for a rather friendly place. Meg wasn't sure she wanted to spend what turned into almost a full day with the amazon beauties, as she'd affectionately termed them while they were waxing her bits, but they were good at their job. Running her hands along the silky edges of her now shoulder-length hair, Meg had to admit there was something liberating and fresh to being polished.

Rudolpho had taken three inches of "dead mess" off her hair and pulled a round brush the size of Meg's oatmeal container through what was left. The result was lighter and softer. She liked it and as a bonus, when she asked him if their color products were tested on animals, he launched into a diatribe about how he personally selected all their products to ensure they were not only humane, but natural.

"Nothing that touches your body in my house is harmful to anyone," he had told her with a kiss on both cheeks before he sent her on her way. All in all, it was an amazing day of pampering. It wasn't that Meg was against pampering, she simply hadn't thought about it before.

She glanced at the clock in the kitchen and decided that before the community garden event at four, she needed some fresh-air time all to herself. Pulling on her cargo pants and a sports bra, she smiled at the blending of polish and her old life standing together in the mirror. She pulled her glossy strands through a baseball cap and reluctantly decided she would need to shower and blow-dry her hair before the garden event. The idea that she was allotting time to blow-dry continued to amuse her as she grabbed her vest and locked her apartment door.

Considering the route she planned to take to the Mount Sutro Loop, she decided she would need to run the whole way if she was going to be back in time. West had texted that he was sending Vince to bring her to the Next Generation offices. The garden was around the corner from there. She had thanked him and ignored the flutter in her stomach when she saw his name flash on her phone. A good hike was in order. Time among the trees would take care of the flutter. At least that's what she told herself.

∽ᓂ ᓂ

"Yes, it's palm oil you want to stay away from. Now, there are some small distributors that are sustainable. They've been growing palms since before the fast-food boom. Generations, right. Oh sure, I'm happy to help." West heard Meg's voice as she left whomever she was talking to and pushed through into the all-glass, all-solar, all-happy-planet meeting room of Next Generation. He was still reading a pseudo-script they'd given him for the community garden shoot they were going to do for *Good Morning America*, which would air the following day.

After their appearance at the smart house, this thing with Meg had quickly escalated. *If Hannah had her way, there would be more than three events,* he thought. He almost said it out loud, but Meg set her bag on the table with a clunk, pulling him from his thoughts. As he glanced up, something new raced through him. It was the physical equivalent of the way he felt anytime she talked about her work or made him laugh. Her hair was shorter and she'd lost the poncho. His eyes traveled before he could stop them, causing Meg to look down at herself. Her cheeks went pink.

"My eyebrows feel a little weird. I'm sure Rudolpho's gorgeous amazons know what they are doing, but I have never had my brows this thin. My face feels a little naked. That's probably what you're noticing."

West didn't catch much of what she was saying, but her eye contact was fleeting, which hadn't happened in a while. She was nervous. He recognized the signs now.

"I... don't see a difference in the brows, but those jeans are tight."

"So?" She jolted back and again looked down.

"So, pretty sure that's what grabbed my attention." His hands gestured of their own free will up and down the length of her. "I mean, I'll take your word for it that your eyes are... naked"—their eyes met on that appropriate word and West realized she was as beautiful with makeup as she was without—"but I wasn't in that vicinity."

"Oh."

"Yeah." Warmth rose through his body. He needed to get a handle on this, or he was going to throw her over his shoulder. He tried to find a character, a role he could play that wouldn't be so turned on he could barely speak.

"Huh. So, the polish is working."

"I don't know about the polish, but those jeans are working. Yes, you should keep those." He went with aloof, clueless. He'd played a young dad distracted by a new TV in a commercial once. Young dad, television, that's where his mind needed to be, but his eyes fell and he dropped character when they found her ass. Before he could look away, she caught him.

Meg turned in a circle, jutted out her hip, and put her hand on her butt. West kept his eyes on the paper in front of him. This was not happening. *B. F. F.* He reminded himself firmly. She was brilliant and adventurous. *But, what about the jeans?* a part of his body nowhere near his brain asked. Shaking his head, he looked back to Meg still shimmying around. Their eyes met.

"Holy smokes, these jeans are hypnotic. Look at your face."

"What?"

"You want me." She put a hand on her hip.

West laughed and added playful and fun to the already long list of Meg's irresistible qualities.

"I do not want you," he lied.

She nodded and stepped closer to him. "Yeah, you do. You are checking me out."

"Easy does it, shiny pants. I think you've been sniffing the polish. I will say that the curves are impressive. I'm a little taken aback. I mean how the hell was I supposed to know all of that was under those rainbow skirts and your poncho?"

Meg turned her back to him and glanced over her shoulder with pouty lips.

Damn, she was pretty good at this.

"Would you mind signing my ass, Westin Drake?"

He shook his head. "Can we review this script please? In less than an hour, you are going to need to be in front of a camera with a shovel in your hand. The world will be watching you talk community garden, and I doubt you'll be so feisty then."

She cleared her throat and went almost white at the idea of being on the other end of a camera again.

"Right. We need to focus."

"Exactly."

She sat down next to him and picked up the notes for the spot with her lines highlighted in pink.

"Why are my lines pink?"

"Going out on a limb here, but it's probably because you are the female."

"Sexist."

"Oh, please let's let it be just a highlighter. I can't do sustainable food and sexism all in one day."

"Fine." After a minute, she wiggled in her seat and flicked her hair, which was now begging West to reach out and touch her.

"Sorry. It's just that these jeans are so... tight." Her mouth quirked and West wondered how one woman could possibly be all of these things.

He was reminded of their first breakfast when she said it was only fair that he was a little dense. The same rule applied when he thought of Meg. It was out of balance for a woman who captured incredible images of the Spirit Bear and the Polar Bear to be so funny. Or for a woman who could discuss regions of the world most people had never heard of and make them sound so fascinating that he wanted to get on a plane. Or for a nationally recognized photographer to giggle at getting her ass waxed. She could not possibly be everything. But he looked at her and her expression danced with the playfulness of a woman who, despite the polish, still wanted to smell like coconuts. He had a feeling she was everything.

You're screwed, the only functioning part of his brain declared.

West had resigned himself long ago to companionship or sex. The two didn't exist together. Now that he knew Meg, he wasn't sure how he was going to go back once she left. There was no way she would survive in his world, even if she wanted to, so he needed to reel this in before he started telling himself stories. He loved a good story, but acting had taught him that fiction was not life and once the director yelled "cut," reality was what he'd be left with.

"You still smell like coconuts," he said before he realized he was speaking.

She wrinkled her face in bemusement. "I never agreed to give up the coconut oil. Besides, Rudolpho said it was a 'fabulous body drink,' direct quote." She extended her arm and ran her hand along the length. "So smooth," she said.

Where the hell had all this skin come from? He was comfortable with her in long and flowy, but he was starting to think the polish had been a bad idea. Now, in addition to wanting to be near her, he wanted on top of her.

West stood up abruptly to look for Hannah. If anyone could bring a cold bucket of reality to the situation, it was her, but of course, when he needed the distraction, she was nowhere to be found.

Chapter Eleven

*A*fter the surreal experience of standing in front of three huge cameras and saying, "Good Morning, America," there was something invigorating about being in the open, windy air with a shovelful of dirt in her hands. This was a project she could get behind, Meg thought as she tried to ignore the click of the cameras. She and West were adding the topsoil to a planter full of radish seedlings. The community garden was one of four Next Generation was opening around the city. The gardens each had a lead crew member—an NG employee—and the rest of the work was to be done by neighborhood volunteers in exchange for a produce box each week. The remaining harvested veggies would be sold to local restaurants and the proceeds would help sustain the garden, as well as fund community outreach.

Red-cheeked and enveloped in the smell of soil and the outdoors, Meg felt, for the first time, that she might have a place in the city after all. That she wasn't only a photographer and there were several ways she could live a life that was true to her spirit. West was charming and chatty so she didn't have to be and when the press sent a question directly to Meg, it was usually something about her travels. She found that practice did ease some of her nerves and she could share parts of her story that were entertaining.

~⋑ ⋐~

"Okay, one last question and then these two need to be going," the CEO said to the crowd.

"West, mind if I ask something personal?"

"Aw, Tony. What's with the manners? You're usually the first one to take a personal shot without asking."

"Guilty, but I thought since it's a community event and all, I should show some respect."

"Yeah? Remind me to hang around community gardens more often. In fact, if I plant one of these at the hotel, will you guys pack up and leave?"

"Not a chance. Do I get my question?"

"Not a chance," West said, placing his hand at Meg's lower back and moving her toward the staging area where the Next Generation marketing team was going to hand them each a T-shirt and then, if all went according to plan, they would get into an electric car provided by the company and be delivered safely home.

Green event number two was almost in the bag when West heard a flurry of cameras behind them.

"Are you two dating now?" Tony the asshole, as West affectionately called him, yelled out.

West, back still toward them, closed his eyes and gave himself a second to soak in his stupidity. The cameras continued as he slowly removed his hand from Meg's back.

"Keep walking toward the entrance. Do not look back and do not answer their questions. Behind you is what I refer to as a swarm."

"As in bees."

"Closer to wasps. I'm sorry. I put my hand on your back, and by tomorrow morning they'll have us picking out our children's names."

"Shouldn't we get married first?" Meg said with a surprising calm. It was a clear indication she didn't understand the power of a swarm, and that need to protect her surfaced again. He wasn't sure protection was possible at this point in the game.

"Clever, but I forgot the ring." His eyes cut to Hannah, who had flown in for the event. She recognized his expression and since she no doubt wanted West to continue playing nice, she intercepted the small group of reporters advancing from the press area.

"That's okay. I'm not a ring kind of woman anyway." Meg kept walking.

"You've given this some thought?" West asked, glad their banter was a distraction. He could hear raised voices behind him.

"No. I can't imagine myself with one of those big... rocks on my finger. Seems like it would get caught on everything. Are they supposed to be following us?"

"No." He moved to put his hand on her again but caught himself this time. "Hannah will take care of it. T-shirts, big smiles, and then we are free. Did you want to go to the pier, or are you busy?"

Meg took the T-shirt offered to her and so did West. They flashed camera-ready grins and right as they were preparing to make a clean getaway, Meg hesitated and turned to face him. He wanted to turn her back around because the cameras were snapping and it looked like they were practically nose-to-nose. Not good, West thought. But her eyes locked on his and somehow in the middle of the community garden party, even with the advancing swarm, he wanted to hear what she had to say more than he cared what was going to be made of it.

"What's going on? With us. Is there an us?" she asked, eyes curious and confused.

Yeah, not what he was expecting, and certainly not a conversation he was going to have in front of hundreds of strangers.

"Let's get in the car."

"No, I mean before you whisk me off again, can I get some clarification?"

"In the car, Meg. Believe me, now is not the time for us to play our little game."

"Is that what this is?"

Holy shit. Paparazzi had slipped past Hannah. The slimy ones always did and West felt at least two at his back. His heart was at a full gallop and she wanted answers. He was sure he'd had a nightmare that went along a similar path, but certainly not starring Meg Jeffries.

He risked the picture, took her by the arm, and leaned into her.

"I'm sorry. We can go home, but if we continue having this conversation, it will be turned into something bigger than it is and you will be all over the gossip rags by the morning. Is that what you are looking for? One more word and we're there."

Meg stiffened as if she'd been awakened from a trance, shook her head, and climbed into the backseat of the car. West quickly slid in next to her and almost slammed some idiot's hand in the car door. He'd been blunt, maybe a little rude, but the need to protect her became more and more fierce the closer the piranhas got to her. She was a grown woman and he knew it wasn't rational, but he felt responsible and she'd become important to him. Christ, how had he let that happen?

They drove in silence as Meg tried to figure out what had happened. One minute she was having a genuinely amazing time and the next, she was standing her ground. All she knew was before she was going to be pushed into yet another car or offered one more amazing city adventure, she wanted answers.

Was he Westin Drake, the blockbuster movie star screwing with her head for an audience, or West, the man whose expressions lately seemed like his next breath might depend on her?

Meg had always been patient. It might have appeared to be a spontaneous act when she took the job with *National Geographic*, but the truth was she'd been waiting her entire life, watching others pass by and leave. She'd spent years taking pictures of the family cat, her room, or a rock in a tide pool. She got her camera by the time they took Sage to college and a pass to use the darkroom at her high school by the time Anna went. She'd been capturing images her whole life, so while many viewed her chosen profession as daring, it was a slow and patient progression. She was rarely in a hurry, but she needed to know what was going on with West in that moment, right then.

The panic on his face had been a first, and again the vulnerability behind it was something she would not soon forget.

"I like you," he said, eyes still hidden behind sunglasses despite the shadows of the setting sun. "I enjoy being around you and I keep coming up with excuses, which is crazy. I'm sorry, I honestly can't explain it."

Meg thought the answer was obvious but wanted to hear some confirmation from him first in case she'd lost her mind and only imagined they were having fun together. She needed to know when he took her around the city or they were joking around that it was real, a genuine friendship and not some sideshow. She knew bullshit was his business, but it wasn't hers.

"I didn't mean to put you on the spot back there, but lately I feel like I'm being sucked into a tornado and dropped from place to place."

"You are," he said.

"Oh, well that explains it then."

West confirmed her address with the driver and Meg was more confused.

"So this is all part of your show?" she asked.

He laughed. "I don't have a show. I have a life that requires me to do some pretty absurd things, but I am a normal human being."

"I doubt that. You seem pretty extraordinary to me." They pulled up in front of her apartment and West handed over her coat.

"Only one more event, Meg. Stand firm. No matter what they try to lure you with, leave it at one more and get back to your life. We have your gallery show last, so at least it's on your turf. Have a good night."

The driver opened the door and Meg stalled by attempting to put on her coat while sitting. It had grown a little colder, and sure it was weird she was putting on her coat to walk fifty feet to her front door, but she needed some time to think.

West reached over to help and she gave up the arm wiggling.

"Do you want to come up to my apartment? I know it's not the adventure you had planned, but my pizza delivery guy has a tattoo that says 'Mom' across his neck, so that's something."

When he didn't respond, she gathered her twisted coat in her arms. "I like you too, West. I think we get along and I'd be interested in having a pizza with you. Do we need to alert the Special Forces for that type of thing, or can you simply... you know, come on up?"

The interior of the car was dark now, save for the muted glow from above them, and Meg felt bad for the driver, who was still standing out in the cold holding the door for her. West took off his sunglasses and stuck them in the pocket of his blazer. He looked out the back window of the car but stayed put.

Meg wanted the comfort of her apartment. It had been a long, smiley day and now it was over. Stepping from the car, she thanked the driver and turned toward her door. She heard the other car door close and West saying something to the driver. As she stood with her key in the main door to her building, West came up next to her.

"Do you have any good movies?"

She laughed, pushed open the door, and knew he was taking a chance on her, on them. She liked him even more.

Chapter Twelve

"Want to see something?" West asked, one large veggie pizza and the director's cut of *Forrest Gump* later.

Before she could answer, he started lifting the hem of the T-shirt he'd brought with him. When West joined her at her front door, he held a bag Meg would later learn was a change of clothes. Turns out, he carried comfortable clothes with him anytime he had to wear dress shoes and a jacket. He had changed in her tiny bathroom while Meg ordered the pizza and thought back to the first time they'd met. Westin Drake was not the kind of man to get caught without underwear.

Speaking of underwear, twisting from her place on the chair next to him, she could now see the waistband of his boxers as he lay sprawled on her couch and continued lifting his T-shirt. Meg swallowed. She'd been around men most of her career, seen them in various stages of undress, but there was no denying that her heart picked up at a glimpse of his dark skin in contrast to the blue of his shirt.

It seemed West was wearing a mask, a persona, from the watch on his wrist to the pomade in his hair. Rudolpho had given her an extensive history of hair-care products, and Meg caught herself examining strangers to determine whether they used gel or pomade in their hair. West was a pomade guy. Everything about him appeared to be calculated for maximum effect, but there was something so unadorned, scrubbed, and touchable about his skin.

"See this?" He was leaning up and pinching his stomach just above the waistband of his jeans.

"What... exactly am I looking at?" Meg's eyes were stuck on his belly button and a light dusting of hair that led places she'd honestly never thought about until that moment. Sure, she'd noticed him, his unfair, almost female cheekbones, his shoulders, the silver ring that looked like a branch on his right hand. She hadn't been completely immune to the beauty of him, but her imagination had not quite traveled this road yet. The road to his body was too obvious a choice. Meg always thought "obvious" lacked imagination.

Since meeting West, she consciously tried to see past his beauty, focusing instead on their conversations and the fascinating contradictions that swirled through their time together. Practically every woman wanted Westin Drake's body. Now that he was giving her a preview, the body was fun too.

West's eyes sparkled at her long stare. "Speak up if you see something you need, Meg?" He lifted his shirt a little more in a teasing way that made her laugh. Turnabout was fair. Although she might collapse if he stood up and started shaking his ass.

"You asked me if I wanted to see something. You have my attention."

"I can tell."

He ran a palm across his now-bare abs. Meg's mouth went dry, but there was no way in hell she was giving in to his game.

"Oh, please. I'm sure there's nothing under there that I can't Google on the Internet. Are you going to tell me why you're pinching your abs?"

"Any time a scene or photograph is taken of me without my shirt on, this is photoshopped."

Meg's gaze combed his body, stopping at some of her newly discovered favorite spots while she tried to figure why anyone would want to standardize all the exceptional planes and edges that made his body so much more than perfect.

"Seriously?"

West nodded and dropped his shirt back down over his stomach. Meg sat up in the overstuffed chair. "That seems like a lot to take in. I'm not sure how they focused on that tiny spot." She waved her hands in the air to encompass his long frame across her couch, his arms tucked behind his head and legs crossed casually but hanging over the edge.

His expression softened and he pulled at his shirt again, as if making sure it was adjusted back to the most flattering position. How was that possible? Meg thought. How could someone so casual, so seemingly at ease with his body, his looks, be insecure about... skin?

"Aw, look at you stroking the ego. According to my trainer, that section of my stomach is where I keep my beer, and I'm not giving up beer."

"Why not?"

"It's practically in my blood. My brothers have a brewery. It's bad enough I left them behind for 'twinkle town,' as my dad calls it. If I gave up beer or started drinking that low-calorie girl shit, I'd never hear the end of it."

"The family business is beer?"

West sat up and nodded. "My brothers, and my dad on occasion, are Foghorn Brewery." He said it with such pride, as if she should recognize the name.

Meg was stumped.

"They're up in Petaluma. The operation is bigger now. They recently took over the old poultry plant. My grandparents had a farm in Petaluma years ago. We're fourth generation."

"You're a farm boy?"

"No. I mean, I remember going there as a kid, but they sold it and retired. I do try to hold my own at the brewery when I'm home. They work long hours and enjoy calling me their little sister."

"That's a little harsh."

"You haven't met my brothers. That's a light tap. In their eyes, anyone who takes a shower or gets a haircut is a girl."

Meg pulled her legs into her chest and listened because she found she wanted to meet his brothers, wanted more of his story.

"So, your brothers don't have a stylist?"

West laughed, which made him seem younger. "No. They're... different. I mean the four of us are similar when I'm home, but their life is built on something tangible. I guess that's the right word. They get dirty. They make something. Do you drink beer?"

"I'm not a big drinker, but that's probably because I've been away for so long. I like water, especially clean water, but if Amy keeps rewriting my TED talk speech, I might consider drinking."

"You have a TED talk?"

Meg nodded. "October."

"Finally, something worthy of your time. And you've gotten the polish without losing yourself. You'll be incredible and away from all of this flash and bullshit."

"So, your brothers are the real deal and you're all about the bullshit?"

West considered for a minute, as if he'd never noticed the framework he put around his life. "I think that's about right."

"Oh, wow. Spoken like a true youngest child. I should know."

"Big shoes to fill."

"Tell me about it."

West grinned. "Said the woman who's been on the cover of *National Geographic* twice."

"Nothing but another magazine in my family."

"Are you kidding?"

"Yes. They are supportive, but of course, they give me the guilt trip that I'm never home. Nothing is ever—"

"Good enough?" West said.

Meg nodded. "Something like that. Look at us, our own little youngest-in-the-family support group."

"And we have pizza. Not bad for our first meeting. So, if I ran to get out from behind my brothers, what are you running from?"

"Who says I'm running?"

"Well, not anymore, but why did you run?"

Meg pulled her legs closer. "If I tell you, do I get a question?"

"Sure."

"I was sick of being left behind. I made a decision that I would be the one walking away as soon as I was old enough," she said, surprised how coherent her thoughts had become.

"Good plan."

"Not exactly. I forgot to look back and I missed some things I shouldn't have missed."

"Is that why you're visiting now?"

Meg nodded. Visiting. She'd leave it at that for now. "My turn. Are you happy?"

"Sure," he said almost before she finished the question with the enthusiasm of someone used to saying the right answer.

She waited, hoping there was more.

West took a deep breath. "My life is different. Happy and sad don't factor in."

"That's not an answer."

"Is there any more pizza?"

"West."

"No. I am not always happy, or in general happy. That's such a huge thing. I'm lucky and I have money. I can pay my bills and help my brothers in that way, but does making action movies and surrounding myself with people who are constantly taking from me make me happy? No."

Meg wasn't sure what she expected his answer to be, but it wasn't that.

"Do you get to do this a lot?" She tapped the pizza box.

"No. But I'm not sad either. I'm neutral. How's that? And I don't eat pizza. The camera does not like pizza."

"I beg to differ." Meg unfolded herself from the chair and grabbed one of her cameras off the dining room table.

West tried not to flinch as if she was holding a dangerous animal. There was no reason not to trust her. Hell, she'd probably have to ask him where to sell the images of him anyway.

It was a screwed-up response, he knew, but it was difficult to find normal when almost every girl he'd dated in high school and college had shared at least one story with a magazine and every other trash news cycle, a random stranger claimed to have partied with him or given him a blow job.

Things were more manageable in San Francisco, but it was bizarre being so hyperaware of oneself. Probably screwed up, but West had no intention of seeking help like so many other successful actors. He wasn't going to be a juice-drinking, life-coached-to-death whiner. His father and brothers would ban him from hunting altogether if they had any inkling he'd gone soft.

He didn't need professional help, but he had decided a while ago to acknowledge his world was unusual. Awareness allowed him to look things in the face and protect himself, especially if they were scary as hell.

He was aware, even on her couch. But if Meg Jeffries and her camera weren't safe, if she could fool him into trusting her only to turn around and burn him, then his faith in humanity would be completely lost. He wasn't the best judge of character, but no way Meg was like the rest of them. His expression must have relayed panic because when their eyes met, she was a little snarky.

"West, this is a camera. Did you want to pet it?"

"Look at you being funny."

"I'll have you know I am an endless source of entertainment for my family."

"I have no doubt. What are you doing?"

"I want to take some pictures of you. Actually, parts of you, if you don't mind."

"Yeah? I would have never guessed you were into kink. You disguise it well behind the poncho."

"Shut up or I will go put that poncho on."

"You kept it?" He chuckled.

"I love my poncho and I am not into kink. You can keep *those* parts covered, thank you. Over by the window."

"Bossy. Do you talk to your animals this way?"

Meg shook her head and twirled a finger in a gesture for him to face the other way. West obeyed. He was curious.

"Look, you're beautiful," she said, turning the camera view screen toward him to reveal a close-up image of the back of his neck.

It was a part of him he never saw, and the fact that she chose something abstract was not lost on him. She was attempting to show him a side of himself the paparazzi were incapable of exploiting.

She took more shots of him, but the click of the camera was slow, rhythmic. He was either losing his mind, or there was something incredibly sexy about her eyes combing over him. West turned and she took a few shots of his face. At this point, he didn't care.

One hand wrapped around her lens, Meg was the one who was beautiful. Still not in the glossy magazine sense of the word, but in an honest and natural light way. God, he'd never met anyone like her.

"Do you miss it?" he asked, needing to take the attention off himself.

"I do, but I'm working on finding new things to shoot. I went back to the stairs you showed me and took some shots at sunrise. I'll e-mail you one."

"Thanks. There's plenty of adventure in this city." He moved toward her and she turned her back to him to set her camera down.

"Do you date a lot, West?"

He laughed and when she didn't, he tried to think of the right answer.

"No. I don't date a lot," he said. "Do you?"

"No, but I'm not you." Her back was still to him, and West wondered if that made it easier to push away what had been building from the minute she invited him for pizza.

"True." He took a step closer, wanting to move the hair off her neck. Put his lips to her skin.

"You should date Amy. She recently broke up with her boyfriend and she's your type."

He barely heard her now through the thrumming in his ears. "What exactly is my type?" He took another step.

"Oh, you know, polished and photo ready."

Inches from her now, Meg finally turned from the dining room table where she'd been stalling with her camera bag.

"That could not be further from the truth."

Their eyes held and he didn't need to tell her she made his heart race or that he wanted to know how she looked first thing in the morning. None of that needed to be said—it was all right there between them.

"Do you want to watch another movie?" She tried to move past him, but West reached out and touched her arm.

He shook his head and even though his mind was spinning with a million reasons why he needed to leave, for the first time, something he wanted was well within reach. Running a hand up her shoulder, her body stilled and he stopped.

She was no longer with him. He wasn't sure where she had gone, but it was clear he wasn't going to kiss her tonight. He'd misread.

He moved back. "I should get going."

Meg closed her eyes for a split second and without a word grabbed his coat.

"Your gallery show is next week, so I'll see you there. Thanks for some normal time, best friend," he said.

She smiled and he started to breathe again. Damn, he thought she was going to drop, and not in a good way.

"You're welcome. See you next week," she said.

"Right. Goodnight, Meg."

West was out in the cool night air before he realized he'd been rejected. It wasn't often he went in for the kiss and the woman on the receiving end shut him down with no more than silence. In fact, it never happened these days.

Rejection was something he knew well. He was practically drowning in it the first year he moved to LA, but it typically came from strangers behind clipboards and tiny lights. This rejection was different and personal on a level that had him searching for an even breath as he climbed into the familiar backseat of Vince's car.

West had thought they were on the same page, but something happened. She probably didn't let people get close to her or she wasn't around long enough to commit. *Or she's not into you, man.*

With any other woman, it would only take one cold shoulder for West to move on. He didn't ask twice. But Meg was unlike any woman he'd ever known and the idea that what he felt coursing between them was going to culminate in a polite goodnight and a pat on the back stung more than it should. Then again, he'd never wanted anyone like he wanted her.

Chapter Thirteen

Meg was losing perspective. She'd spent the last three days in a fog of "what if." On a purely physical level, she had wanted to kiss him, but right when she felt his warm breath—somehow still enticing after eating pizza—whisper across her lips, she panicked. The entire day had been a shift in what she knew to be true.

She was working with a celebrity, Westin Drake, in a combined effort to promote Next Generation. That was what his agent had said so professionally in the meeting. Meg was getting paid more than she was ever paid for a real assignment.

Real. There it was, she thought, standing in the back of the Plimpton Gallery as the doors opened and people began filing past her photographs poised on easels and washed with gorgeous light. What *was* real?

She had asked herself that exact question moments before West leaned in to kiss her. If he was playing a game, if the show was all he knew, Meg wanted out before the kiss. She never worked with artificial light. While many photographers applauded the benefits of artificial light, Meg preferred things in their natural state.

All of this started when he helped her onstage and kissed her on the cheek. That was an absurd way to form a connection, but then she'd gotten to know him, right? Is that what they were doing, getting to know each other? Or was the whole "get the misfit polished up, show her around town, and then move in for the kiss" all part of the picture? That's what she'd been asking him at the community garden before she acquiesced and climbed into the back of another car. Then she'd invited him into her apartment and still didn't have an answer, or did she? Was the move to kiss her an answer?

Christ, she was minutes away from her first show and trapped in a mental vertigo as all the pieces jumbled in her head.

Taking a sip of wine from the chilled glass in her hands, Meg was certain she'd never had a problem telling real from fiction before. She didn't swoon after a romantic movie like Anna, and on occasion, Sage.

She understood that the only way to get a polar bear to look as regal as the one in her cover shot was to lie on her stomach and shoot the picture from below. They naturally held their heads low—that was the reality she had distorted a bit to convey their power. She explained that to people during discussions. It was the truth.

Meg couldn't tell what West was distorting for effect and what was real the moment he wasn't joking around and seemed to want more than a best friend. It scared her the way her body reacted and that her heart all but climbed into his eyes without question. She'd had three days of distance since the pizza and several conversations with herself, most of them ending with—*Oh come on, who cares what's real, take that man.*

"Meg," a voice that used to be as familiar as her own cut through the cocktail chatter. The stem of her wineglass slid along her fingers and when the ball of the glass hit her palm, she barely kept it from dropping to the floor. Her heart racing from the near crash, Meg turned and crashed instead into her very real past.

Now that she was no longer on assignment, she was certain she'd never see David Cupo again. He looked good, for David. Her body no longer responded to him as a lover, and what was left was an almost painful awkward she already wanted to escape.

Briefly turning toward the crowd to compose herself, Meg caught West approaching from the opposite end of the room.

The perfect storm.

She tried to smile.

"David," she said, turning as West joined them. David, Meg's ex-partner and ex-lover, held his own, even standing next to West, which was no easy feat. His hair was shorter, which usually meant he'd recently returned from assignment, but she didn't know him or his schedule anymore. Didn't want to.

He surveyed West in that way he assessed everything and then his expression became distracted, anger-tinged. Meg took another sip of wine, knowing it wouldn't help. No wonder she was having trouble sorting things out. Everything already felt like one of those mirror rooms at a carnival, and now the universe had added David. Was this karma for something she couldn't remember?

"I heard you were dating an actor." He extended his hand to West.

If Meg could have crawled under the expensive Oriental rug they were standing on, she would have seized the opportunity.

West shook it. They hadn't even had a chance to say hello and there he was standing up as the imaginary boyfriend. Meg was sure Hannah and Amy were high-fiving one another over espresso.

"I've seen your movies. I'm David Cupo."

"Good to meet you too. Are you a photographer?"

His laugh was barely there and touched with the pain of someone forgotten. Meg tried to meet his eyes, hoping to smooth the edges with the good parts of their time together, but it was too late. He finished his whiskey in one gulp and nodded. "Yeah, you could say that."

"David was my mentor. He's a big deal."

"Sure. I think this might be the third or fourth time I've put my foot in my mouth since I walked in. Sorry about that," West said.

Meg wanted to smile as she switched from wine to water.

"This must be a lot for someone from Hollywood to take in. Meg, are you showing him around our world?"

West's brow furrowed with confusion, and then Meg saw the moment he realized he was dealing with more than a snotty photographer. West had an expressive face. It was how he made his living. Meg wondered if casting agents ever saw his range, but she was pulled from her thoughts when he answered.

"It's not that complicated. Gorgeous photography. A worthy cause. Meg has even been helping with some public appearances for Next Generation. Fairly simple, even for us Hollywood types. How long were the two of you together?"

"We 'worked' in the Arctic on and off for a year," he said, the sarcasm evident in the aggressive air quotes around the word—worked.

"Nice."

"It was. Clearly she's talked about me a lot since." If David had a mustache, he'd be twirling it right now, Meg thought.

"Not exactly cool to talk about exes." West mocked a flinch, and Meg felt like the woman tied to the train tracks in those black-and-white silent films.

"Wow. He's pretty and witty, Meg. Well done, you." David summoned the circulating wait staff and ordered another whiskey.

She looked at West, who seemed perfectly fine with the tension. He wasn't taking shots, merely defending himself and allowing David's annoyance. West was downright relaxed. At first Meg marveled at how he managed it but was quickly reminded of his body sprawled on her couch. Without a word and out of sight as the crowds grew around her images, West set his hand at the small of her back. It wasn't a gesture of possession or meant to piss anyone off. He was holding her steady.

Meg had to wonder: why hadn't she kissed Westin Drake?

David's last comment washed right over him. If this prick thought calling him pretty was more than a glancing blow, he needed to spend some time in LA. West kept his hand at Meg's back and took in the room. He was in awe of her work and prepared to let any remark go, but the guy ordered another drink and moved in for his next shot. Meg beat him to it.

"Why are you here, David?"

West put both hands in his pockets and stepped out of the way to watch round two. Meg didn't appear to need his help. West found that impressive, sexy even, but he wondered if being so self-contained left much room in her life for anyone else.

"I wanted to see your work. The ones from Canada are decent additions. Every career has an arc and from the looks of your exhibit, you peaked in the Arctic."

Yeah, this guy's a real prince.

Meg didn't flinch, her tough skin in place even without the poncho.

"Besides, we're a tight community. I wanted to contribute to the cause."

She spun toward West, presumably to leave, when a woman far along in her pregnancy joined David.

West had a feeling this might be the blow that would hurt.

"And, I wanted to introduce you to my wife."

Meg wasn't facing them, which was good. It was a clever strategy to lose the stunned expression first. There was a hint of pain in her eyes and one more time, West stood in unfamiliar territory. He was jealous.

Meg pivoted back to them, her lips almost lifting into a smile, and shook hands. West moved to her side and admired the raw acting ability.

"This is Candace. She's an assistant editor for the *New Yorker*."

"Part-time assistant editor soon." She touched her belly and beamed.

"Good to see the *New Yorker* caters to work-life balance," Meg said, obviously trying to move the conversation to a speedy end.

Asshole leaned over and kissed his wife's neck. Another whiskey and poor Candace would be sharing a cab home with a blithering idiot still hung up on his ex. *Lucky girl.*

"It was a pleasure meeting you, Candace. Thank you for coming and congratulations to you both." Her eyes locked on David. "I am happy for you."

West had a feeling she *was* happy for him, which was incredibly generous considering he had stopped by for the sole purpose of pissing on her parade.

"Yeah, we were married off the coast of—"

"Would you... I'm sorry to interrupt, but I need to get back to my show. It was good to see you, David." She shook the wife's hand again. "A pleasure. Best of luck to you both."

She left and rounded the corner near the caterer. West followed but kept his distance. She was leaning down, hands on her knees and clearly trying to get it together.

"He's gone," West said.

She nodded and took in a deep breath. No tears, which was a relief. He only dealt in fake tears, and what had gone on over there was not fake.

"This is probably not the time to offer acting notes, but that was a genuine performance. Polish firmly in place when you shook the little wife's hand. Twice, I might add. Well done."

A laugh teased her lips as she stood and gently rested her head back on the panel separating them from the rest of the gallery.

"Thank you."

"For what?"

"Being you."

He went next to her. The panel was wobbly, so he took a step forward as the servers flew by them with more drinks.

"You're welcome. I'm guessing things didn't end well with you two?"

When she didn't answer, West supposed he should leave her and head back out to the crowd exclaiming, "Oh, this is so lush," every time they moved to another photograph. He thought he might puke out there, but Meg probably needed space. Again.

"He wanted to get married. Correction, he wanted me to quit my job and start a family. I hurt him, so now he's bitter," she said quietly right as West shifted his weight to leave.

"Did you love him?" He moved back, lately never missing an opportunity to know more about her. He did take a quick look around to make sure there were no bees buzzing in the vicinity.

"No."

"Ouch. Good thing the poor bastard left. Ruthless, Poncho. Completely ruthless."

She laughed, grabbed another glass of wine, and looped her arm under his. West should have made a joke and created distance. Instead, he kissed her hand and returned it to his arm as they walked back out to the crowd together. This was her night, and there were not enough photographers to keep him from being there for her.

Chapter Fourteen

*A*fter the gallery had sold the last print and West had posed for what Meg hoped was his last selfie of the night, she was exhausted. She had no idea how he kept up a sense of humor about the constant attention.

Thanking the gallery owners, Meg slid into her coat and walked past West as he held the door open for her. Meg looked around for Vince as West pulled up the collar of his coat, took her hand, and began walking. She was struck by how far they'd come and that their time together was almost over.

"I never told him I loved him," Meg said. "It was a bad situation in the end, but I never lied to him. I don't lie," she added as he swerved them past a puddle.

"We all lie."

"Correction. I don't lie to people I care about. I have lied about paying a bill online or when Amy asked me to join her bridge group, but other than that, I don't lie. I'm good at the truth."

"You don't like bridge?"

"Everyone in my family plays bridge. My sister, Sage, teaches it at the community center. Our grandmother taught us all when we were little. I've played enough bridge for one lifetime."

"Who tells someone that?" he asked as they stood on the corner with a few other people. West's eyes flicked almost imperceptibly at the group and back to her. She supposed he was constantly assessing.

"That I don't like bridge?" she asked.

"No, that you don't lie. That you are good at the truth."

Meg shrugged, and the wind picked up as they crossed the street. She was old enough to know that honesty was a rare commodity, but West seemed downright shocked at the idea of being told the truth. She wasn't trying to sound noble. Ever since her second-grade bake sale, she'd made a vow never to lie.

She didn't have many rules for herself. They were stifling, but she held fast to the truth. Even as a little girl she'd wanted to tell her mom that her corn bread was awful, but when she'd offered Meg a piece to try after she walked home from the bus stop, the kitchen was covered in canisters, a mixer, and almost every wooden spoon they owned.

The entire scene was dusted in a film of flour, as if it had started snowing inside their house. To Meg's almost eight-year-old eyes, her mom looked sad, so she swallowed down the glop of bread and even with it sticking to the top of her mouth, she nodded and told her mom it was delicious. Despite her mother's initial beaming and humming around the kitchen for the rest of the night, Meg hated that she'd lied.

She had no way of knowing at the time the impression a bake sale would have on her, but seeing her mom among the other moms had hurt her heart. That was how she would forever remember it, and that night she made the rule.

No one bought a piece of the corn bread, not one. Meg had heard some of her classmates and even a couple of moms whispering.

"First, who brings corn bread to a bake sale," the mom that looked like a mouse said to the mom wearing the red lipstick.

"Correction, who brings awful corn bread to a bake sale," Red Lipstick had cackled back. Meg wanted to say something, defend her mom, but she was only eight so she quietly helped pack up.

They sang along to the radio just the same as always on the way home. Once Meg was older, she realized her mother probably never cared if anyone bought her bread. She might have been relieved the whole thing was over. If the Whispering Pines Elementary School bake sale had hurt her mother's feelings, she never said a word.

The following year, her mom took baking classes and started making cakes from scratch. She even presented their father with a crème brûlée for his forty-fifth birthday a couple years after that. Their mother was a master baker now, but that bake sale had changed Meg. She never again wanted to send someone she loved out into a sea of strangers on a lie. There was no way she would have understood it fully as a little girl, but the night after the bake sale, she wrote in her diary, the one with the unicorn and the heart-shaped lock—I don't want to be a liar. She'd cried, wiped her eyes, and had been pissing people off ever since. She wasn't cruel, merely honest. She owed that to the people she cared about.

Obviously, not everyone in her life saw honesty as a virtue. When David proposed to her almost three years ago, Meg would have given anything to go back and erase her diary entry. In the grown-up world, Meg learned quickly, there was no way to be honest with a man who looked at her as if she was the moon without hurting him as she had. She cared about David. They'd shared some incredible adventures together, but it wasn't love for her, and it certainly wasn't something that would hold them together after he stood up from one knee.

They were different people. He wanted a wife, someone who was going to quit her job and raise a family while he continued taking pictures all over the world. Meg was not that woman. But David, too, had changed her. He had said some things in anger the last time she saw him that all but knocked her over.

"You're a hider." That's what he'd said. "Someone who runs from real human contact." He'd raised his voice, thrown his duffel bag in the truck, and finished with, "It's not normal, Meg. You're not normal."

There was no point in arguing with a wounded man, but those words, similar her mother's corn bread, were tucked into her being. She supposed, looking at West now, his gorgeous face lit by the street lights and still waiting for an answer to his question, every person she met had shaped her. Her relationship with West, if that's what this was, would leave its mark too.

"Animals are drawn to the truth. I think they can sense fake. They don't like it, so I guess that's why we get along. They're okay with my honesty."

"And they can't talk." West smiled, and Meg was struck by how imperfect and wonderful his face could be when he wasn't trying. "Truth telling is not advised here in the human world."

"I don't know. I think we could all benefit from honesty."

West considered her answer. "Does that mean I can ask you anything I want and you'll give me a straight answer?"

They stopped, and he pulled her out of the way as a group of people approached from behind. She was up against the building and West had subtly kept his face hidden. He was inches from her face, their puffs of breath mingling in the evening.

"Does it?" he said quietly. "Can I ask you anything, Meg?"

A shiver traveled the length of her body and she pulled on her coat, knowing full well the weather was not the problem.

"Are you hungry?" she asked.

He laughed and stepped back now that they were alone again. Meg decided his laugh was one of his best features, which was saying something since the man had an abundance of best features.

"I could eat." He offered his hand, gloved in leather.

"Let's do that, let's eat." She put her hand in his, and that felt even more intimate than his arm. Another puff of air escaped her lips.

"Are you asking me on a date?"

"Sure. I'll buy," she said.

"Oh, I'm there. Mexican?" West took out his phone.

"Do you eat falafels?"

"Are the little fried things they put in them fresh?"

"Those are the falafels."

"Huh, what's the rest of the stuff?"

"It's a falafel sandwich, or you can get a plate."

"It's the sandwich on the pita. That's what I want."

"I know the perfect place. Are you calling that car again? We could grab a cable car. The place is right on Market."

He typed a quick message and returned the phone to his coat pocket. "Why do you need to give me a hard time? I ride the cable cars, but only during weekdays after lunch."

"What?"

"Not a lot of traffic then, and the people on the public transportation during that time couldn't care less who I am. They're my kind of people."

Meg smiled.

"Don't worry, Poncho. I'm not missing out on life. I simply have to plan more than the average person. It's ten thirty on a Friday night. Take me on a cable car and it will be a drunken selfie freak show. You'll never get your falafel."

There was no way this was an act. She'd watched one of his movies when she couldn't sleep the other night, and he wasn't *that* good of an actor.

This was real. He was asking her to like him back.

Meg faced him and smoothed her hands up the front of his soft and probably expensive coat. As if she'd already done it hundreds of times, she rose on her tiptoes and kissed him softly on the lips.

West had gone to St. Barts one year after Christmas. It was the year the first *Full Throttle* came out and he foolishly went home without a plan. Photographers followed him and his family to the edge of where they'd cut down their Christmas tree and then hid out in his mother's oleanders. It had scared the shit out of him and when he called Hannah, her advice was to leave.

"This isn't dying down anytime soon, hon," she'd said.

As much as West desperately needed to be home and grounded, his dad couldn't even pull his truck out of the driveway to get more firewood. So Hannah sent him his first of many cars and he left before Christmas. That was the last time West did anything without a plan.

There was an upside, though. St. Barts was warm and gorgeous. As his tongue slid past Meg's cold and delicious lips, he was reminded of sinking into the warm ocean, safe and removed from a world he didn't understand. Kissing her had the same effect and as he wrapped his arms around her and pulled them from sight, he wanted her with a force that was unfamiliar.

The lights of Vince's car cut through the dark, damp alleyway and idled on the street. West slowly pulled back from her mouth and was aware of nothing but her peaceful face and the rhythmic dripping of water from somewhere farther down the alley. Meg's eyes slowly opened and her hands rested on his arms.

She held on and put her forehead to his chest before whispering, "I think you might need to find a new best friend."

"Nah, in the movies, this is what we call a plot twist. If I'd known alleyways were your thing, I would never have tried to put the moves on you at your apartment," he said over the top of her head, which promptly fell back in laughter.

West wanted that sound in his life, but when the car flashed its lights, he was reminded that they were not two people stumbling over their feelings after a night out on the town. He was a puppet and her heart was happiest in faraway places. Before reality could sneak between them, she squeezed his arms.

"Exactly what kind of gym work goes into these arms, Westin Drake? Professional inquiry, of course."

He wrapped an arm around her waist, lifted her off the ground, and moved toward the waiting car. Rewarded with more laughter, he set her on her feet and they climbed into the backseat.

"So, you *do* notice the arms. I need clarification since so far, you've appeared completely immune to my body. Truth please, Poncho."

"Okay. Yes, your body is… it's impressive. That's all you're getting."

"I'll take it," he said.

"What's the secret?"

"Work. And falafels only on special occasions." He wanted to kiss her again.

"That's a shame. But I suppose you need restraint if you're going to be the sweaty guy driving fast cars."

"You watched?"

"You're sweaty in the pictures on Google, but I confess I did watch one."

"My arms were sweaty too, eh?" Mocking his image somehow felt like a game now that she'd let him know she saw past his shine.

"They were. I swooned a little."

"I'm sure."

"Oh God," she said. "The ego on this one. Vince, could you please take us to the Falafel House on Market Street?" She leaned back in his arms as if she too felt the comfort of seclusion. Or she cared about him enough to give it a try.

"How did you know his name?" West wondered what other details she was picking up along the way.

"I pay attention." She shrugged against his chest.

"Yeah? Can I get some more attention?" He pulled her onto his lap.

Meg huffed dramatically. "Damn, celebrities." And then she took his mouth in another kiss, and West slipped right back into the crystal-blue water of her again.

A short car ride later, Meg stood in line while he waited in the car. Every now and then she would make a camera with her hands and he shook his head. He'd forgotten how fun sneaking around could be. She was so alive and the only thing he cared about was being near her. He asked Vince to wait and joined her in line.

Leaning slightly into her back, he wrapped his arms around her and when someone took their picture with a phone, he ignored it. They were next in line and if anything got out of hand, Vince was right there. West mentally planned, and then dropped his mouth to the curve of her neck.

She wasn't the kind of woman who handed everything over to anyone. He knew that, and even if she did, his life would suffocate her. Meg thrived in fresh air and a life with her family and friends. His world provided him with opportunities and an obscene amount of money, but that didn't mean he could have her under the glass bowl. That was fine too. She was merely passing through anyway. But before she left and ruined him for all other women, he wanted all in.

Chapter Fifteen

S pices filled the car as they sat across the street from the Fairmont San Francisco.

"Side entrance?" Vince asked.

"Yes. Wait until the last group of cars leave the roundabout. I've texted Towner."

"I thought we were going to your place," Meg said.

"We are." West seemed distracted.

"Wait, you live in a hotel?" She turned his face to meet hers as Vince pulled into traffic and made a quick U-turn.

"I don't live in a hotel. I'm staying in a hotel."

"For how long?"

"Until September, when I go back to LA. Can we discuss this later? I need to get you inside."

Meg wished she was an actor. Her feelings were all over her face and she knew he saw them.

"I'll be back and forth," he clarified.

"I don't... it's none of my business. I'm not sure why I asked."

The next thing she knew, West was out of the car and grabbing the take-out bags from her. The other door opened and the largest man Meg had ever seen looked in on her. Even his watch was huge.

"Good evening, Ms. Jeffries. Welcome to the Fairmont." His voice was deep. "My name is Clay. Mr. Drake will meet you in the suite if you'll come with me."

Meg's mouth must have fallen open for a moment during what resembled a movie scene. She was waiting for someone to yell "cut" when the tall guy in all black offered her his hand and she slid from the backseat. Clay had one of those Secret Service hearing-aid-looking things in his ear. Glancing at Vince, who seemed to be scanning the alley as if they were on a tactical mission, she noticed the gun holstered inside his jacket. It all felt like a Bond movie.

"Clay," she said as they walked through a door that suffered tremendously in comparison to the opulence of the front entrance.

"Hmm?"

"Is this the part where you tie me to a chair and hook those sticky things onto my head? Because I'll save you the trouble. What do you want to know? I'm an open book."

The edges his mouth faltered slightly and Meg thought she might see a smile, but he was back to composed by the time they stepped through the steel elevator doors.

"This is nuts."

"It is," Clay said, running a white card across a raised square in the elevator and pushing the button for the twenty-second floor.

"It is almost one o'clock in the morning."

"We received a Google alert with a photo of the two of you kissing at a falafel shop."

"A Google alert?"

He nodded. His neck was easily the size of a small tree trunk.

"Shortly after that, three sets of photographers showed up in the lobby. Most women think this is sexy or intriguing, but it's honestly for your own safety. Those people are relentless. I'm glad you get that it's nuts. Makes my job easier."

When the door to what Meg assumed was a hotel room opened and she saw West, shirt now open at the collar and shoes off, "most women" was still swimming in her brain. *Did he stage this performance often?*

Meg rested her shoulder against the wall of the entryway. Christ, being around West made her dizzy, and she had to wonder if he brought some of it on himself. One minute he was looking at her as if she were the only person on the planet and the next, his security guy handled her like some groupie being shuffled about for a quickie and an autograph. Surely there had been other women and the world knew about all of them. By the time he finished talking with Clay and closed the door, she wanted to leave.

West paused for a moment, checked the lock, and turned to her, exhaustion all over his face. "I am truly sorry about that. It is usually easier to get up here, but I guess tonight things were a little crazy."

"It's the Google alert," Meg said, torn between wanting to touch the side of his face and running for the street.

"Clay has a big mouth." He guided her gently through the entryway of the room, as if he sensed she was ready to bolt.

Not a room, her mind buzzed as she took in the deep navy-and-gold-accented space that was easily the size of two of her apartments. She noticed doors to other rooms too.

"I'll get napkins. Do you want a beer or water?"

Meg stopped in the middle of the room, jolting him to a stop next to her. Their falafel bags sat on the shiny wood table with the curly legs next to not one, but two full-size couches. She wondered if that's how she looked compared to the polish of this world she'd been thrust into—like a crumpled take-out bag.

"What's wrong?"

She shook his arm off her elbow. She'd never liked being led around, and it seemed he was doing that more and more. "Could I get a minute to take all of this in? I understand that you have to keep moving, but you need to give the rest of us time to catch up."

He said nothing.

"This is an incredible place you have here."

"Thanks. It's the Tony Bennett Suite."

"Very funny."

He raised his brow.

"You're serious?"

He nodded, disappeared around the corner, and returned with two beers and two bottles of water.

"I left my heart in San Francisco. That Tony Bennett?"

He put the drinks on the table and touched his nose to indicate she was correct. Meg sat on the couch and heard her mother's voice in her head inquiring about a coaster for those drinks on the nice wood. She absolutely did not have time for her mother's thoughts. Meg had enough of her own.

West hit a button on the wall and the white blinds beneath the gold swaths of fabric framing them began to move. When a 180-degree view of San Francisco appeared in front of her, Meg gasped like a little girl and ran to the window, remembering not to touch the glass. *Someone has to clean that, young lady*, her mother's voice chimed in again. *Yeah, thanks Mom. You can leave now.*

She turned to find West sitting on the couch, opening the little containers of yogurt sauce.

"Have you caught up yet? I'm starving," he said, glancing up as if they were sitting at one of the cracked linoleum tables back at the Falafel House.

Most women clung to the bells and whistles of West's world like catnip. Meg, on the other hand, seemed like she might run, so he kept moving things forward. He popped open their bottles of beer and tried to pretend he was a regular guy hoping an incredible woman would agree to wake up in his arms.

All he wanted to do was eat falafel sandwiches and fall asleep on this couch. He honestly was up for any plan so long as it didn't include her walking out that door.

Meg sat back down next to him and he handed her a paper plate. Their eyes held and concern was right there in the beautiful curves of her face, but she said nothing. Simply unwrapped her sandwich, took a big bite, and closed her eyes in pleasure. West could get used to that expression too.

"So a couple of things," she said, washing down her food with a swig of water instead of beer.

"Only two?"

"Well, two pressing things. When we were coming up in the elevator, Clay mentioned 'most of the women.' Without going into disgusting detail, how many notches are on that bedpost?"

"I've never understood that phrase. Is that a Wild West thing? Why am I putting notches on my bedpost? And with what? My pocket knife?"

She held his gaze and kept chewing. She wanted an answer. Right. Start simple.

"I am male."

"Yes, you are." She took another bite.

"And single."

"Another truth, good, you are on a roll."

"I have slept with some women, and the people who help me navigate my life have seen a few come and go."

Meg nodded and set her plate on the table. West thought she might get up and walk right out, but she reached over and grabbed another napkin.

"Why are you eating with me? Why did you show me street art and the stairs? Why are you always pushing me into your car?"

"Wow, that's a lot of questions for one breath. Let's see, I am on a break from filming and I enjoy food. That is why I eat with you. We went on the art drive as an alternative to walking down the street in broad daylight *and* I thought you would appreciate it. The stairs, because I wanted to share something private with you. I push you into my car, actually there's no pushing, but I do that because I want to be near you. All. The. Time." Those last three words trickled out with hesitation. He couldn't read her expression or where she was leading with her questions.

One of those must have been the right answer. Meg took the plate from him, set it on the coffee table, and climbed onto his lap. Her hands were on his shoulders as if being this close to him helped her judge his sincerity.

"Are you going back to Los Angeles? You said you were."

"I have to be on the set by September eighteenth, and then it will be three to four months of filming. I will be back here full-time. I need to buy a house."

She said nothing and appeared to be weighing things in her mind.

West had questions too. "My turn. Why do you eat with me? Why do you let me push you into the car? Most importantly, why did you kiss me?"

Meg dropped her head to his shoulder and took in a deep breath. "You make me feel," she said so softly he barely heard her.

West lifted her face in his hands. "I make you feel what, Meg?"

"There's never been a time when I haven't had chaos inside of me. I'm curious. It's one of the reasons I became a photographer, why I move around a lot."

"I know you're leaving. Is that what this is about? It's fine. I'll take what I can get."

Meg's laugh was laced with nerves. "Why would you ever take only what you can get?"

"Stay on topic. Things are getting good. What do I make you feel?"

"You make me feel safe. It's as if you have all day to sort through my thoughts and while you are sorting, you look at me like…"

"Like you're everything?"

Meg bit her lip and nodded. "If this is a game, if I'm a notch, please tell me now and we can go back to being friends. I liked being your friend. That was working."

"It's not a game, Meg." West leaned in to kiss her, but she held her fingers up to his lips.

"Good. In that case, I would love to see you naked, but I have a few questions before we go there."

His heart thundered in his chest as she sat straddled across his lap. She had no clue the effect she had on him. She wanted to clarify the rules for sex, simple as that. He was either having a heart attack or he was falling in love with her. West had played love a few times, but this must be the real deal because what was racing through him had nothing to do with a sweeping soundtrack and everything to do with being pulled into a riptide.

His body was ready for whatever was next, but his mind scrambled for how he was ever going to make this work. He had a feeling once he took her to bed he'd need a plan, because there was no way in hell once was going to be enough.

Maybe, his rational mind kicked in, he didn't need a plan. Meg might be staying put for a little while, but after her TED talk, she would return to her life of adventure. That was fine, he lied to himself. They would see each other when they could. People did the distance thing all the time.

She shifted on his lap and much to his body's disappointment, West opened his mouth. "I can't believe I'm saying this, but it's almost morning. Why don't we save your questions for tomorrow? Instead, I could kiss you stupid and we could fall asleep right here."

"You want to cuddle with me?"

He nodded.

"Westin Drake, if you are a phony bastard, I am going to be so mad at you," she said, and then she kissed him again.

He didn't want to let go. Her mouth softened and he continued taking. In that moment, he was more than enough and she truly was everything. Surrounded by the skyline, he shifted her onto the couch and ran to the bedroom for the comforter. Her eyes were heavy as he tucked in behind her and covered them both. She folded her arm under her head.

"I'm going to buy you a poncho," she said, barely above a whisper, and fell asleep in his arms. West smiled into her hair and kissed the back of her head.

While his heart struggled for a way to keep her close, his brain knew he should have kept his distance, ignored the fact that she smelled like a tropical island and had a way of reminding him that he was once a kid who played flag football with his brothers or the man who caught his first tuna with his dad off the coast of California.

He'd moved to San Francisco for a little perspective, but from the moment she told him she'd forgotten her underwear, nothing was off limits. Now, holding her in his arms, he wanted everything, which was ridiculous. No one got everything. Life always came down to choices and what he was willing to give up.

It was late and before West convinced himself he'd throw it all away for the woman in his arms, he pulled the covers farther up, drew her closer, and fell asleep.

Chapter Sixteen

*M*eg's eyes opened at around five a.m. as far as she could tell from looking out at the darkness. She'd slept outside for so many years that she considered it a bit of a game to guess the time and place upon waking. West's body was firmly pressed against her back, making the where and with whom part of the puzzle easy. They'd fallen asleep on his couch and looking out through the wall of glass windows, she felt like they were camping, surrounded by the night sky. If the outdoors had down comforters and cashmere robes, that is. She softly kissed the arm holding her close and slipped out from under his warmth.

The suite was so quiet she could hear the hum of his laptop on the table behind her. They were in the middle of a city, suspended over it to be exact, but she couldn't hear any of the real world. Meg was reminded of the first time she met Westin Drake. They were suspended then too. She was beginning to wonder if his feet ever touched the ground, if it was even possible for someone who was comfortable with his face on a passing bus to ever go to the grocery store or pump gas. She'd seen movie stars on the covers of rag magazines since she'd been home. Some of them were pumping gas, albeit in unflattering sweatpants or looking painfully hungover, but their hands were on the pump like everyone else.

Meg wasn't sure he could even drive. There were a lot of things she didn't know about him, things not found on Google, she thought as she crossed her arms, hoping to hold herself in place. The carpet beneath her bare feet was plush and she noticed papers near the pulsing light of his open laptop. Glancing at the stack, she read the title—Preliminary Shoot Schedule. Her eyes skimmed down. Table Read – *Full Throttle: Floor It*. She stopped there and realized the date below was tomorrow. He needed to be in LA tomorrow and they were eating falafel? Hadn't he said September? Was a table read different from filming? How long did a table read take, and why hadn't she realized he was leaving? She turned away from the desk as if her back would somehow keep the information from sinking in.

While she tried to refocus on West's sleeping face, the next inevitable question made its way to her brain—*What the hell am I doing?* Her gallery show was finished and while she was sure the profits were enough to pay her rent through the next year and keep Amy in incredibly high heels for a bit longer, Meg didn't have a next step. There were still a few last-minute tasks for Anna's wedding, but that wasn't a job. After that, what was her plan, her next assignment?

She did not know and the fact that she was in Westin Drake's hotel room like one of his many conquests made things worse. Her thoughts were thick with self-criticism and a reminder that she was a photographer who hadn't picked up her camera in almost two weeks. She'd gone downtown to photograph some of the old buildings and hadn't even downloaded the shots. She was normally frantic to see her work after a day out. When had that changed? Probably around the time she'd let Amy pressure her into polish and hanging out with celebrities. Is that what she was about now?

And then there was David last night. How could she forget about that? The memory of his smug face as he paraded around his expecting wife like a prize he was dangling under her nose. She didn't love him and she certainly didn't want to change places with his wife. Meg worked for a living and preferred being alone. She wasn't even sure she wanted a partner. Wait, she *knew* she didn't want that, didn't she?

She'd given her life to her career, and while she'd returned for her family and a sense of stability, that didn't mean she wanted what her sisters had. They were different. So instead, she was what? Sneaking around an overpriced hotel suite that doubled as a home for a man she'd let slide into her life and who was now leaving? How was that any different than settling in with David?

Holy crap, she couldn't breathe.

Barely aware she was moving, Meg gathered her things. She took off the sweatshirt West had loaned her, folded it, and placed it on his bed like an item she was returning to the store. Had she truly been escorted to his room last night through the back elevator? Who lived this way? Certainly not her, she thought, slipping into her shoes from the night before. Meg's roommate in college often spent the night at some guy's house and she used to return home in the early hours of the morning. Mascara smeared, she'd whisper "walk of shame" and crawl into her bunk. Meg had never participated in that college ritual, but here she was like a groupie. She stopped, purse in hand, and wondered why she was being so hard on herself. They hadn't slept together.

It occurred to her that all of this started when she read he would be in LA tomorrow. There it was again, the urge to leave before being left. She would think about what all that meant some other time. Right now, she opened the door and made her way to the service elevator.

West woke up alone on the couch. He was on his stomach, which meant Meg was not blissfully tucked against his body. Rubbing his eyes, he called her name and after a quick look around the suite realized she was gone. He checked his phone and saw her text:

Thank you for dinner and your couch. It has been great working with you these past few months. Good luck with your movie. Safe flight to Los Angeles.

Working with him? West read the text again. Yup, that's what it said. What the hell had happened? He replayed the evening in his mind, lingering on the parts when they were kissing, which only left him more confused.

Working with each other, my ass.

He was poised to text a clever response but stopped. Setting his phone down on the table, he ran his hands over his face. They had finished her gallery show and technically he had no more business with Meg Jeffries. Aside from the fact that his heart was throbbing in his chest, they were done. That was how she wanted it. The whole covert ops thing coming up to his hotel was understandably too much for her. Wait, how the hell did she get home?

West called down to Towner.

"How did Meg get home?"

"Well, good morning to you too. If you are referring to the woman your security team bumped into getting off the service elevator, Vince drove her home."

"When?"

"Around five thirty this morning."

After a thank-you, West hung up, glad Meg was safe but still stunned by the brush-off. She'd left at five thirty and texted him at— he turned his phone over—seven. What was that, guilt relief for leaving without a damn word?"

He had never been responsible for anyone but himself. Looking out at the city below, he realized someone usually swept in right as life or responsibilities loomed close to his shoulders. He was left with his parents and their almost empty nest by the time Patrick and Cade left for college, but right as his parents started talking chores and responsibility, Boyd was back from Oregon with his young son Mason. The family dynamic was turned on its ass and two years later, West was gone to UCLA, his youth intact and any share of the family weight left firmly back on his older brother's shoulders. Hell, even as far back as when they were kids, West would talk himself into trouble and one, usually a couple, of his brothers would wear the black eye.

He'd been so self-centered most of his life. It could be that acting wasn't a calling at all but more the only way of life he knew. That was until he stepped backstage at the convention center. It was hard to believe it had only been a couple of months since Meg managed to plant herself firmly under his skin. If he kept this up, if he called her and asked to meet, what then? Was he going to make a life with her? Drop down to one knee and offer to buy her a house in the hills? Neither of them wanted that, did they?

No. It was his ego scrambling to bring her back to his couch. Things would end eventually; she'd simply beaten him to it. That's what he was going with. That's what was working in some weak, pathetic part of his brain at the moment he tossed his phone on the table.

She would be on assignment soon and he had a movie to make. They'd made no commitments to one another. This was clean. She'd closed it up for him. He should be in the shower and halfway to packing for his flight. There was no room service or awkward good-bye. Good.

West sank back down onto the couch, held the pillow to his face, and smelled coconut. As hard as he tried to force the time he'd spent with Meg into the mold of any other project or overnight guest, he couldn't. They hadn't even slept together. Closing his eyes and opening them when the sight of her tucked into his arms flooded his memory, he felt like he was losing his mind.

She'd left before he had a chance to decide what he was willing to give up. She wasn't interested in anything more, and anyone with an inside view of his world wouldn't blame her. Good. Fine. A clean break, that's what he told himself as he stripped off his clothes and walked under the hot spray of the shower. More coconut oil.

Shit! He hoped like hell that stuff washed off.

Chapter Seventeen

*T*hey were running but wearing regular street clothes. He was holding her hand, but the frantic race of his heart pulsed all around her like one of those movie theaters with the reclining seats. Meg was trying to figure out what was wrong or where she and West were going in her dream when the Black Eyed Peas burst through her haze singing about their humps. Meg slapped the alarm clock.

Rolling to her back, Meg realized she wasn't running and West wasn't holding her hand. He'd been in LA for almost a week now and had moved on with his life. She hadn't heard from him. It wasn't fair that she expected to, she knew that. But it turned out women created stupid expectations and sometimes played stupid games when they were... whatever the hell it was she felt for West. After leaving his hotel, she'd been filled with empowerment. She'd cleaned her apartment, bought a toaster, and reaffirmed that she was not the kind of woman a man snuck up the back elevator. Ever.

Anna's wedding was next weekend and Meg intended to spend this weekend relaxing. She still didn't have a next assignment, but "something is right around the corner," Amy assured her. Meg had resisted the urge to e-mail her boss at *National Geographic* under the guise of seeing how things were going.

She lived in San Francisco now. Her life was settled. She propped herself up and pulled her laptop in front of her. The heart foundation's follow-up e-mail sat in her empty e-mail box with its little red flag calling to her. She wasn't sure what she was going to do with their project. She'd been avoiding it and now she was running out of time. They'd already given her an extension and agreed to move her deadline to November. Surely the wedding would inspire her, or maybe she'd go through some of her first photographs and create a progression of images. Something would stick by then.

After quickly texting Anna to make sure she was still vertical and not obsessing over the weather report, Meg threw on some clothes and went for a hike. There was time for that now. The gym membership hadn't worked out, but she had managed to find a variety of challenging hikes in the city that not only got her heart racing but fed her need for green trees. It wasn't until the turnaround to head back down Strawberry Hill that she thought about him.

After the first anxiety-fueled day of getting back to her life, he slowly crept back into her thoughts until his face was there the moment she opened her eyes in the morning. Today she'd gone almost four hours before she'd wondered how he was doing, or allowed the memory of his lips on her body to grab her breath. Progress, she decided.

Things would be back to normal next week. She had to admit she didn't miss being shuffled from one black sedan to another. And, she felt fantastic. More water, and the salad chop-shop around the corner from her apartment instead of the falafels. Last night she made soup. She was firmly in a routine, a life. The fact that her heart was still restless, still telling her she needed to do something, was irrelevant. The last time she went with her heart, she had gotten fourteen stitches. West was where he belonged, and so was she. Meg switched out her hiking boots for her tennis shoes at the base of the trail and decided to walk home. It was another sunny September day. Keep this up, Mother Nature, and Anna's wedding was going to be perfect.

After finishing a smoothie and taking out her earbuds, Meg

turned onto her street and stopped cold. The black Lincoln Town Car was parked outside her apartment and while it could be anyone's car, she knew Vince was sitting in the driver's seat. She decided to ignore it and her feelings, which worked as she climbed the steps and opened her door. And then she heard his voice.

"Meg."

Closing her eyes, Meg gave herself a minute and spun to find a thinner, tanner version of Westin Drake.

"Incredibly unfair that in a week, you've managed to lose all that pizza weight and get a tan." It was all she could think of to say. Her heart was clamoring and she wanted desperately to appear as though she were over their time together.

"I tried to call." He closed the car door and stepped closer.

"Oh." Meg pulled her phone from her pocket, mainly for something to do. "Sorry, I was hiking."

"Glen Canyon?"

"No, Strawberry Hill."

He stepped closer and she met his eyes. "I need to talk to you."

"Okay." *Breathe, damn it, and don't lock your knees.*

"We can talk here, or I'm back at the Fairmont for the weekend."

"You get the weekends off?"

He smiled like he'd missed talking with her. She knew the feeling. "Yes."

"That's good. Well... um. Here is fine. What did you want to talk about?"

"This." He gestured between the two of them.

Meg held her hand up. "I'm doing well. I bought a toaster."

"Yeah?"

His eyes were their own heat source, so Meg looked away. "How are things with you?"

"Awful."

Her chest thumped and Meg put her keys back in her pocket and walked to the car. Once again, she climbed into the backseat. This time, no one was pushing or rushing. She wanted to go, wanted to hear what he had to say.

⤜ இ ↄ ⤛

West had envisioned the scene being way more complicated on the plane ride home. The second day on set, he knew his plan to let her cut and run wasn't going to work. He needed her for as long as she'd have him and if that meant putting in some effort and making some choices, he was willing to do that.

The expression on Meg's face when she saw him in front of her apartment was not encouraging, but now she was sitting next to him, waiting for an explanation he'd managed to misplace in the simple joy of seeing her again. Wondering if "I need you" sounded desperate, he opted to start slow.

"How was your hike?" *Jesus Christ, there was slow and then there was lame.*

Meg furrowed her brow, hands twisting in her lap. "What's this about, West?"

"I wanted to see you."

"Okay. I'm here and it's nice to see you too."

"Nice?"

"What do you want me to say? I liked spending time with you. Our lives are different."

He reached up and closed the divider behind Vince.

"I'm going a little nuts here, Meg." He swiped a hand across his face as if that could somehow get rid of the exhaustion of the past week. "You left me without a word."

She was going to say something, but he held up his hand. Now that the words were finally flowing, he wanted to get this out.

"You were right to leave. Everything says we're done working together. We're different and we should get the hell away from one another, but I tried for a week and I can't let go. You're probably going to kill me. Screw everything up in my going-through-the-motions world, and I'm holding on to you like my stupid life depends on it."

"What am I supposed to say to that?" She'd stopped wringing her hands.

"I have no idea, but I need you."

He took her hand and she didn't pull away. A good sign, he thought.

"You should have led with that."

"Yeah?"

"Yes. Always lead with 'I need you.' It's a knee weakener. Don't you watch movies?"

"This is serious, Meg. I can't sleep and now I take this fucking mental inventory while I'm lying in bed alone. Am I being the best man I can be? What should I be reading or where should I be shopping? It's exhausting and when I finally close my eyes, I see you. Christ, I'm not used to this. I have a movie to make. One of my lines this week was 'Babe, bring that sweet ass over here.' How the hell am I supposed to deliver that with any authority when I'm asking the hotel restaurant if their salmon is farm raised? I'm ruined."

A smile teased her lips. His first thought was to lean forward and pull her bottom lip between his teeth, but that was followed closely by the idea that she was mocking him. "You think this is funny?"

She shook her head. "I'm sure it is difficult. That line is, well, I imagine it's... challenging to deliver on a good day. Who speaks like that? And while we are on the subject, which actress is your 'babe' this time?" She held up her hand. "On second thought, I don't want to know. Oh God. Is there some nasty garage sex scene where you have strategic oil all over your bare chest?" She cringed.

West couldn't help but laugh. It felt good to be home, back with her. She made him feel and want to be the "best version of himself," as his mother frequently advised. He'd tried to stay away, do the smart thing, but he couldn't figure out how to turn any of it off. He didn't want to.

"My shirt is on," he said, still laughing.

"Well, that's a relief."

"Open, but on." He shrugged. "There might be some oil."

West pulled her in and kissed her as if his life depended on it. He was no longer sure it didn't.

He'd read this book on the Crimean War during his last year of college. Every other page had a word he didn't know, so he kept a dictionary handy. It was insane, but when he was finished, he walked around for weeks feeling like the smartest man in the world.

Meg was a hell of a lot more fun than that book, but there was nothing easy about starting a relationship. He kept kissing her, hoping his brain would shut off.

After pulling up to the alley of the hotel, they went through the same procedure getting up to the suite. He drew her close as soon as she closed the door, and if she'd have him, he wasn't letting go all weekend.

"Do we need to go over your lines?" she asked as her hands moved over his shoulders and laced behind his neck. "Maybe Towner could send up some dark eye shadow we could use for oil."

"You're hysterical. About finished?"

"Almost. Do you want to play lonely, frustrated car guy? Electric car, of course." Her eyes were mischievous and so damn sexy, West locked the door while he could still breathe.

"This will change things," Meg said as they stumbled toward the bedroom and began clawing at one another's clothes.

He nodded, and while her mind needed to figure out what that nod meant, her body had moved on to wanting him no matter the answer. He must have sensed her thoughts because after he pulled off everything but the cotton camisole she had underneath her hiking clothes, he stilled. The fact that he was reining himself in to make sure she was there with him somehow made her want to throw him to the floor even more.

West ran a finger along her shoulder, stopped at the strap of her camisole, and gently pushed it away. Meg enjoyed sex, but she could not remember feeling sexier than she did outside his bedroom door with her sweaty clothes strewn on the floor.

How did he manage to make her feel something that usually eluded her with a single touch? His expression was almost desperate—as if she alone could give him what he needed.

"I never watched these scenes in your movies," Meg said, once again unable to keep her thoughts to herself.

"Believe me, this has not been in any movie." His lips skimmed her neck. She wanted to let go, but now that they were about to fall into bed, or onto the floor, she wasn't sure she'd survive. She still had questions. Big shock. Turning wheels at the most inopportune times ran deep in the Jeffries family. Damn her parents for raising thinking daughters.

"I mean the love scenes. That may have been when I knew."

"Knew what?"

"Knew that I might want to get naked with you."

Laughter rumbled through his lips and hummed along her collarbone. West met her eyes. The heat in his gaze practically knocked her over.

"That was the moment, huh?"

"I guess. I didn't want to see some other gorgeous woman having sex with you. If I didn't want you in my bed, that wouldn't have bothered me, right?"

She felt some of the tension slip away. Honesty was great that way.

"Those scenes are more in line with synchronized swimming than sex, Meg."

"You know every actor says that, but you guys sure look like you're having a good time."

"Acting." He went back to kissing her neck, but she pulled away so she could think, which was silly. *Look at him*, she all but yelled at herself.

West release a slow moan as his head fell to her shoulder. "I'm not that good of an actor, Meg. You'd know if I were acting with you. It's my job. That's the only way I can explain it. I make a living in make-believe, but I have my own life when the cameras are off."

"Who's the actress?"

"Which one?"

Meg almost snorted a laugh. She hadn't thought of multiple. Wasn't this a franchise?

"That didn't sound good." He looked at her. "Let's bring this into your world."

"Yeah, good luck with that."

"When you take a picture of an animal, you connect with them through your camera, right?"

Meg nodded.

"But you're not touching them."

"Rarely."

"You can see them, get a reaction, but you are you and they stay where they are. It's understood."

"I suppose it is."

"Crystal Farr was in my last movie. She's married to a stuntman and they have three little boys. There were two men in the shower with us."

"The shower?"

West almost blushed. "Focus. Two men in the shower scene with us. Sean, he's the lead camera man for all the installments. He's well over six feet tall, hairy, and wears T-shirts with camera directions like 'Look Over Here' and 'A Little to the Left.'"

Meg chuckled.

"He's a good guy. You would like him. He was in there with us during what moviegoers went on to vote 'the hottest love scene of 2016.' In fact, I remember him joking that my wet ass cheek soaked his jeans when he went in for a close-up."

"You don't need to explain."

"No, I do." He tucked her hair behind her ear. Meg felt naïve and more vulnerable than she'd ever been in her life. "It's a weird way to make a living. Especially the shit I do."

"It's not shit."

"Aw, look at you. Did you want to join the fan club?"

"There's a fan club?"

"I'm not helping myself here." West rubbed his temple.

She was ruining the moment, but she couldn't help it. He was right. It was weird and while she hadn't watched the actual scenes, she'd seen pictures of him. Not the him she knew, but some other hot-as-hell guy. It was confusing.

"Yes. There's a fan club. Yes, women think they know me. They don't, and what I'm trying to say is the guy in the shower on-screen is not me. I don't make love to women that way. I'm a horrible driver, ask my family. And if I didn't have to project some image, I'd wear T-shirts for the rest of my life and probably have a beer gut. I get that you live in the real world and mine, is well... not that, but I am real, Meg. This"—he touched the side of her face—"is real."

She moved closer. "But it is part of you, a part I'm not asking you to be ashamed of or downplay. You're an actor and from what I saw, a good one. You're right, that guy isn't you. I'm a little intimidated, I suppose. Not by the pretend sex with women in front of the camera."

"Then what is it?"

"I don't know. It's kind of ironic. I photograph beautiful creatures all the time, but I'm at a safe distance. Like you said, they stay in their world and I return to mine. Touching you, having you touch me breaks that fourth wall a bit, you know?"

"Dear God, please take me to bed." He rested his forehead on hers.

She laughed.

"We can put the fourth wall back up if you need that, but I want you and I'm not sure how else to get us through that door and onto that bed."

Meg gave in to the sensations racing through her and decided there were no more questions. She was going to sleep with him. If it turned out to be a mistake, she would pick herself up and move on.

"I should probably warn you since you're mostly experienced in pretending to have sex," she said. "I can get kind of wild."

"I believe that." He followed her lead as she opened the bedroom door.

"I enjoy sex."

"There is a God."

She laughed again. That was twice in less than fifteen minutes. It didn't matter how long she had him or where this—whatever *this* was—went. She was falling in love with him while he still had his jeans on, so by the time those hit the floor, her heart and her body were not turning back.

Chapter Eighteen

Meg was in nothing but her underwear and West almost fell to his knees. He was the one nervous now, so through a thick haze of lust, he managed to find his sense of humor. "Underwear this time."

"Barely," she said, running her fingers along the thin pieces at her hips. She grabbed him by the front of his T-shirt, pulled it off, and threw it to the floor. As they moved closer to the bed, West noticed a scar on her side and ran his finger along it. Her body tensed and her hands stilled on his bare chest, which was a shame.

"Barbed wire," Meg whispered. "It was stupid."

"And *you're* intimidated?" He leaned down to kiss the scar and slid her underwear to the floor. "I want to hear the barbed wire story, but first..." He filled his hands with her body. Meg's eyes closed and West imagined there weren't many people allowed this close to her scars.

He got rid of his boxers and took her to bed. Their bodies at first shivered in the cool sheets but quickly warmed as he traveled over her. Skin so soft beneath the smell of coconut and the salty outdoors, that by the time he touched another scar on her thigh, he'd lost the ability to think.

He brought her up gently, and when he couldn't take it for one more touch, he grabbed protection off the nightstand and slid into heat as her body rose to meet him. Her hands moved over him as if she sensed every need and met it with more than he could have imagined. He took his time, desperate for one more sigh, but when his name fell off her lips, he completely lost his mind.

There would always be the physical part of sex. A release in being stripped down and yearning for a touch, but Meg was a mind and a body West had never experienced before. When he took them both over for the last time, he knew he would never be able to go back to one without the other and all the questions that came with it. What he told her in the car was true: she'd ruined him.

⤙⤚

Meg lay across his chest hours later, running her hand up the bend of his arm. No tattoos. She wasn't sure why she was surprised. West's body was a work of art, part of how he made his living. She supposed tattoos defined a person too much for make-believe. Glancing out the bedroom window, she knew it was Friday and the sun was still up, but for the first time, she had no sense of time and didn't want anything other than the man beneath her.

"Barbed wire?" he asked.

She nodded into his chest. "It was a calf."

"A cow?"

"A baby moose. We were in Alaska and when we spotted him, he was tangled up in barbed wire."

West touched her hair, held her to him as if he sensed her pulling away.

"We're supposed to leave things as they are. It's an unspoken rule. Well, a rule yelled at a photographer when she steps over her professional boundaries."

"Would he have made it out without your help?"

"No."

"Then how were you supposed to leave him there?" His chest rose and fell.

"It wasn't my place. I should have left him and if he died, that was his path."

West leaned up to look at her. "That's bullshit. Barbed wire isn't natural, someone put it there."

"That was my argument."

"After that nasty gash in your side, did he get away?" He lay back down.

"He did, but his leg looked broken. He probably didn't make it, although we did see him hobble back to his mother."

"So, if he did die, he wasn't alone."

"True."

"I think that's incredible." His chest tightened when he leaned up again, as if he needed to see her.

"Well, you are alone in that opinion. The guys I was with reported me, and let's just say my assignments dried up for a while."

"Isn't compassion part of your job? If you don't connect on some level, can you truly capture them?"

Thinking back to when she told him it was only fair if he was dense, Meg realized the universe smiled down on Westin Drake because the man was far from stupid.

"We do connect on some level, but as observers. We do not participate."

"Sounds cold."

"It's for their survival. We are not part of their world, and they can't ever become dependent or comfortable. It's damaging."

His hand stroked up and down her back.

"Did you ever see *Old Yeller?*"

Meg shook her head, finding it hard to concentrate on anything other than his touch.

"Don't."

"Okay." She climbed up his chest until they were eye to eye. "Is the acting that bad?"

"It's not the acting. The dog dies. Worst movie of all time. My dad loves it. Calls *Old Yeller* the best movie ever made." He scrunched his face in dramatic disagreement. Meg sat up, taking a part of the comforter with her.

"One afternoon, I think we were off school for the summer and he was in charge while my mom was at work."

"What does your mom do?"

"She's a bookkeeper. Works for the only accounting firm in historic Petaluma. My dad is a contractor, so his hours are more flexible."

Meg nodded and tried not to look surprised. It was a stretch for her mind to imagine that the Westin Drake of big billboards and magazines grew up in a neighborhood, let alone that he had two hardworking parents. She'd imagined him eternally polished, born to a glossy family, but that was silly now that she was next to him in bed. He'd been more than a polished picture even when she'd first seen him in the conference room.

"So, we came in for lunch after riding our bikes. Kraft singles and sausage on crackers, guaranteed. It's the only lunch my dad knows how to make. I must have been eight or nine. We were all ready to head back out when Dad decides we should watch a movie. Why are you smiling?"

"I just am. Go on."

"He tells us it's about a dog. We had two dogs at the time, so we were all psyched. Popcorn, the dogs next to us on the couch. It was a good day to be a kid."

"I bet."

West shook his head. "Two hours later we were all bawling. Not a dry eye. We kept doing that guy thing where you look up or away with your eyes wide, hoping the tears will disappear before they fall."

"Girls do that too."

"Nothing worked. It was a disaster. My mom came home and we were still crying."

Meg laughed but covered her mouth. "Sorry, it's not funny."

He pulled her under him. "It is funny now, but at the time, man it was rough."

She looked up at a face she'd never seen before. His guard was gone. No lights, no camera, and no paparazzi. It was intoxicating, and she could tell by the warm creases at his eyes and the soft curve of his mouth that happy was his natural state.

Meg had known people who were miserable and faked happiness. West was the opposite. He layered indifference or polish over his happy. She'd been given a secret, a full view of his happy. He kissed her, pulled them under the covers, and she felt a deep need to keep the man behind the glossy finish safe. They would need to leave the Tony Bennett bed eventually, but for right now she held on.

Chapter Nineteen

Meg woke to West watching her sleep and stroking the hair off her face. The weight of his stare was that of someone having a complete conversation all by himself. She pulled up on her elbows and asked, "What's on your mind?"

"You."

"Why aren't you asleep?" She looked down and noticed he was on top of the covers and fully dressed in jeans and a button-up shirt. "Why are you dressed?"

"Disappointed?"

"Incredibly." Meg pulled one of the pillows close. "I had another dream about you."

"Yeah?" He leaned in and softly kissed her neck. "Was I wearing a poncho?"

She swatted his shoulder and then kissed him gently. The smell of warm morning man caressed her from head to toe. She held back the comforter and motioned for him to come back to bed.

"It's still dark out."

"I want to take you somewhere," he said.

She yawned. "What time is it?"

"Four thirty. We need to get going."

"Can't we go back to sleep and order up pancakes or cinnamon buns much later?"

He shook his head and Meg finally sat up, still wrapped in the warmth of down feathers. "Please don't tell me you're an early-morning runner. If you are, I am no longer your BFF and I will not be joining you."

"Get up," he said, playfully pulling at the comforter Meg clutched like a child who didn't want to dress for school.

"No. I want to go back to bed."

"You don't. There are some jeans and a sweatshirt right here." He patted the foot of the bed. "All you have to do is put these and your hiking boots on. I promise it will be worth it."

Meg crawled forward and lifted the clothes. "Where did you get these? Oh God." She sat back on her knees in animated shock. "Do you have a little store for women when they come over and you rip their clothes off?"

West laughed and dropped her boots by the bed. "Yes. You've figured me out."

She lay back down, wondering where anyone needed to go at four thirty in the morning.

"Towner bought them for me. Don't ask how the woman works her miracles. She's the concierge and you can meet her later. But we are wasting time. Get up, or I'll have to carry you there."

"I am not a morning person."

"How can that be? Don't you capture the best shots at sunrise?"

Meg finally climbed out of the bed. She thought about wrapping the sheet around her body, but he'd visited every curve multiple times last night. There was no point in being modest now. Besides, she felt satisfied and sexy. She didn't want to cover that up.

"Yes, but animals have the decency to wait for the sun." Meg walked to the bathroom.

"You sure look like a morning person." He pulled her back and kissed her stomach.

Mischievous eyes looked up at her, and the last thing Meg wanted to do was get dressed.

"You'll be a morning person after this. I promise." His hands slid from her body.

"What is with you and the confidence all the time?"

He took her hand and led her inside the bathroom.

"Oh, I'll bet there's an assortment of toothbrushes in here too." She was teasing him and so happy it didn't feel real.

"Only one, but it's pink since you're a girl. Please hurry up. There's a car waiting. Think of poor Vince who had to get up early to drive your perfect ass all over town. Now, get in there, you, before I lose control of myself and you ruin my surprise." She breathed into her hand and rolled her eyes. No one had good morning breath.

"Are we walking?" she asked, following him back out of the bathroom.

He turned her back toward the room. "Go."

"Fine."

Meg brushed her teeth, got dressed, and then sat on the couch to tie her boots. Whoever Towner was, she had an excellent eye. The jeans fit her perfectly. Just as the bed beckoned her back, West threw a puffy black jacket at her. Resigned to meet the crisp morning, she took a baseball hat off the hook by the door and pulled her hair through the back.

"That was quick," he said.

"What can I say, I'm all about quick. There'd better be coffee and breakfast on this adventure. I'd hate to scratch your pretty eyes out."

"There will be." He tipped the brim of the hat back and pulled her in for a kiss that was starting to feel familiar. She knew his taste now and the slow campfire burn of his heat. As her knees began to buckle, West pulled back and put her cap back into place. She was sure her face was completely giving her away and there was no point in hiding her feelings from him anymore. She was trying to formulate something to say when he took her hand and pulled her into the service elevator.

Vince dropped them off at the entrance to the Golden Gate Bridge, and before Meg could mention that the bridge was closed this early, the arm of the gate rose and he drew her into the tendrils of fog as they twisted through iconic red steel. She had to remind herself they were in the middle of a city. Apart from the occasional car horn, it was silent. She could see nothing but West's arm and shoulder as they moved through the fog and farther onto the bridge.

Meg instinctively reached for her camera and realized she had nothing. She couldn't remember the last time she'd been caught without her camera. Sliding her hand into the pocket of West's coat, she could now hear the water below them. It wasn't waves or lapping as she had noticed before. There was a rumble below them, as if the bay wasn't a morning person either and the fog was carefully stirring the current awake.

Meg guessed they were about a half of a mile onto the bridge when West stopped. She still couldn't see him and was reminded of when she noticed the fog from his agency's office window. It seemed so intimidating at the time, but now that she was in the middle of it, instead of watching from a distance, it was simple and so beautiful. Moving her hands through the condensation, she heard West's voice as he materialized in front of her. She wiped her face, damp with moisture, and wrapped her arms around his neck.

"How did you do this? It's closed."

"There are perks."

"To being one of the sexiest men alive?"

"Look at you waking up. No. Perks to being friendly. Ryder let us in. He was a crowd extra when we shot some scenes on the bay for the last *Throttle*."

"And he works the bridge?"

West nodded and touched his lips to hers, as if he couldn't wait another minute.

"We became friends," he said, easing out of the kiss.

He played with a strand of her damp hair.

"How long do we have?" She turned to keep walking but he held her in place.

"The bridge opens at seven."

She pulled his arm and West finally budged. The fog grew even thicker as they continued. Meg glanced over at him a few times and could barely make out the sharp lines of his face. It was as if she was pulling him deeper into a thick forest instead of standing on a famous bridge. Still so quiet and unclear, it reminded her of watching photo paper float in the developer. Everything starts white and then the exposure appears through the ripples of water. About a mile onto the bridge, she stopped this time.

"Thank you."

He held her without a word, the steady rhythm of his chest practically in sync with the water below.

"This is your best adventure by far. I grew up in this city and never saw it, or at least I've never noticed the details. I was missing the corners, so thank you."

He rested his chin on top of her head. "Yeah well, I live for the corners. You're welcome. Forgive me for getting you out of bed early?"

"I do, but after you feed me. I would be interested in an encore on that extremely large bed in the Tony Bennett Suite." She took his hand and continued walking.

"Well, he did write the song," West said.

"How does that one go again?" Meg looked coyly over her shoulder.

"Nice try. Everyone knows the song."

"Do they? Because I can't seem to remember."

"If I sing it while we finish walking, will you stay in the Tony Bennett bed with me until Sunday?"

She nodded as the end of the bridge came into sight. "You know music really... motivates me."

"Is that so?"

West, whose hair was now soaked and sexier than anything she'd seen in his movies, belted out a rather impressive performance of "I Left My Heart in San Francisco," complete with snapping.

Her sides hurt from laughing by the time Vince opened the car door.

He was in love with her. It was the simplest and most complicated thought all rolled into one. He'd assumed he had it all figured out when he was waiting outside her apartment, but he didn't have a clue. Meg naked and giving a part of herself to him almost destroyed him. And when she'd said she was motivated by music, the heat in her eyes was enough for him to break out in song. Imagining her back in his bed, panting his name, had him dropping his fork with a clatter while they finished up breakfast.

Meg crooked her head to the side. "You okay?"

West grinned and picked up his fork. How was he supposed to answer that question? *No, Meg, now that you mention it, I'm not okay. Every time I look at you I want to crawl farther inside.* Should he say that in the middle of a busy diner? It was sure as hell how he felt. He dropped his fork again and went to stand but banged his leg on the table instead. The dishes jumped.

"We need to go." Tossing some money on the table, he heard the faint murmur of voices. *Shit.*

He'd been so wrapped up in wanting to peel those jeans off her body that he hadn't even noticed the sun was up and they were now surrounded by people.

Meg was still sitting and smiling up at him until her eyes drifted below his waistband. She dipped a finger in the syrup that had pooled on her plate and sucked her finger into her mouth. West managed to stand as the rumbling of an audience he could feel watching them grew louder. Camera phones were now out and flashing while Meg continued her demonstration of sugar porn.

"Time to go," he said, a little more urgent this time.

"Oh, sorry. Should I leave the tip?" she asked as she stood slowly.

Yeah, she was screwing with him now.

"I should probably use the restroom before we go," she said, wide-eyed and innocent as a smirk teased her lips.

Don't look at the lips, idiot.

"Excuse me, are you—" West heard over his left shoulder and held up his hand to stop whichever standard question was about to invade his space.

"I am, but we were just leaving."

Meg pursed her lips. "I'm sure we have time for a—"

"Oh, for crying out loud." West hauled her over his shoulder like a sack of potatoes and the diner erupted in applause. It could have been a movie scene, but usually the heroes in films weren't frustrated beyond reason.

He deposited a now crying with laughter Meg into the backseat of the car and all but pounced on her as Vince closed the door and drove back to the hotel.

"Oh," Meg finally said through her laughter. "You are going to be in big trouble with Hannah when those photos pop up on the Internet."

He kissed her neck, his hand sliding under the damp layers of clothing.

"Do you think you'll be scolded for not being polite?" Her eyes were hooded with lust now.

West raised the divider to close off Vince and dove under her sweatshirt. As his mouth gratefully closed around her breast, he heard nothing but the labored panting of her breath as she arched into him and her hands dug into the leather of the seat.

No wonder Tony left his heart in San Francisco. If West didn't get her back to bed, he was sure his heart was going to jump right off the bridge.

Chapter Twenty

Meg thought she was dreaming again, but the persistent knock on the door finally woke her up. It took a minute before she remembered where she was and whose warm body was stretched out next to hers. A smile slid across her face as images from last night floated through her memory. The knocking continued so she put on West's shirt, cliché she knew, but it was right there and still smelled like him.

"Who is it?" she asked.

"Room service for Mr. Drake."

Meg should have noticed the peephole in the door, should have woken West before he was startled awake by the noise and forced to charge from the bedroom in an attempt to keep her from being humiliated, but none of that had happened. Instead, still in a daze of untouchable warm and wonderful and with her stomach growling at the thought of breakfast, Meg opened the door. There were no pancakes.

Pops of flash. Yelling.

As she tried to close the door, a hand blocked it while the cameras continued clicking. West was behind her by this point, yelling back something she couldn't quite make out as one arm struggled to push the door closed and the other pulled her back behind him. Meg blinked, trying to restore her focus as West snatched the last camera from a hand that would not retreat and threw it into the hallway. He slammed the door. Both hands were on the now-closed door, his chest heaving.

"Are you okay?" he asked, not looking at her.

Meg stumbled back and fell into the chair. "Yes. I'm... what was that?"

"My life," he mumbled, rubbing the back of his neck as he grabbed his phone.

"Good morning. I'm sorry to bother you, but the piranhas somehow made it to my floor again. There were at least five of them. Where the hell is security?"

West glanced over at Meg, his face now placid and resigned as he disappeared into the bedroom and returned with a shirt on.

"Yeah, we're fine. No, she's staying."

She commanded herself not to be scared as hell, but the truth was probably all over her face. She had been in some dangerous situations before, but nothing could have prepared her for what happened. Closing her eyes, she took in her first confrontation with the piranhas, as West called them. She'd noticed them from a safe distance for the first time after she'd met West for lunch early on in their collaboration. As West paced the floor talking at varying degrees of frustration, it was hard to believe they'd come so far from that day.

Meg had been nervous at that meeting, not because of the photographers, but being with him had been so new back then. She closed her eyes at the memory, which was already a simpler time.

"Where do you source your chicken?" she had asked the waiter at Brook's Bistro, a restaurant West had recommended. It had a back room too.

"Sorry?" the tall, young man said.

"I'm looking at the chicken salad, but I need to know where you get your chicken."

"I'll... ask." The guy backed away slowly.

Meg returned to her menu. If the restaurant had ethical sourcing, the waiter would have known. She would stick with vegetables.

"Is that not a good sign?" West had asked, genuinely curious.

"He'll come back and say something like Sunvale or Brixmill. Massive farms with disgusting practices."

The waiter returned with their drinks. "Okay, I asked our manager and he said we utilize a network of farms throughout the area all under the umbrella of"—he glanced down at his pad—"Sunvale."

West coughed, but Meg heard the undertone of laughter and she remembered wondering for a minute if he was laughing at her. Even if he had been, she was used to it. While the environment was now trendy, the practices and pieces that made up a healthier planet weren't exactly mainstream. If caring for the earth had hit the majority, fast food would have been out of business years ago.

She remembered smiling at the waiter. It wasn't his fault. "Thank you. I'll have the mixed greens and the vegetable soup."

"Can I get you tofu on your salad?" The waiter had kind eyes and an arrow tattoo on his forearm. She'd made him nervous, and that certainly wasn't her intention. She simply had questions.

"Oh, no thanks, I'm not a fan of tofu."

"So you're not a vegetarian?"

"No. I limit my meat."

"I gotta know since you're the only person that has asked about our meat. Is Sunvale bad? Like, was that the wrong answer?"

"Their practices are not to my liking."

"Cool. That's cool. Hey, do you have a boyfriend?"

West had snickered, not bothering with the cough cover that time. Meg barely knew him back then, and the added awkwardness of being asked out by the waiter had her head spinning.

"Sorry?" she asked.

"Are you dating anyone?"

"No."

"I get off at—"

West, who had been quietly observing, took off his sunglasses and put his baseball hat on the table, probably to save the guy some embarrassment. Looking back on it now, especially considering the ordeal she had just experienced, it was a larger gesture than she realized.

"Oh, holy shit!" The waiter had looked around, making sure his outburst didn't cost him his job. "You're... wow, are you her..."

"BFF? Yes, I sure am."

A sound, possibly meant to be a laugh, escaped the guy, who began to jump and dance around. That was the first time she'd witnessed West's celebrity other than a picture or request for his autograph. The waiter became completely unhinged simply at the sight of him. It was unreal.

As they left the restaurant, West pointed to a cluster of photographers across the street.

"Who? What are they?" she had asked.

"Good question. They are a special kind of wild animal that has no boundaries. They're predators in bad leather jackets."

"There is no reason for them to take pictures of me," she'd said.

West had remained quiet, giving her time to understand the connection.

"They think we're together, so I'm fair game too." She had leaned close to the window as they drove past. "Wow, that's a Canon CN-E lens. How much money do these guys make?"

"A lot."

"So I'm the animal now? All from one afternoon and a peck on the cheek?" Meg had asked, so simple she realized now.

"I'm sorry," West had said, his sincerity sprinkled with the same sense of powerlessness he seemed to have now as he was wrapping up his conversation with his security team, Meg guessed.

Months ago, she had been bewildered by the interest and West had warned her, but she had not processed a few guys hanging out across the street as threatening.

Now, as West sat next to her, she realized she was shaking. Those same photographers, most of them grown men, had tried to push their way into his private room. Meg was trained never to make contact with her subjects, let alone scare the life out of them. Obviously, not all photographers played by the same rules.

∿

Dealing with paparazzi was nothing new, but finding them that close to her had made his blood boil in a way he hadn't known was possible. When he saw her in nothing but his shirt trying to keep them out, he could have killed someone.

Towner said his security guys had caught them in the lobby and were calling the cops. They'd swiped a key card from behind the front desk. West's stomach curdled. This wasn't simply a matter of a public life anymore; it was harassment and ten times worse when they were after someone he loved.

He planned every moment with his family to shield them, but there had been a few times the assholes managed to get to them too. Fortunately, his family possessed a thick skin and a sense of humor, but Meg had looked terrified, and an apology seemed less than adequate as he took a seat next to her.

"Are you sure you're okay?" he asked again.

"I'm fine. I have a scar from barbed wire, remember?" She kissed him gently, but her hands were still trembling. He took them in his and searched for something to say.

"It won't always be like this."

"What does that mean?"

"The media is fickle. At some point, the photographers will move on. I have had easier times, months even when no one gave a shit what I did, but I think things are heating up now that we've started filming."

"I understand," she said, but he could tell her mind was racing, probably questioning why she'd let him back into her life. He couldn't blame her, but he needed to find a way to keep her with him.

A knock on the door caused Meg to jump, and his heart squeezed as he looked through the peephole and opened the door for Towner and Graham, one of his room service attendants, pushing two breakfast trays.

West shook Graham's hand and tipped him before he wheeled the cart back out into the hallway. Towner stayed behind.

"Meg Jeffries, this is Towner. She asked me to call her Alice when we first met, which wasn't an option unless I wanted to hear a lecture from my mom. There's no Mrs., Miss, or Ms. allowed, so we've settled on Towner."

"Like Madonna," Towner said, extending her small hand to Meg.

She was surprised to find Towner was a woman, West could tell, but Meg took her hand. Everyone fell in love with Towner eventually.

"It is lovely to meet you, Alice."

Towner's eyes sparkled behind her glasses. She was wearing the green ones today. "Oh, I like her."

"Me too," West said with a look of need Towner appeared to understand.

"I apologize for what happened this morning, Meg. Those little shits will stop at nothing for a payday. We have changed all the access keys, per protocol. Westin has said you are staying for a while, but he's used to this craziness. Did you want me to arrange for safe transportation home for you? I need to let you know there are still photographers outside the hotel."

This was the moment. West was certain Meg would say "thanks, but no thanks" to him and take Towner up on her offer. Right as he was preparing to let her go, Meg gave Towner a hug.

"Thank you for your concern, but I'm fine. Nothing happened and honestly, people have endured far worse than a few pushy photographers."

Towner asked a few questions about Meg's work and declared that she loved TED talks and would be sure to watch for Meg's. After another hug, West walked her to the door.

"Why don't I ever get a hug?" he asked Towner.

"Because you're a boy."

She gave him a quick hug and a pat on the back. "There, that's all you're getting for a while. Look at me," she said as their eyes locked by the open door.

"I am. The green frames really make your eyes pop."

She swatted him. "I'm serious." She lowered her voice to a whisper and West almost laughed but knew better. "I don't know what your plans are with that young lady, but I will throw you out on your tuchus if you don't marry this one."

West's eyes grew wide. "Okay, let's take things one step at a time, insane matchmaker."

"Her photographs have been on the cover of the mother-of-all photography magazines."

He grinned, almost forgetting the situation that brought her to his room. "I might have heard that. Hey, I didn't know you were Jewish, Towner."

"Of course I'm Jewish," she exclaimed as if he should be able to pick that out without the help of the word "tuchus." "This isn't about me. I'm telling you that a man only gets one of those women. Lock that down."

West couldn't hold the laughter back this time. He promised to give her advice serious consideration and closed the door behind her. Meg was curled up on the couch in what West would now refer to as "their" comforter. In fact, the day he left the Fairmont, he was taking that thing with him.

"Look what I found," Meg said, clicking the television remote. The screen filled with the opening credits for *Full Throttle: First Gear*.

"Oh, will you look at the time."

Meg grinned and carried the two breakfast trays to the coffee table. "Oh no you don't, mister. It is Sunday and we are hiding out from the bad guys. I think that calls for a movie marathon."

West plopped himself down on the couch next to her, reaching for the remote while she was distracted by food, but failed when she pushed it between the cushions on her side.

"There is no way in hell I am watching my movies." He folded his arms across his chest, as if that would somehow give him authority.

Meg stuck a piece of croissant in his mouth and he turned to mush again.

"Just one. I haven't seen the first one and you look so young. I heard you have a fanny pack in this one."

"Where did you hear that?"

"Clay told me."

"What? When?"

"The first night I came to your suite."

"I'm employing all my covert ops to make sure you're brought up safely, and you're chatting with Clay, who by the way never talks, about *Full Throttle* and my 2005 wardrobe disasters?"

Meg nodded and ate the rest of the croissant.

"Unbelievable."

She shrugged and crossed her legs like a kid getting ready for movie day. West was giving serious thought to never leaving the room again. He had everything he needed right on the couch. His family could come and visit. Whatever it took to keep her from the ugly parts of his success. Eager to return to where they left off, West questioned whether the scum that had barged into their weekend would eventually ruin the happiness dancing in her eyes. He couldn't let that happen.

"We don't have to watch the first one. I've only seen two. There are several others to choose from. You can pick. How 'bout that?"

West let out a breath, torn between the agony of watching himself on-screen and keeping her in a playful mood. He closed his eyes and gave in.

"Fine."

"Yay!" Meg bounced on the couch, the sarcasm thick. "Which one?"

He realized he didn't often say the titles of his movies out loud. There was a reason. "Let's go with the second one. There are some gorgeous scenes in Italy." He poured them both coffee and grabbed a bagel off the trays.

"Would that be *Downshift?*" she asked in a voice that was a little more sarcastic than peppy.

West nodded and dimmed the lights. She scooted close to him and he realized he would watch anything if it meant being with her a few more hours.

"Lock that one down," he heard Towner's voice in his head. He would give it his best shot, he thought as music filled the room and he cringed as the movie began.

Chapter Twenty-One

"I liked it," Meg said a couple of hours later.

West shrugged, and she was again surprised that the cocky persona she'd seen strutting around and driving a modified Nissan that shot flames out the back was the same guy on the couch next to her. She leaned over and kissed him. When he pulled her close, she backed up, knowing if he took her back to the Tony Bennett bed, she would never want to leave again.

But you will leave, her mind whispered. They both would. He had a flight to catch in a few hours and Meg had to pick up her dress for the wedding. As West stood to put their dishes back on the room service trays, life began to creep into their slumber party weekend. She could practically see the responsibility return to his shoulders, between his eyes.

"When did you start acting?" she asked, needing to know why he put up with all of it.

"I was one of the T-birds in *Grease* my junior year in high school." He grabbed both napkins off the coffee table. "I auditioned on a dare. We did four shows and when that audience clapped, I was hooked. It was the way Boyd described smoking. He'd lit a cigarette in a parking lot with his friends, and a week later was buying two packs at a time. The audience energy, the thrill of a live show was heady. I took acting over the summer and during senior year. I was in three other plays."

"Why didn't you stay in theater?"

"I tried. I promised my mom I wouldn't move all the way to New York, so I went to LA for college. Eventually commercials were faster than monologues and voice and movement. I guess I took the easy way out. If you ask my brothers, that's a pattern with me."

"So geography was Plan B?"

"Yeah. My parents called it a backup plan. I remember being incredibly insulted that they even thought I needed one, but if my son said he wanted to be an actor, I'd do the same thing."

"Mine was a teaching certificate. My parents made me promise too."

West sat back down. "By my second year, I didn't mind. I enjoyed geography, but now that I think about it, it's not much of a Plan B."

"Um, could you see me as a high school teacher?"

"No." He held her legs on his lap.

"I guess it's a good thing our Plan A worked out."

"I guess." West ran his hands along her calves and seemed lost in thought.

"Are you close?" Their eyes met and West was back from wherever he'd gone. "With your brothers?"

He nodded. "I mean as close as brothers can be. Weird that we're both the youngest, don't you think?"

Meg agreed and they continued on like that through another pot of coffee and eventually sandwiches ordered from room service. They both stuck with the vegetarian since the poor room service attendant didn't even bother to ask his manager. He was so thrown by the "where do you source" question that he came right out and said he "had no clue." Meg had to appreciate that a guy shuffling dozens of orders didn't have the luxury of worrying about their meat. It wasn't his job. West agreed to talk to the manager and Meg left it at that.

Hours went by and right when it seemed they'd learned enough about each other for one day, one of them would insist on another question. They both knew what was happening, could feel the looming inevitability of the real world.

"Okay, I know that you don't eat berries because of the seeds and that your father broke his wrist when you insisted that he hang a tire from the tree in your backyard, but I don't know how you started taking pictures. I think that's an important one."

They were now lying on opposite sides of the couch with their legs making a bridge between them.

"I... well, I started taking pictures of the crazy things I was doing. I used to go rock climbing and hiking, bungee jumping, cliff diving, you name it. If it had an edge to it, I was there. So, I started that way and then I kept pushing myself. I wanted to do more, see more. Somewhere along the way, it became less about me and more about animals. They are the ultimate thrill seekers."

"Neither of you does well in captivity," he said as if the parallel had occurred to him.

Meg didn't have an answer and he was certainly one to talk—it wasn't as if his life was moving anywhere near a picket fence. The guy lived in a hotel. Meg let her legs drop, needing to rip the discomfort of leaving off like a Band-Aid.

"I need to get going," she said, swallowing a growing lump in her throat. An hour's worth of questions ago, she was ready to move into one of those cute little historic homes near Berkeley and spend every morning with him.

That was never going to happen. And while she talked a tough game after the photographers barged through the door, Meg wasn't sure if she could ever get used to the bubble of his life. When West came up behind her and wrapped her in his arms, the lump in her throat grew. She wished Westin Drake had stayed in theater. At least then they'd stand a chance.

"We are blowing up a bridge on set next week. Who's excited?" he said into her neck.

Meg laughed and turned to find him smiling at her. That need to protect him, to love him despite the obvious complications, bloomed in her heart again. *The heart wants what the heart wants*. Meg remembered that quote hung in Annabelle's room when they were growing up, so someone important must have said it.

❦

"Do you want to be my date for my sister's wedding next weekend?" Meg blurted out as if she might change her mind. West wondered which of the "we could do this" scenarios she was running through her head. He had a whole list of his own, but after the morning they'd had, the list was getting smaller.

"I... don't think that's a good idea. It's their day," he said as carefully as he knew how to be.

"It *is* their day and I can bring a date. I want you with me."

He hesitated and saw whatever minute leap of hope she had that he was simply a man and she was simply a woman slip between them.

"Can I see you after the wedding?" he asked as a pathetic consolation.

"Where? Here in the Tony Bennett Suite or huddled in the backseat of a car?"

Here we go.

"There are other things we can do. What do you want to do, Meg?" He tried steady and controlled since she was about to launch into the "none of this is fair" portion of the weekend. But also because his heart was begging him to buy an SUV, text Hannah on the way out of town, and take her to some small remote place until they found some other guy to take over his public life. He needed to maintain control.

"I'd like to go to the farmers market or the Sunday Fun Days they have down by the Wharf. I've heard Kite Park is fun. I want to get on a cable car at eight in the morning."

West said nothing, so she went into the bedroom to grab her things.

"You can do all of those things. Are you sure you even want to? You'll be leaving soon too, Meg. Don't put this all on me."

"I want to go to my sister's wedding with my—"

"Your what?"

"My boyfriend. Isn't that what you are, West?"

He was still facing her, but he closed his eyes in resignation that he would never be something so ordinary ever again.

Meg threw her bag over her arm and put her hand on the door. "Forget it. This was a fun weekend. Thank you." She opened the door and West lunged forward.

"What are you doing? Let me get my shoes on and I'll drive you home."

"Drive me? Or ride with me?"

"Come on. This isn't fair. I haven't pretended to be something I'm not. You knew what you were getting into before you climbed into my bed."

That came out harsher than he intended, but he wasn't sure where this was coming from. Her work with him was done too. She'd be jet-setting around the world in a matter of weeks. Neither one of them had normal lives, so he was trying to figure out why with his life, as ridiculous as it was, he needed to be the bad guy. He loved her, not that he was ready to share that yet. He hadn't pursued this alone, but he must be missing something—she seemed to want more than either of them had to give.

"I'm sorry. You're right. It's frustrating."

While that response was unexpected and far too easy, West took it. He'd be up to his ass in pyrotechnics by tomorrow. He'd take easy if Meg was willing to give it for now.

"I know, and I'm sorry too. Let me take you home."

She nodded and seemed defeated, which made his chest hurt. What the hell were they doing?

Chapter Twenty-Two

West was physically on set by nine o'clock Monday morning, but his heart was in San Francisco. He was beginning to think it was some cruel joke that he lived in the Tony Bennett Suite.

After his flight landed, he'd texted Meg but received no response. She was pissed and nothing he could say would change that, so he stopped trying. Since the thought of losing her was not something he was prepared to deal with on four hours of sleep, he was three espresso shots into his morning and standing in a makeup trailer while one of the makeup interns shaded and dusted his nipples with an airbrush that looked like it should hurt.

"The fucking bridge will blow up today and it will blow up correctly, or I'll have someone's ass, is that understood?" Gary bellowed after the third squib failed to ignite, instead causing a sparkler parade rather than the massive explosion following the car chase that would end the movie. They'd started with the end scene because it was massive. Nothing was filmed in sequential order on action films. West had learned that after only a few days on his first movie set.

"I'm finding it difficult to follow Nick's character arc on this shoot schedule," he'd said to Gary eleven years ago. It had only been his second time directing a blockbuster. He had more hair back then and wasn't quite the eternally pissed of guy who only minutes ago reduced the explosives team to a group of first-year ballerinas. Although, even back then he had bite and a sense of humor.

When West had expressed his character concerns, Gary had pulled him aside and told him exactly what he could do with his character arc. West had been stunned into silence, made worse when Gary refused to talk to him for the rest of the day on set. The next morning, three dozen pansies were delivered to his trailer. The note simply read—Good luck with your arc. Lesson learned. West had not asked Gary another question, apart from clarifying intent and blocking, in eleven years.

West had been drawn to the creative freedom acting allowed. It only took a few years before he'd become part of a machine that was the furthest thing from creative or freedom he'd ever known. After the fourth movie, West had some box office clout and Hannah agreed to get him some smaller independent films to work on over the summer. He did a couple and loved the experience but soon learned it was difficult for people to see him as anyone other than Nick Shot.

Something shifted inside of him when he signed on for the fifth installment and he'd been resolved ever since. The money he made with *Full Throttle* helped finance his brothers' brewery, paid off the home he grew up in, and funded a new traumatic brain injury center at San Francisco Memorial Hospital in honor of his Aunt Margaret. *Full Throttle* had been good to him and the people he loved. It wasn't creative, not what he'd planned for his career, but it was his job. Over the years, the movies had come to define him a bit more than he liked, but back home he was a success. A shining star on the McNaughton family tree. West wasn't sure he could ask for much more than that.

So he understood the pressure a guy in Gary's position was under. The *Full Throttle* franchise wasn't about compelling stories or character development. It was about money and marketing. He needed his actors to look good, not get hurt, and focus on the spectacle. When the third installment failed to hit number one opening weekend, there was talk of finding another director who could deliver. Gary pulled off record returns with the fourth installment and had been a demanding ass ever since. West was all right with that. He supposed they both had bills to pay.

"Drake, I need angles and your stunt dummy seems to be taking a powder break. Do you mind?"

West put his T-shirt on over his airbrushed nipples and headed to work.

It was time to buy a house, he thought hanging from a bar placed in front of a green screen. He had no clue where the thought came from, but he wasn't sure what kind of a guy lived in a hotel either. Dropping one hand and his head to his right shoulder as instructed, he had another thought that almost caused him to lose his grip.

He should go to the wedding with her. She'd asked him and before he'd even realized the leap of faith that must have taken for her, he became wrapped up in his own self-centered world. When had he developed such a fear of everything?

"Drake, both hands back on. And can you pull up a few times?" Gary called out. "I've got a million-dollar-a-minute actor hanging here, moron, do I need to come over there and film the movie too?" Gary said as the guy on camera three shook his head.

West smirked as he pulled his weight up and dropped back down as instructed. He'd have to thank his trainer again. There was no way in hell he'd have the discipline to develop this strength on his own. West's thoughts drifted back to fear. He wasn't about to be a victim of his own life. They were shooting through the night on Friday. He could leave by eight on Saturday morning and sleep on the plane. He could get there in time to be her date for the wedding. No one was going to take his picture at a private reception, and if they did, so what? She wanted him there.

"You know what? You're an asshole."

You're right, West thought and then glanced up at Gary, who was standing next to West's stunt double. Doug, whose resemblance to West freaked him out a little, was finishing up a sandwich from craft service. Doug was the asshole.

"Drop, Drake. Your stunt dummy decided to show up to work," Gary said and redirected his attention to camera four.

Doug pounded West's fist and with one effortless jump was hanging in West's position.

Meg had said her sister was marrying a football coach. There might be security at the reception, or he could bring his own. Her life was just as important as his own and West was getting tired of explaining himself. That's why he'd told her he couldn't go. Of course he wanted to be there for her, to meet the family she so clearly loved.

Then there was that look in her eyes again, the one that hinted she might need him to be there. Lead with need, that's what she'd said. Christ, that look was haunting him, especially coming from Meg. She hung out with bears for a living. How was it possible she needed anything?

In all the years she'd been gone, the UC Berkeley Campus had barely changed, at least from what Meg could see of the outside. Anna wanted to meet her for lunch between her last class and a faculty meeting. Her sister, Middle Two as they all called her, was a Shakespeare professor when she wasn't obsessing over seating charts and helping Dane plan their honeymoon.

"I swear to God, I'm going to have so much time on my hands when this is all over, I'm not going to know how to act," Anna said after they ordered. "You too, sis. We are heading into the home stretch. Barring fire or flood, I think you have survived your first assignment as maid of honor."

"Only," Meg corrected.

"Oh, come on. You don't want to be the woman in *27 Dresses?*"

"I don't know who that is, and I don't want to be involved with anything that has twenty-seven dresses. I'm retiring from M-O-H duties, as your obnoxious wedding planner put it, on Saturday night."

"She is awfully cranky, isn't she?"

Meg nodded and bit into an egg roll. If she didn't need to slip into a form-fitting dress over the weekend, she would be giving serious consideration to eating her feelings. There were so many of them and she didn't know where to put them.

"Your new office is beautiful. How's the new job that goes with it?"

"Thank you. Not much different from what I was doing before. More meetings, which I don't mind. At least I know what's going on now. I'm still working my way around the politics, but it remains my happiest place."

Meg had no doubt. Her sister was practically glowing already and the wedding was still two days away. Anna's happiness, like Meg's, had been self-contained and she doubted that had changed. Middle Two still made her own happy. Dane was the icing on the cake. Gorgeous icing and incredibly sweet, but Anna was a full show all by herself. Meg liked that about her, probably patterned her own life after her big sister's in some ways, although their career choices were opposites.

"What's up for you next? The gallery show was incredible. They're delivering the black and white of the Spirit Bear to our house after the wedding. Our house, that sounds odd," Anna said.

"You bought a picture? I would have given you one. You don't need to buy it."

"I knew you would say that, so I didn't. Dane bought it."

Meg shook her head.

"I wanted to. It's gorgeous and I'm so proud of you."

Meg had to look away, do the wide-eyed thing West had described so perfectly in his story. Her sister's words hit her straight in her heart. They were so simple, and yet to Meg they meant so much. Her parents must have said they were proud of her when she was a child but that acknowledgement left after high school sports and report cards. No one said they were proud of an adult. No one except Anna, it seemed.

Her sister reached across the table and took her hand. *Not helping with the tear control, Middle Two.*

"Are you okay?"

Meg nodded. "I don't know why, but it means something that you're proud of my work."

Anna smiled. She looked so comfortable with her love these days. She'd always been a loving sister, not quite as syrupy as Sage, but then again no one was that agreeable. Anna was more at ease, though—in love and happy. It spilled off her and across the table to Meg as if Anna sensed her baby sister needed a little extra.

"I didn't say I was proud of your work. I said I was proud of you."

A tear slipped down Meg's cheek and she quickly wiped it away. "Cut it out."

Anna handed her a tissue.

"I don't need that. This is supposed to be your last lunch as a free woman. We should be talking about all the new sex positions you are going to try with that mountain of a man you're marrying. This is not the time for warm and fuzzy."

Anna didn't say anything. She held her gaze.

"What?" Meg finally said a little louder than she planned.

"Nothing. I simply wanted to tell you I was proud."

"Okay. Thank you. We're done now."

"And I wanted to say that everything is going to be okay."

"Isn't that a song?"

"Probably. I'm serious, Meg. With you and West. If it's supposed to be, it will work out."

"What, no Shakespeare quote this time?"

"Well, since you asked." Anna's eyes widened.

She was forever quoting Will, as she called him, in everyday situations. Occupational hazard, she told people. Will's bits of wisdom were often educational and frequently annoying. But there Meg was, asking for one. Nothing made sense anymore.

"The fault, dear Brutus, is not in our stars, but in ourselves," she said with the ease most people only felt when reading a grocery list.

"Brutus? Didn't he kill Caesar? That's not exactly romantic."

"He did, well with the help of forty other senators, but yes. It's a powerful quote all the same."

"Uh-huh. Translation, please."

"We are responsible for our own actions. West may be a star, but he was a man first and I believe he'll sort that out. Eventually."

"Before he kills me?"

Anna laughed. "He's not going to kill you. Caesar was stabbed. You wouldn't allow him that close. The quote works for you too, sis."

"Okay. Thank you for that, but I'm finished talking about the Greeks."

"Romans."

"Whatever. Let's talk about something normal."

"Since when have we been normal?"

Meg agreed but told Anna that she might be willing to try some version of whatever Anna had if the right opportunity presented itself.

"You want to get married?"

"I... not right this minute, but I might. What I want more than that, though, is to feel grounded, tethered to something that isn't going to fly away. I need finish making a place for myself."

"Here?"

"Yes."

"Mom was right. She said you would stay, and none of us believed her. That's amazing news."

"Yeah, I guess. I need to get going on this heart for the hospital foundation before they knock on my door, but after that, I'm thinking of trying my hand at artistic portraits. Different animals, same concept."

"It could be. I think that's a terrific idea. You know so many people. I'm sure you could work with politicians or even..."

"Actors. You can say it, Anna. I'm not allergic to the word—only one in particular at the moment."

"Actors, athletes. There are endless opportunities. Any idea what you're going to do with your heart? The foundation one, not the one in your chest."

"No idea, for either of them."

They paid the bill, and Meg walked Anna back to her office. Taking the long way around campus to her car, Meg knew she had always been good at taking risks as long as they involved enduring rope burns or rolling off a dive boat. She'd returned to her family with a backpack full of memories. Some of the highest awards for her craft were now perched on her bookshelves, and yet loving people and letting them love her in return was something she was still working on. She wondered if West was too.

Chapter Twenty-Three

Meg had once dangled from a cliff trying to capture a Common Murre flying back to its nest on Saint Paul Island. It was probably the most dangerous shot she'd ever attempted, and the result landed on the cover of *National Geographic*. She was twenty-six, the youngest photographer to make the cover in the history of the magazine. It was a big deal, complete with a ceremony and a round of toasts. Meg barely remembered the evening. She'd been exhausted and leaving for Kenya the following day.

A huge accomplishment by most standards was muted by her rush toward the next thing. As the woman with a pixie cut and embroidered flowers on her shirt stood to tune the rest of the string ensemble in the garden where her last and dearest sister would be married, Meg took in a slow breath at the realization she had been running for most of her life. She'd never seen it that way before. It was disguised as drive, ambition, "pure stamina," as her boss once put it. But with the sun warming the morning chill and members of the UC Berkeley orchestra continued their warm-up, Meg allowed that she'd been running away from things she was desperately afraid to want her whole life.

That didn't diminish her work or her accomplishments. They were the result of her choices, but in the end, they were only photographs. The lions she captured were living a life, even her precious polar bears barely noticed her and moved on with the essentials of family and survival. All this time, she'd thought she was the tactile one, the adventurer of the Jeffries family, when in reality she was observing right along with Anna. Granted, hers was hands on and she couldn't remember the last book she'd read that wasn't a travel guide, but it was the same thing.

If Anna had continued being wallpaper, sitting on the sidelines of her life, she wouldn't be slipping into her glittery shoes and preparing to marry the man who would still watch *The Notebook* with her long after the newness of their relationship wore off. Meg knew her sister, knew what it took for her to let someone in, especially someone like Dane. It was dangerous, and it turned out her sister was made of cliff-dangling material too.

"Meg." Her mother tapped her on the shoulder and handed her a bouquet of blush and ivory flowers, snapdragons included. "Everything all right?"

Meg nodded and recognized the musicians were now in full play and the sun was higher in the sky. Her mother kissed her gently and Meg noticed the tears pooling at the edges of eyes that looked so much like her own.

"It's time," her mom said and turned to join the rest of the wedding party under the tent. Meg pulled herself together and remembered she was the maid of honor. Once again there was work to be done. As she headed back toward her responsibilities, Dane finished talking with his sister who was also his best woman. She was in a black-and-white dress with her daughters, the presently reluctant flower girls, each holding one of her hands. The groom approached with a smile Meg registered as pure joy. No matter how everything unfolded today, the whole damn event could fall apart, and Dane would leave with the only thing that mattered to him: Anna. Men were wonderfully simple that way, Meg thought.

"You ready?" she asked Dane, who towered over her and cleaned up even more handsome than usual in a tuxedo.

"From the day I met her," he said.

Meg slapped him on the shoulder. "You're such a liar. You couldn't stand her the day you met her, remember?"

He shook his head.

"Reality has been replaced with all that mushy love crap, hasn't it?"

He practically beamed and Meg could have sworn his eyes were glassy already. Amazing that her tiny sister could bring such a big guy to tears. Meg was sure it wasn't the first time.

"She gets right in there with all her poetry and glitter, doesn't she?"

He nodded and Meg wiped the lapels of his tux. "Well, you look dashing, so let's get on with the party."

"I knew I liked you, little sister. See you in there."

"You will, I'll be the one standing next to the bride. Not that you'll notice a thing once you see her."

Dane put his hand to his chest and walked through the arch of flowers and up the aisle. The music grew louder and Meg knew the moment Anna arrived. She could feel her sister's energy bursting through the morning air. She glanced up and their eyes met, Anna flawless in lace and silk. She nodded, her arm draped through their father's as she stood in the moment they'd been talking about and planning for months.

Hollis handed Ansel over to his father. Matt kissed his gorgeous, impatient wife and then joined Garrett, Sage's husband, who was guiding Olive as she toddled toward their seats. Sage smoothed her hair and even in the first trimester with her second child managed to look calm and delighted.

Meg considered her three big sisters, three different women united in a childhood of memories and the adult lives they'd fumbled through. She had spent her life trying to outrun and outperform each of their shadows, but she'd grown up on her adventures and returned home with clear vision. All she saw now when she looked at her sisters was light. Fractured and difficult to capture, no doubt, but still the most glorious perfect cast of warmth she'd ever witnessed.

"Are we going to get this show on the road?" Hollis called to her. "Or are you going to keep us waiting per usual?"

Meg shook her head and took her place in front of her sister, not before kissing both her and their father on the cheek.

"You're looking a little nervous, Dad," Meg said.

"I'm concentrating. No more talking or I'll cry before we get to Dane."

"Get thee a good husband, and use him as he uses thee," Meg whispered in her ear. Anna's face, creased with the details and expectations of the day, softened into laughter and she kissed Meg back.

"Was that Shakespeare? Did you honestly look up Shakespeare? That's sweet, Meg. It's so—" Sage didn't finish her sentence before she began to cry. Anna handed her a tissue and then they heard the music change and it was time to go.

"Thank you," Anna said as they all approached the arch. "For everything."

Meg reached back and squeezed her sister's arm. "Thank you right back. For everything."

"Could you two pay attention?" Hollis asked from her obviously distressing place at the end of the line.

"Hollis, don't ever leave Matt," Meg said right as the strings and piano began playing the song Meg thought she recognized from a movie but had forgotten to ask Anna about. All of them burst into laughter, Hollis included, and that would forever be the memory of the Jeffries sisters, delivering one of their own down an aisle of glitter to the man she loved.

Annabelle and Dane Sivac were married in the Shakespeare Garden at Golden Gate Park a little after ten in the morning under a perfect fall sky. It went "off without a hitch," as their father exclaimed shortly after, save Olive wiggling free of an exhausted-looking Garrett and running to Sage's side. Not that Olive could ruin anything. Sage scooped her up on her hip without missing a beat. Middle One turned out to be a natural.

Meg held both bouquets as Dane delivered a kiss, complete with a dip that made Anna laugh and would not soon be forgotten. Meg hoped the wedding photographer was paying attention.

The smell of flowers and the chatter of people filled the garden as guests congratulated the couple and made their way to waiting cars that would take them to the rooftop restaurant at Dirty Habit. When Meg had seen the proofs for the invitations, she'd burst out laughing at the name paired next to the Shakespeare Garden and decided she loved her new brother-in-law even more.

Meg spent an inordinate amount of time alone and rarely felt lonely, but standing on the curb in a beautiful dress she would probably never wear again, she felt a bit isolated. Perhaps it was that familiar feeling of being left behind. Her mother had often tried to explain that her position in the family held an "inherent sense of abandonment," although Meg usually scoffed at that. Sure, Meg had seen three sisters go off to college and one by one leave her with an extra set of chores. It had been difficult when Hollis first changed their family dynamic, but Sage leaving had been the hardest. The dinner table felt weird after that. Quieter. It was a foursome—Anna, Meg, and their parents—and for the first time in Meg's life, they could all fit in a standard booth at a restaurant.

By the time Annabelle left for Berkeley, Meg had all but shut down. She made it her business to keep herself active from there on out. She had been busy for the last ten years away from home and now, as it began to drizzle a bit and Meg tipped the string quartet (another maid of honor duty), she wondered if she'd stayed away so long as punishment for being left behind. Was that possible? Did the experiences of childhood run that deep? It certainly wasn't anyone's fault that life moved forward, but pulling a wrap over her shoulders and grabbing a purse one of the guests left behind, Meg was lonely.

"Excuse me," a deep, familiar voice called out behind her.

She turned to find a sleek black car, pulled to the curb, window rolled down.

"Do you know where I can find the Jeffries-Sivac wedding? I'm late."

Meg held her hand up, squinting in the sunlight peeking its way through the clouds, and almost melted into the grass. How had he known that she needed him at that exact moment? He seemed to find a way to her, into the places she tried to lock down.

Meg walked up to the car window. "Wait, OMG, are you Westin Drake?"

He flashed her a smoldering Hollywood expression. "Why yes, yes I am, sweet thing."

She leaned into his car. "Where did you come from? And you're driving all by yourself. I wasn't aware you even had a license. Please tell me your picture is as horrendous as the rest of us."

"That's way too many questions. Get in. You look gorgeous, by the way."

Meg couldn't move. Even though she'd begun envisioning him in her life, the impact of loving him hit her right there on the curb with a force that rendered everything else, including which actress was in his next shower scene, silly.

"I love you," she said without hesitation, as if it was urgent he know right then.

West stepped from the car and Meg realized she was looking around in an effort to protect him in case someone popped up from the bushes. All worry was quickly washed away when she took in the full sight of him. Navy suit, plaid shirt, and an open collar. He was effortless style and genuine polish. Outside beauty lit from within by the mischief and energy in his eyes.

"Did Tamara get this for you because —" She was silenced as his hands slid around her face and his mouth took hers in a kiss that she knew had nothing to do with his training and everything to do with his heart.

"Say it again." His voice was low and his eyes were reaching into a soul Meg saved only for herself.

"I love you."

"I know." He kissed her again and she started to laugh. They both did as she smacked his shoulder and he held her tighter.

"Not your line, movie star. Now we're going to have to shoot that whole scene again. From the top. Get back into your car." She squirmed to turn in his arms, but only managed to crane her neck. "Is that a Tesla?"

West nodded.

"Oh, you are pulling out all the flash today, aren't you?"

His expression grew serious. Meg blinked.

"I love you too, Megara Jeffries. My heart figured it out right away, but I've always been a slow learner."

She kissed him and, resting her head on his chest, tried to regain her balance. "That was good."

"Yeah? I wrote it myself." He eased his hold on her and Meg felt the cool breeze blow between them. "I'm sorry I'm late."

"You're not late." Meg smoothed her dress. "You said you weren't coming."

"I changed my mind. Decided to stop playing the part of the pretentious and paranoid dick."

She laughed. "I see. Well, I'm flattered."

"Good. Now, as fun as kissing you crazy on the street curb is, I'd like to meet your family."

"That's a big step."

"It is. Get in my zero-carbon-footprint car, Meg." He held open the door for her.

She tucked her purse and the few left-behind items under her arm and gathered her dress. Before she ducked into a car she'd only ever seen in magazines, she kissed him one more time. Already anticipating the eyes that would be on them once they arrived at the reception, she wanted him all to herself for one minute more.

"Zero footprint. Look at you talking clean to me."

"Like that?"

West closed her door and quickly circled around to the driver's side. She let out a deep breath and admired the beauty of the Tesla's interior. Incredible what could be created without hurting anyone, she thought.

"Here we are in the front seat like grown-ups," West said as he stretched a seatbelt across his chest and pulled away from the curb.

"That's right. Did Vince get the day off?"

"He did. I'm breaking all the rules today."

Meg took his hand and acknowledged he was downplaying a gesture she knew firsthand could lead to chaos. She loved him even more for taking a chance but couldn't ignore the concern hanging in the air.

"I'm not sure what kind of security—"

West squeezed her hand. "Your sister is married. From the sound of the place they're holding the reception, I think I'm going to get along with the happy couple. This is a time for your family, and I want to be the only man dancing with you. Please let me worry about the baggage I bring to the party."

"I know, but I don't know everyone there and—"

They stopped at a light and he kissed her. It was a move to shut her up, but the taste of him kept her from protesting.

"Clouds are rolling in. It might rain. That's good luck."

"The reception is on the roof. How is rain good luck?"

"They'll have covers, and it is good luck when it rains on a newly married couple."

"Where did you hear that?"

"I don't remember, but personally my best memory so far happened among the clouds. They're good like that. Take my word for it."

Meg wrapped herself in the fog of their moment on the bridge and told herself, rather convincingly, that things would be fine.

West must have heard her mind. He reached over as they pulled into the valet line behind the other guests. "Normal, Meg. We are normal for today."

She held tight to his hand. It was a lovely bit of fantasy, she thought, but he wasn't normal. Neither one of them were and while she knew she'd asked for this, pushed him with her need to have more of a life with him, she had a sinking feeling that wasn't realistic. Glancing over at him, she pretended he could pass for any other wedding guest. He was a fantastic actor bent on getting the part, so the least she could do was play along.

Chapter Twenty-Four

*W*est had requested one plainclothes member of his security team for the lobby and another placed in the reception. His guys were experts at blending in. And while there was no reason Meg needed to know, West did put a call in to Dane, the groom who now sat a few chairs down and was all but bursting with love for Meg's sister. West needed to make someone aware so Maxwell, who was keeping an eye on things and hitting on the bartender, didn't get kicked out for crashing their wedding. They were an hour into the reception and so far, the focus was on the happy couple and Meg's family. Right where it needed to be.

West loved weddings. His brothers were all still single, so he had not been in a wedding that truly meant something yet, but he had been in two weddings on the big screen. Nick Shot married his first wife on the big island of Hawaii in the first movie, but by the end credits, she'd been killed off by a crazy drug dealer with a mechanical arm. Fortunately, West's on-screen alter ego found love a second time around with his feisty car mechanic.

Not exactly original, but West liked Ali Strump. Being her pretend husband for the last three films wasn't nearly as difficult as he imagined the real commitment would be. Their on-screen fights could get intense, but once Gary yelled cut, they made faces at one another and both agreed Cheetos were far superior to Doritos. Not that either of them could afford the calories during production, but it was fun having someone willing to food-dream with him.

Reality, at least the one he wanted, was sitting next to him, holding his hand under the table as the groom's sister tinkled her glass to announce a toast. West didn't have a whole lot of experience with commitment and he'd never been in love before Meg, but he knew *of* love. He'd watched his parents navigate bills and deal with his brothers and all their different phases. They raised four boys and still appeared to enjoy one another. They laughed a lot and when they fought, they went hard and made up quickly.

West had not realized he'd been taking notes, but he supposed all kids learned how to love from their family and friends. He'd never thought about a family of his own, and he wasn't exactly entertaining the idea now, but he did know that he wanted Meg in his life along with the freedom and fun she brought to it.

He needed to bring something to her life if this was ever going to work. The wedding was a start. The guests clapped as the best woman speech ended with laughter. West glanced over at Meg. Her dress was incredible, but honestly he'd missed her so much during the week, he'd have wanted her even in a burlap sack.

"Everything all right?" Meg leaned in, coconut mixing with the champagne on her breath. When he didn't answer, she stole a tomato off his salad and searched his expression.

"Have I ever taken you on a date?" he asked.

She nodded and took another sip of champagne. "The bridge was the greatest date of all time." She leaned in closer, her breath on his ear. "And then there was the weekend date on the Tony Bennett bed—that's a favorite too."

His whole body went on alert as his mind filled with thoughts he was not able to share with her while several hundred people were around and expecting their best behavior. "I meant a real date. Dinner, a movie."

"You know, now that you mention it, there is this new movie I want to see next year. Hot guy, fast cars."

He took her hand, above the table this time. "I'm serious, Meg."

Her smile dropped and while he was sad to see it go, he was surrounded by her family and friends. His life, the crazy moments they shared so far stood in stark contrast to the abundance of warmth, date nights, and dog walks in the park that swirled around them. West needed to know if he'd given her any of that and if not, he needed to get to work.

"No. We have never been on a real date."

The truth hit him with a slap, but then again, her honesty usually did.

"Now, if it's any consolation, I've never asked you on a proper date either until this wedding, and you're here. I think wedding dates count for five regular dates." She took another tomato. "So, you're ahead of the game. Best boyfriend ever, in fact."

"Yeah?"

"Yes." She kissed him, held his face, and took more. "No complaints, Mr. McNaughton."

His name, his family. How did she know what he needed or where his mind was? She was a photographer, used to observing instead of showing and that must include him too.

Maybe she could keep her travel assignments to one week. Maybe this last installment of *Full Throttle* would be the last. That was a lot of maybe, West thought as he considered the guests who were laughing and enjoying normal.

"So, Westin Drake." Meg's oldest sister Hollis switched seats with her husband and assessed the man she thought West was. He was used to getting the "once-over," as Aunt Margaret liked to say when she first saw him on one of her visits. "Let me look at you, Wes. I need to give you the once-over like in the John Wayne cowboy hat movies." The fact that his aunt was wearing a flowered party dress and drawling like a western icon might have seemed strange to most people, but she got a kick out of putting things together like that, stuff that didn't belong. West's mom said it was how her brain healed after the accident, "kind of jumbled," as she put it. The whole experience of growing up was jumbled for West too, so he and Aunt Margaret had gone well together.

The woman assessing him now was not Aunt Margaret. Hollis Jeffries was a powerhouse. She had a commanding air, similar to West's oldest brother. It was the first-in-everything air. But in an arm wrestling match, West had a feeling Hollis would kick Boyd's ass. And yet with all that attitude, West knew from Meg that Hollis had a soft inside. "She'll bite you if you ever try to touch it, but it's in there," Meg had said one night when she was showing him pictures on her phone.

"Hollis Jeffries Locke," West replied, hoping his acting skills were masking his need to be liked, especially by Meg's family. He tried to muster up a John Wayne stare for Aunt Margaret, but she'd been gone awhile now and he couldn't remember.

"Not a huge fan of the car movies," she said.

West looked to Meg, who glared as if she were trying to set her sister on fire. Ah, you gotta love siblings, he thought.

"I did, however, love you in that movie you were in before the whole hot and dangerous thing took off."

"I..." West was at a loss. No one ever talked about that film. Ever.

"You owned a pet store. It took place in Brooklyn and there was something wrong with your character."

"Schizophrenic."

"Yes. That was a brilliant film. He made all those weird lists on scraps of paper."

West nodded.

"Why haven't I seen that?" Meg asked.

"It was never in theaters. I saw it at Sundance and I remember looking for it, but it never came out. You weren't Westin Drake back then."

West's brow furrowed and he glanced at Meg again. "She does have superpowers."

Meg's smile grew wide and she nodded. "I told you."

"How did you know it was me? That was the first and last film that I was billed as Wes McNaughton. I was picked up for *Full Throttle* six months later."

"That's a shame."

"You think?"

"I know."

"Hollis, not today," Meg said.

"It's the truth. You should appreciate that, goddess of truth. You must see this film. It took everything at Sundance. Why wasn't it released?"

"The production company folded. They were stretched too thin. Entered it and then by the time Sundance came around, there was no money left to move. A big studio was never going to take a chance on a film like that, so it died."

"Another shame. Well, I wanted to come over and tell you to be kind to our baby sister. She thinks she's a badass, but she's not."

"Can't imagine where I get that from," Meg said.

"Probably Sage." Hollis stood.

Meg snorted a laugh, a champagne haze filling her beautiful eyes now.

"West, help her with project normal, will you?"

"Project normal?" *Hadn't they just been talking about being normal?*

"Yes. We provided the guilt to get her home, to quit her job. Now all that's left is for you to sweep her off her feet and we won't have an empty seat at the Thanksgiving table."

West could feel Meg's exhale of breath across his neck. Drawing on Mr. Hernandez's voice and movement training, West smiled, giving the air he knew Meg had quit her job. Knew that she wanted to make a life, a home, in the city. Of course he knew. They were a couple. She loved him. Didn't she say she never lied to...

West tried to remember where the men's room was and stood from the table without another word. Hollis had left them and he needed air. They were on an open rooftop and he needed air. Not a good sign.

Technically, it wasn't a lie. Meg attempted to justify through the happy bubbles in her head. Leave it to Hollis to drop a bomb at a perfectly magnificent reception. West seemed caught off guard, but that quickly morphed into downright stricken. She couldn't tell if he was nervous that she wouldn't be jet-setting off soon and therefore preserving his own schedule, or if the tense shift in his jaw was because she'd lied. Withheld the truth, that sounded better. Meg knew better. No matter how small, no matter how unintentional, lying was never a good idea.

She'd known it the first day in his car when she'd lied to bring her ego on par with his. She'd had fleeting feelings when he made comments about her flying off or when he said, "you'll be gone soon too."

It was a power thing, she knew that now. If she still had one foot out the door, real or inferred, she would be willing to throw it all away, throw him away at a moment's notice. Traveling Meg was safe. Adventure Meg wasn't thinking of buying a house, wondering if she should drive down to LA and surprise him on set. Exciting Meg wasn't just a little out of reach and not letting Westin Drake anywhere near her heart.

That's why she'd withheld the information that she was jobless, sappy over her niece and nephew, and had recently downloaded a copy of *Grow Your Own Garden* onto her e-reader. Loving West was a nonissue for *National Geographic* Dynamo Meg. The problem was, she no longer wanted to be that person. She simply hadn't figured out how to tell him who she was, and now he was gone.

Meg swallowed, looking around as if everyone in the room had read her thoughts. Placing her napkin on the table, she went to find her date.

"He went that way." Two women Meg didn't recognize pointed toward the stairs. She nodded and kept walking. Oddly helpful when everyone in the room knew your date, Meg thought with annoyance. Her humor was gone.

She finally reached the lobby and still no sign of West. She slid down into a chair that resembled a big fuzz ball under a mirror next to the bathrooms, prepared to wait, when West took the seat next to her. Meg closed her eyes.

"It wasn't a lie."

"But it was." His voice was steady and a touch cold.

God, she hated lying, and being caught in one, no matter how unintended, sucked.

"I came home to try to make a living with my photography. I wanted to be closer to my family and I was... well, I needed to... buy a toaster."

West said nothing for what felt like an eternity, so she glanced over at him.

"Why didn't you tell me?"

"I don't know. First it was to balance out my ego in your backseat and then things became complicated and I... don't know."

"Hard to have a toaster in a tent, I'd imagine."

Humor was a good sign, she thought, nodding.

"Is it that I'm not as exciting anymore? You know the whole idea that I'm making a life and you're... not wanting that. Is that why you're pissed?"

"I'm not pissed, and I have a life. It's a bizarre one, but it's mine. You had a life when you were gone, too, Meg. You want something different now. That doesn't make what you had wrong."

"Different from what you want, though?"

He seemed thrown by the question, and Meg decided that might be an answer.

"I don't know. I'm still wondering if you love me."

"What?"

"You said you don't lie to people you love. So, I'm confused."

"That's a little gray."

"The love or the lie?"

"The lie. It was withholding information and you assumed."

"Ah, so it's my fault." West propped his feet out in front and crossed them at the ankles, as if they were sitting on a park bench in the middle of spring.

She faced him, touched his arm. "I don't want to be left behind."

"No one wants to be left behind, Meg."

"Well, I do things to keep that from happening."

He said nothing.

"I love you. That's not a lie. But, I did lie about my job, which I never do, just to clarify, but I lied this time probably because things feel good and I'm scared to change anything. It's like snowboarding. You and I are on a sweet run and if I change direction, or you realize I was never going in your direction, I'll fall on my ass."

"And take me with you?"

"Probably."

West sat up, faced her, and pulled both of her hands to his lips.

"I haven't been snowboarding in twelve years. Insurance—while I'm under contract—forbids it, but if I remember correctly, the best part is moving down the mountain, through the trees. If you, if we, fall, I think we can simply get back up."

"I'm sorry."

He stood, offering his hand, and Meg took it in a way that felt as if she was committing to more than a simple ride in an elevator.

"I know. I love you." He pulled her hand under his arm as they walked toward the elevator.

"I love you too. I think they took our dinner plates."

"There's still cake," West said as the metal doors closed behind them. He held her from behind and kissed her neck.

"I thought you couldn't have cake while you're shooting?"

He switched to the other side of her neck and Meg felt them slide back into their normal rhythm.

"I've been thinking that Nick Shot should go through a rough patch for this movie. Pack on some weight, get all fat and happy."

Meg laughed as the elevator opened on to the rooftop in time for them to see Anna and Dane take to the dance floor.

"Is that a character choice?" Meg pulled him toward the music, ignoring a couple of iPhones strategically pointed in their direction.

"I think so. Nick Shot, normal guy." He took her in his arms and they danced slow and then fast, silly and serious. Meg held on, felt a soft breeze swoosh past them, and remembered she was a good skier.

Chapter Twenty-Five

*L*ess than three days after sending her sister and Dane off for a surprisingly short honeymoon and kissing West until he almost missed his plane back to LA, Meg stood offstage at the Herbst Theater in downtown San Francisco waiting for her introduction.

Hers was the second TED talk of the evening, so she had some time. She preferred the more intimate setting of the historic theater. No platform, no theme music. Meg smoothed her hands down the cashmere poncho West had surprised her with the Sunday after the wedding. The tag, from some fancy store in Beverly Hills, described it as an "infinity cape," but when West whipped it out of the shopping bag, he declared that if she was staying put, she needed a California poncho too. Deep purple and so soothingly soft, Meg had a hard time taking it off. Even Amy approved when she met her early at the theater and introduced her to a man in a turtleneck who wanted her to take some photographs of his football players. Meg was gracious and asked him a little more about the project. He told her he was the manager for the USC Trojans and had heard from Dane Sivac that she was looking for a challenge. Amy was practically dancing in her high heels and Meg found she was, in fact, ready for a challenge. They shook hands and Amy walked him up the center aisle of the theater to do what she did best: "close the deal."

Things were starting to fall into place. Meg could feel it.

She'd gone to Rudolpho for a little polish before her big day and to her surprise, he left her hair wavy. "Suits you," he'd said. "A little spritz and you're off to change the world." It had been five months since she'd walked into R House, intimidated and unsure. She now knew Rudolpho wasn't some Oz-type figure behind a curtain. He was a man who understood the importance of details, Meg thought as she stood in the darkness watching the small chandeliers casting buttons of light on the audience.

Normal people were no different from actors. No matter where a person came from, they were strangers, veiled under a mask of their choosing. The human part, where people connected, was in the details.

R House was the shiny cover of a man born in Portugal, who moved to the United States alone and learned to cut hair. His salon was luxurious. That's what made him a success, but Meg counted herself lucky that she knew Rudolpho had a pug named Curly and a fairly unhealthy obsession with the LA Lakers.

Her photographs were often lauded for their connection and the way she managed to make the viewer feel as if they were right there. "They were intimate," one reviewer said of her gallery exhibit. Despite their mass, Meg found it easy to connect with animals. She respected their boundaries and they climbed right up her lens and into her being. Animals didn't know how to be anything other than what they were and they had a shared respect, a willingness to accept, that Meg had found fascinating.

Humans were a little trickier. One, in particular, allowed brief glimpses behind his mask, but not often, and Meg was starting to think it would never be enough. She couldn't blame West for being careful. She wasn't exactly comfortable baring her soul either, and no one was hunting her with a camera or a microphone hoping she'd screw up. She understood why West never told her about the independent film Hollis raved about, and she even pretended not to notice the flash of panic when he realized she wasn't going away. He loved her, Meg knew that, but love wasn't the same as intimacy. She needed to know him. That was how she was wired and since returning home, the need to connect had only grown stronger. West would have to let her all the way in and Meg had a sinking feeling he'd been behind his mask for so long, he wasn't sure how to come out.

Are you wearing underwear?

Meg jumped at the text that came across her phone. She thought she'd turned it off but looked down and was glad she forgot. West. She almost said his name out loud, but instead walked farther into the wings for some privacy.

M: Who wants to know?

W: Your man.

She lost her words and wit for a moment at the thought of West's body. If she closed her eyes, she could almost feel him against her, but that was not a good idea right before a TED talk.

W: I'm having my nipples airbrushed again and I thought of you.

M: That should be on a Hallmark card.

W: Yeah? I'll have Hannah call them.

Meg chuckled and remembered where she was.

W: So, are you?

M: Yes.

W: That's a shame.

M: No, it's really not. I don't think the older guy that's introducing me would be as generous as you were.

W: Did you just call me… generous?

Meg shook her head.

M: Don't celebrities need to worry about people hacking their phones?

W: No fun. Ooh, you're almost up. The talk on meditation before you is winding down. That guy confused the hell out of me, BTW.

M: How do you know that?

Honestly, did he have a live feed of the show? Was that even possible?

W: I have connections. Now get out there, Poncho. Break a leg.

M: I'll try.

W: Panties firmly in place. Remember the knees. Sorry I can't be there this time.

M: Me too.

A few beats passed and Meg heard the rumbled applause of the audience. Thumb hovering over the power button, the phone vibrated again.

I love you, Megara Jeffries.

Her heart reached out from her chest. The man crawled right inside her every time.

I love you too, Westin McNaughton. Now get back to your nipples.

After a deep breath, she pushed the power button and moved back to the edge of the stage.

"Please join me in welcoming Meg Jeffries." The audience came to life as she once again walked on stage for the animals, human and polar bear, that needed her most.

West had had some shit days on set, but this one might go down as the shittiest. Leaning against a table in his trailer while a doctor stitched up his right shoulder, he no longer knew what he was doing. It had been coming and going for a while now. But looking around at the frenzy of people dedicated to making sure he was comfortable and "had everything he needed," made him nauseous. What were they all doing? How had he gotten so deep into something that once the cameras stopped was little more than a joke?

And now that he had Meg what he did for a living seemed even more absurd. The need to be with her, there for her, strangled him every time he hung up the phone. Last night, in between being hung from a chain in an abandoned garage and beaten within an inch of Nick Shot's life, West watched her TED talk via a live link one of the AV guys had made possible. She was so fantastic that he'd floated back to his rental house sometime after two in the morning and watched it again. He was bruised and stained from the makeup, but she was surrounded by an audience that sat attentive, laughing at all the right parts, eventually clapping and filling the theater with all the love she deserved. All of it—she deserved all of it and all of him, the guy he was underneath all the thick makeup he'd applied over the years.

"West," someone said, but he ignored it. He was wrapped in the memory of Meg in nothing but his sweatshirt jumping on her bed while she read through her speech with him over Skype. It was a trick he'd taught her to help with her breathing and pace, something he'd learned along the way that he could share with her. When she had finally collapsed on the bed, his heart was begging to be next to her, but he had a job to do, so as they had for almost a month now, he let her go.

"West!"

"What!" his misdirected annoyance snapped.

"Sorry, but Gary wanted me to ask you how long you think you'll be?"

West faced the doe-eyed production assistant and prepared to release an epic actor temper tantrum, even though it wasn't her fault. He needed somewhere to direct all his frustration.

Empty your angry bucket, he heard Aunt Margaret's slurred and labored voice. She'd been in his head a lot lately but like a whisper in a hailstorm, he found it hard to pay attention. That wasn't an excuse, and West managed to pull his shit together before he said something he would regret.

The doctor finished taping the dressing on his shoulder.

"Give me fifteen minutes."

"Absolutely. Wow, quick recovery. I'll let Gary know. Thank you. Do you need anything else? Water, a beer?"

He shook his head, pulled out his phone, and stepped from the trailer for some privacy. After trying to text Hannah with his right hand, he winced and rolled his shoulder. He'd done two cold readings for the woman casting *The Messenger*. It was indie but managed to get the backing of some pretty heavy-hitting production companies, so Hannah was more on board than she normally would be. West was starting to think the time was right to turn off his stint with *Full*

Throttle. He'd proven himself already. He'd been paid enough money. Now, like the mafia, if he were being dramatic, the public and "his team" needed to let him go.

Aside from *The Messenger*'s brilliant script, three-quarters of it would be shot in San Francisco. The director, who West also admired, was a local to the Bay Area and wanted as much of the revenue as possible to stay in the city. The project was perfect and he was so right for the role, he could feel it. Hearing the roar of engines, West needed to get back before Gary forgot they'd almost cut off West's arm and began barking again.

He texted Hannah one word— *Well?*

After waiting a couple of minutes for the little blue bubble to appear, he gave up and slid back into Nick Shot's world. He would bide his time. He could get this part and finally hand Nick Shot off to another hungry actor who had no clue what he was getting into. Maybe he'd do something fulfilling and get to take Meg to Kite Park in broad daylight.

"West, we're burning gasoline, man."

There he went again with more maybes, West thought as she tossed his phone in his trailer and went back to work.

Chapter Twenty-Six

Meg all but launched herself at West when he showed up at her apartment door the following Friday morning.

"Pretty sure you didn't check before you opened that door," he said as he carried her back into her apartment, kicked the door closed, and locked it. Habit, Meg realized amidst the thrum of need pulsing through her body.

"How would you know if I checked?" Her lips found the warm skin of his neck. "You were on the other side of the door."

"I sense these things." He set her on the counter in the kitchen but stayed between her legs.

She managed to break free of her need to touch him long enough to consider his face.

"What's wrong?" she asked.

West shook his head and kissed her, firm and urgent. His lips flew right by "hello" as his hand tangled in her hair and his tongue took over. The kiss was different. Meg now knew love, lust, passion, and even comfort when he touched her, but this was none of those. He was searching her mouth, running his hands along her body as if he was frantic, starving. Her body wasn't complaining, but something was wrong.

"You weren't supposed to be back until—"

His mouth pulled her back in while his hands lifted and carried her to the bedroom. He undressed them both, his eyes barely meeting hers.

"Hey," she said, putting her hand on his chest. When his gaze, thick with need and heavy with something he couldn't manage to put into words, met hers, her heart stopped.

"West." She touched his face.

He swallowed and it looked like he might say something, but he held her face instead, asking with his eyes if he could have her without explanation, sink into her until the words stopped spinning through his mind and made their way to his mouth. She slid her hands over the plane of his chest, hoping that answered the question she knew he'd ask but never needed to. His weary eyes fell closed and his body collapsed onto the bed, taking her with him.

"I've missed you," she said. Putting her worry away for the time being, Meg welcomed him into her body. Moving over him, every stroke seemed to chase away whatever had brought him to her door. West leaned up and pulled her closer, burying his face in her neck as if he could somehow breathe her into his lungs. Despite the sadness blooming in her chest, the rhythm of their bodies shut her brain off and threatened to take her breath. He met her eyes and she clutched his hands intertwined with hers as they both broke apart and collapsed onto her bed.

"Have you been to the Tobin House?" West asked as they lay together, bodies straining for steady air.

Meg kept her face to his chest, stayed wrapped around him, but managed to shake her head as if they were having conversation over morning coffee.

"It's half a house. The guy built it for his daughters, but one of them didn't want it. Can you imagine? She wanted to live in the country, so she walked away from half of this mansion in the middle of the city. No one does that."

"People walk away all the time," she said.

"You did. Reinvented yourself. Flawless TED, by the way."

She kissed his chest, still not sure where this was going. "Thank you."

They lay in silence and Meg slowly slid off his body. He rolled to his side and held her close. They lay face-to-face and she waited for him to tell her why his eyes were rimmed in red.

"Did I ever tell you about Aunt Margaret?"

Meg shook her head.

"She was..." He broke eye contact as if he couldn't look at her and share at the same time. "She was my mom's younger sister. They were a few years apart and when she was seventeen, she was hit by a drunk driver. T-boned, so the story goes."

Meg tried not to gasp but failed. West rolled onto his back as if his own pain was all he could manage.

"I was four, so I don't remember the accident. My first memory of her wasn't until I was six or seven. I mean I knew something happened to her, her brain, but short of my parents visiting her, I didn't know her."

"Did they catch the person who hit her?"

"He died at the scene," West said with a chill reserved for deep injustice. "Got off easy."

A couple of minutes passed in silence before he quickly stood and pulled on his jeans. "Are you hungry?" he asked and walked out to the kitchen before she had a chance to respond.

Once, on assignment in the Daintree Rainforest in Australia, Meg got turned around and eventually realized she was lost. She'd been embarrassed at the time. She prided herself on a good sense of direction and in the male-dominated world of nature photography, the last thing a woman wanted was to call in for a rescue. She didn't call for help. Instead she sat down, and for about an hour, took things apart, retraced her steps, and slowly found her way back to camp.

Climbing from the bed, she put on some sweatpants and a T-shirt. She was lost again. He was all over the place and she was afraid if she touched him, stopped him, that he might crumble right in front of her. She couldn't let that happen, but at the same time, she wasn't sure how to help him. Slowly walking out to the kitchen, she remembered he was on set last night.

He normally called, but it wasn't unusual for the shoot to run late after she'd fallen asleep. There were stunts and something about a warehouse, but those were all the pieces she had. When he'd first taken off his shirt, she noticed the bandage on his shoulder, the bruise across his thigh when he took off his jeans, but none of that was out of his ordinary. She'd learned that the first time she flinched at a scrape that took up half his back. None of it led to West at her front door for sex and breakfast. Meg leaned against the wall of her tiny kitchen and hoped he'd fill in the details.

The toaster popped and he threw both halves of a bagel on a plate. "So, Tobin House? Are you up for that?" He was looking back and forth as if he'd forgotten where he put something.

"Cream cheese is in the fridge," she offered.

He pulled open the door. "Happy cows at this"—he turned the container in his hand—"Organic Valley Farm?"

"Yes. Happy cows."

"Good. I don't eat dairy unless it's sourced from a small and ethical farm."

Meg managed a smile. He still wasn't meeting her eyes. Instead, he was intent on the bagel. It looked as if the simple task of smearing cream cheese was all he could handle.

"No filming today?" she asked carefully.

West turned, half a bagel in his mouth, and shook his head. He seemed to be riding the wave of caffeine or adrenaline. Meg recognized both—she'd seen them staring back at her in the mirror more times than she could count in her life.

"Did Gary cancel?"

"Oh, come on." He took another bite and set the plate down. "I did not drive all the way up here to talk about Gary."

"You drove?" *How was that even possible?*

"I did, so let's get some breakfast in you and—" West's arm clipped the plate and sent it crashing to the ground. He stood, frozen, and rubbed his tired eyes.

Meg pushed off the wall and went to him, sliding her arms around his chest. Anger or frustration, she couldn't be sure, seethed beneath his surface. Pressing her lips to his back, she held on.

"I'm fine." His voice was barely above a whisper.

"It's okay if you're not."

"I didn't go to work today," he said after a beat.

"Called in sick?"

"Didn't call at all. I'm sure they'll send me the bill."

"Okay."

He turned in her arms and brought her body in under his chin. Meg kept holding him.

"I don't know what I'm doing."

Meg pulled back so she could see his face. "You have come to the right place."

"Hannah texted me."

Meg had never known Hannah to text. Since West had been in her life, Hannah was a phone call, often two or three times if she didn't get an answer, kind of woman. West often commented on the piranhas that followed him around hoping to catch a glimpse of him "doing something exciting like grocery shopping or leaving the gym," but she wondered if he realized Hannah had teeth too.

"They gave the lead in that indie film to someone else." Sensing he needed space, she let him go and picked up the pieces of the plate.

"I can get that," he said.

Meg held up her hand and finished cleaning. She wanted him to keep talking. "*The Messenger?*"

"Yeah. How do you remember these things?" he asked, walking into the living room.

"I—"

"Pay attention, right. I know." She heard him from the other room.

Meg wanted to tell him she was sorry, that he deserved the part, but he didn't want pity and this felt deeper than one missed role. West had been in his business for a long time. She found it hard to believe he'd gotten as far as he had without a fair share of disappointment. Tossing the broken plate in the trash, she dried her hands and joined him in the living room.

"My Aunt Margaret was the one who said I should go into acting. Her speech was pretty bad after her brain injury, so we would practice different voices while she served tea. She was special and she saw me in the shadow of my brothers. I was her favorite."

"Smart woman." Meg sat next to him on the couch.

"She was, but in a way completely misunderstood by most people. She had a way of seeing things."

"Did she get to see you on stage or in your movies?"

"She came to two of my high school productions. Standing ovation and one time with a huge flower hat and her cowboy boots."

"My kind of woman. I'll bet she would have appreciated the poncho."

"No doubt." He flashed her the first real smile since he'd walked through her door, and the vise of tension seemed to loosen.

Thank you, Aunt Margaret, Meg offered up and felt the threat of tears. This was his pain, not hers, so she swallowed and stood to get them some coffee.

"Aunt Margaret is the reason I became an actor. She died my senior year and I guess I thought I could honor her that way. I guess I thought if I got that part it might bring me back to what I set out to do. After the text last night, I tried to finish. I've never not been one hundred percent on a set, but I walked right off," West managed around strangled laughter.

Meg handed him a cup of coffee and curled on the couch next to him.

"Why didn't you ever tell me about the movie Hollis mentioned at the wedding? *Careful Consideration.* From what I saw, you were incredible."

"You watched it? How did you..."

"Not the whole thing, but there are clips on YouTube. Did you know you're all over YouTube?"

"I do *not* want to know."

"If *Careful Consideration* is the type of film you want to do, then do that."

He scoffed as if what she was asking was not only naïve, but impossible. "It doesn't exactly work that way."

"Well, then how does it work? You can't keep doing something that makes you miserable."

The expression on his face turned to annoyance, and Meg wondered if West was truly trapped. Or was he bound by things he simply needed to find the strength to let go of? She knew that feeling, that leap into the uncomfortable, but she had no idea what kind of baggage his level of celebrity carried.

West had ignored his phone so far. Now the damn thing was going nonstop in the pocket of his jacket. Gary must have finally reached Hannah and Regis and anyone else who would listen to him rant about the tens of millions of dollars he was wasting. West could practically hear him, see the vein pulsing in Hannah's head while she listened to him. The fury born of what seemed unfair last night and emboldened him to walk away from the set now seemed impulsive and childlike in the clear light of morning.

It was possible West was finally having a breakdown. It wasn't exactly his style. He'd worked since he was fifteen years old. And in far worse jobs than the one he'd turned his back on. As the minutes and hours ticked by, he could tell Meg was doing her best to understand, but by the time the battery of his phone died and he was finally left in peace, West felt like an obnoxious and privileged whiner. He wondered if the tabloids would wait even twenty-four hours before plastering—Westin Drake Loses His Shit—all over the stands of local grocery stories.

"My job, my life for that matter, isn't exactly a hardship," he said, refocusing on Meg since he had no answers for how he was going to undo what he'd done yet.

"I know, but it might be for someone like you."

"Like me?"

"You're tender and kind. You're so far from 'get your sweet ass over here.'"

West scratched his head and glanced around out of habit. "I know you've been out in the fresh air for a while, but tender and kind are not exactly words guys relish hearing. Besides, it's called acting for a reason. If I were like Nick Shot, there'd be less challenge than there is now."

"But having to play against those traits must be difficult for so many films. That's a long time and the public perceives you that way too, so you can't exactly escape it during your off time. That has to be frustrating."

Yeah, he was a whiner.

"It's not. It is a job. Do you think every barista at Starbucks or garbage man or guy in a tie in some cubicle somewhere wants to do that? That shuffling papers or dealing with some asshole's latte order plays to the essence of who they are?" He shook his head. "It's a job, Meg. People have bills, they need to make a living. I may not have wanted to take my shirt off for every other scene in a movie, but it pays my bills and has afforded a cushion for a lot of people in my life." He stood, blinking his tired eyes, and decided he needed to figure out how much damage he'd caused. He plugged in his phone.

"Who'd they cast?" Meg asked with the calm, careful tone of a hostage negotiator. He loved her, but he felt stupid.

"You don't know him."

"I suppose that's the point? Aren't indie films all about unknown and unpolished?"

He grinned at the reference. It was clear that no matter how empty he felt, she could make him whole, as least for a little while.

"Let's not talk about this anymore. Can I take you home?" His phone turned on and West glanced down at the screen. "After I answer Hannah's twenty-five texts and take my punishment like a man, will you drive home with me?"

"We are home. Well, here in my dinky apartment. We could call your place home. Sure, it's an incredibly overpriced hotel that serves mass-produced truck food in their restaurant and has beauty products in their bathrooms that are tested on animals, but it's your home."

His eyes grew wide. "Have you been holding all of that in?"

"I have given up working on my restraint. I'm a hopeless truth talker."

"I meant my family home. I want you to see where I come from."

"How much trouble are you in? Don't you need to go back?"

"A fair amount." His thumb glided over the messages. "But, it's too late to do anything right this minute. We might as well take the weekend. Can you get away until Sunday?" She glanced around her apartment, and he could see her trying to find order for the both of them.

"How are you so calm about this?" she asked.

"Lots of experience being in trouble growing up. I'm sure my brothers will tell you all about it. Is that a yes? I need to breathe and the air is better up there."

His phone rang.

Meg nodded and took the coffee cups into the kitchen, leaving him to clean up his own mess. West tapped the screen of his phone and held it to his ear. There was no need for a greeting, Hannah was already at her full volume.

Chapter Twenty-Seven

They drove in silence, nothing but intermittent thuds when West changed lanes. she was worried about him. Crossing over the Golden Gate Bridge, she noticed the clear blue sky in stark contrast to the red steel of the bridge. There were no soft edges, no blending or dreamy fog like the morning West woke her before the sun. It was a completely different bridge in the bright sunlight.

Meg pulled out her camera from the bag at her feet. She flipped through the pictures she'd taken on the back patio at Blue Plate. It was a neighborhood restaurant West took her to on their first official "date" after he'd given her the poncho.

Iron lanterns with yellow glass, mossy-green walls and uneven brick paths. The owners were more than happy to tuck them into a back corner at a small round table with an iron frog in rain boots. It had been charming, everything she knew West to be, and nothing pretend or hidden.

To her objective eye, the pictures were interesting, a couple of them worth some editing, but the memories were a vivid tableau she didn't bother capturing. They'd talked about everything from bad auditions to the upcoming election. Effortless, that's the word that came to Meg's mind as they wound up the freeway, the landscape whipping past the window going from brick to green. The last image of the bunch was the one the owner took of the two of them. Arms around one another, candlelight against a dark and tucked-away sky. They were smiling and could have been mistaken for any other couple out for a night. Except they weren't.

West usually signed things on his way out the door. Occasionally they were interrupted, but not always. Despite the attention, there were times they were left alone in public and there were times Meg forgot she had to share him. It certainly wasn't normal, but it was working. At least she thought it was until this morning.

Almost an hour later, they reached historic downtown Petaluma. Meg remembered driving to Petaluma for a music festival when she was in college, but apart from that, she'd never been to the town where West grew up. She supposed Petaluma was bigger than a town, but it seemed small especially compared to San Francisco.

His parents lived in a single-level home on a large piece of land. There were cobblestone walkways leading off to a separate garage and what appeared to be storage areas. Large bay windows from the outside framed rooms with dark wood floors, and cream-colored walls displayed pictures and paintings. Curved flower beds lined the walk that led to a sizable front door with two panels of stained glass. There were little garden characters, a snail, some birds, and a small duck family scattered among the flowers. The sound of wind chimes and trickling water from a fountain or water fixture somewhere nearby reminded Meg of the fixture at the Fairmont. Again, a contrast stood looming as West knocked and a dog barked from inside the house. He took her hand and kissed her wrist.

"Nervous?"

"Should I be?" she asked.

He kissed her. "Probably." His warm breath sent a shiver down her arms. In the time it took her to slap his shoulder, the front door swung open and a large golden dog ran past them. Three men crowded the doorway, each of them a slightly different version of the other. The tallest grabbed West and pulled him into the house in a headlock. Once he was released with a toss of his hair, the other two hugged him, grabbed at his shirt, and teased him about everything from his workout schedule to his shoes.

"And I'm the girl? What the hell, were you guys sitting by the door?" West asked still laughing.

All three men looked at one another, breathing heavily, and nodded. Meg imagined they looked about the same when they were younger and in trouble.

"You going to introduce us to your woman?" one of them asked.

"I was hoping we would be greeted by sane people."

"Yeah, you came to the wrong house for that," the tallest said, extending his hand. "Patrick. Sorry about that. Welcome to the McNaughton Nut House, Meg. West calls one of us practically every night and talks about how much he loves you and wants to kiss you all the time. Sometimes he even cries. Boyd, didn't you say he was crying the last time?"

The brother with the full beard nodded. "He was, bawling if I remember. *Titanic* playing in the background."

"Wow," Meg said, looking at West, who was shaking his head and warding off the other brother with a tattoo on his arm that from a distance reminded her of Jack and the Beanstalk.

"We're kidding. Not about the crying. He does cry, but he wasn't watching *Titanic*."

Meg was laughing by the time the brother she assumed was the oldest extended his hand and confirmed she was right.

"Boyd. It's good to meet you, Meg."

"You too." She was still laughing.

West finally managed his way back to her side. "You are all assholes."

"True, but we're your assholes. Cade, introduce yourself to the love of West's life," Boyd said.

Meg's brow rose in surprise. She wanted to play along.

"He said that, love of his life," Patrick mouthed with fluttering eyelashes as West began to laugh too.

The man in the T-shirt that read "Foghorn Brewery—We're Proud of Our Cocks" stepped forward and brought Meg's hand to his lips. "It is a pleasure, Meg." His eyes were bright green, almost glass. Before he could say another word, West took off his cap and smacked the brother she knew was closest to him in age over the head. Hard.

"Mine."

Cade threw his hands up and stepped back, but not before he winked at Meg and flipped off West.

Her face ached from laughing. "It is great to meet all of you. I'd like to say West prepared me for his brothers, but he didn't."

"You would have never agreed to come," West said.

"Oh, I don't know. I like rowdy boys."

"Is that so?" Patrick offered her his arm and Meg was more than happy to accommodate. "Well, you have come to the right place. We're having dinner on the patio, but first, you must meet the parents. After dinner, we'll be sure to whip out the family albums. You're a photographer?"

Meg nodded.

"There are some potty-training shots of West that you need to see." Patrick smirked over his shoulder at West, who was close behind.

"Oh, yeah, don't forget to show her the year you sported the mullet and Boyd tried to grow a mustache," West said.

Meg turned to the oldest brother, who was running his hand along his impressive facial hair. "It came in eventually though, didn't it? All that matters. That's all you brought? Trick's bad hair and my peach fuzz? Weak, Hollywood. You're out of practice. Hey, are you still waxing your ass?"

They finally reached the kitchen in the back of the house. West pushed Patrick and took his place next to Meg. As his parents approached, West took her in his arms and kissed her. Right there in front of everyone.

"Back up," he said in mock command. They all laughed and Meg's face flushed. She'd already lost her balance and she hadn't even met his parents yet.

"Meg Jeffries, these are the only civilized people in my family. My mom, Sara and my dad, Rich."

"Meg! It's so nice to meet you," his mom said, kissing West on the cheek and hugging "the love of his life," as Boyd had accurately put it.

His father shook Meg's hand and then wrapped an arm around him. West had seen his parents about a month ago, but every time he came home it felt as if he'd been gone for a while. Too long, sometimes.

"Did you do something different with your hair?" he asked his mom.

She touched the sides of her dark, chin-length hair. "I did. Thank you for noticing, Westin." She looked around at all the other McNaughton men and West wondered who was going to jump in first.

"Ass kiss," Cade said, not so cleverly disguised by a cough.

Their mother shook her head. "He is no such thing. He is an observant and attentive young man. Ask Meg."

"Yes, Meg. Tell my entire family how attentive I am."

Meg was crying with laughter again. "I honestly did not know what I was getting into. You guys make my family look—"

"Normal," Boyd said.

"Boring. I was going to say boring. Thank you for having me."

His mother guided them down the hall toward one of the guest rooms. After her tour, all the towel and extra blanket locations, they set their bags on the bed and his mom returned to the others.

"Okay?" he asked.

Meg stood up on her toes and kissed him. "More than okay. They're fantastic."

West felt the smile spread across his face. Even though there was no doubt his family was nuts, he loved them, and for reasons that made his heart race, it was important that she loved them too.

"Let's eat," his father called from the grill on the patio.

Grabbing drinks and chips from the kitchen, they were all finally seated around the long wooden table that seemed so much larger when West was a kid.

"So, West told me your name is Megara. That's beautiful," his mom said as the food was passed around the table.

"Thank you. My parents were... creative." Meg sipped the glass of water near her plate.

"She was conceived in Greece," West said.

Meg shook her head. "Couldn't leave that one alone, could you?"

"It's an excellent story."

"Sounds like a perfect way to commemorate a special time," his dad said with a glint in his eye. West handed him the potato salad.

"Yeah?" Patrick said. "Why aren't any of us named after places where we were conceived?"

Their mother blushed and looked as if she might say something, but his dad spoke first.

"Honestly, there was so much lovemaking going on, it was hard to know which one stuck."

"Okay. Wow. Thanks for that, Dad," West said.

"Christ, we're eating." Cade dramatically dropped his fork.

The whole table cracked up. It was so good to be home. With her and surrounded by his normal, West almost forgot about the shit storm waiting for him on Monday.

Chapter Twenty-Eight

*M*eg woke the next morning to an empty bed. How was it possible she already loved his family too? They were worn in and genuine like a favorite sweater or the rich smell of coffee first thing in the morning. She looked around the bedroom she and West had shared last night. They'd lain in bed talking for hours while he freely shared stories of his childhood and she did the same. There was something about being in the home he grew up in that provided a certain freedom she had not experienced since meeting him.

It was also incredible to see him within the context of his brothers. Meg walked to the dresser and picked up a framed image of all four men. They were teenagers in the picture, but they didn't look all that different. The pecking order had already been established.

They were all good-looking men, versions of the same features and yet completely unique. Boyd was husky, with dark wavy hair and the beard West had teased him about. He seemed to be the most mellow with a dry sense of humor. His eyes were dark green. Meg had taken pictures of a lot of bears, and West's brother Boyd had the same soulful eyes of a grizzly. Buried behind deep lashes and a furrowed brow. Boyd had a son, Mason, who was dropped off by a friend right as they were finishing up dinner. Mase, as they all called him, was almost thirteen and seemed to be well on his way to rivaling his uncles.

Patrick was the most cleaned up of all the brothers, although Meg doubted he waxed his nose, so maybe West won the most groomed. "Trick," as they all called him, was the tallest and he smelled good. And then there was Cade. He and West were separated by two years and from what Meg gathered last night, Cade was being put in charge of the Tap House that would be completed in a few months. She was promised a tour of the brewery, but since she woke up alone, she wondered if the tour had started without her.

They'd asked about her job, her photographs. Patrick pulled out his iPad and there was Phelps, still magnificent even on the small screen.

"It is a close-up. How do you get right to the edge like that? That can't be a boat."

Meg shook her head. "It's not. I'm in the water. I do everything I can to ensure I don't mess with their environment. I think of myself as a polite guest."

"That water has to be freezing."

"It is. The miracle of wetsuits, but it's still cold."

"Incredible," Patrick said as all four men looked at her. Meg liked to let her work speak for itself. Except for her recent lectures, she didn't discuss the details of her job with many people, but they were genuinely interested and she was comfortable. Having grown up in a sea of women, she enjoyed the testosterone of the McNaughton house.

West threw the last bag of whatever the hell it was into the storage room and walked back out into the brewing area. The brewery would be nearly twice the size once the Tap House was finished.

"She's great," Patrick said, handing him a beer.

"I know." West took his first cold pull and looked at the label.

"This year's amber."

"It's on point. Warmer than last year's."

"I agree. I'm not convinced our dear brother did that on purpose, but you know he swears there's a method to his madness."

"Can't argue. He knows how to make beer. I like the label too. That's all you, right?"

"I never get enough love around here, so I'll take credit for it. Speaking of love."

West sipped his beer and looked straight out over the brewery floor. Copper vats and tubes went in every direction. Seemed as if there was more of everything in only a month. It was a workingman's laboratory. Recycled wood on the walls and old barrels, no longer used, were there for Boyd, who loved the history and the tradition of his trade. A large loading door, leftover and refurbished from the poultry plant days was rolled up, which opened the whole space up to the outside.

"What about it?" West finally said.

"You're in it."

He nodded and couldn't control the corners of his mouth from creeping up.

"Are you going to marry her?"

He looked at his brother and was somehow thrown by the actual word—marriage. West had thought about spending his life with Meg. Mostly how the hell he was going to make that happen without destroying them both, but the idea of suits and dresses seemed like something for other people.

"Inquiring minds must want to know?" he said.

"Well, it would make it a little easier on the rest of us. If you want to add Brother of the Year to your titles, throw in a bouncing baby a year after the wedding."

West laughed. "She has a grandson."

"Yeah, but he's almost thirteen now and she's already looking around for her next victim. The woman is tiny, but damn she can deliver the guilt."

"I'm the youngest. You guys should show by example, pave the way, don't you think?"

"Yeah, I haven't been on a date in almost a year. Cade is mentally approaching kindergarten, and Boyd..."

They glanced at one another and Patrick rolled his eyes.

"Still Boyd?" West asked.

Patrick finished his beer and turned the bottle in his hand. "Still Boyd."

"Huh, well I wish I could help you out, big brother, but I'm trapped in the puppet show right now and Meg is... not puppet material."

"Is she having a problem with all the attention? You know a couple of days ago I saw a meme of you on Twitter. Do you have any idea how fucking odd it is to see my brother in a meme?"

"I'm not even sure what a meme is, Trick."

"This one was a clip from one of your movies and it said something like, 'When your girl tells you to stop by the grocery store.'"

West waited to see if there was more, glanced at his brother, and realized that was it. "I don't get it."

"You have to see it."

"I'm okay."

Patrick bumped his shoulder. "Anyway, the meme is not my point. Meg seems to be dealing with your... situation. Am I missing something?"

"I walked off the set Thursday night. Broke the cardinal rule of being a puppet and drew attention to myself. I'm sure it's all over the Internet by now. With that and the extra buzz of a new *Throttle* coming up, the swarms are getting larger. I flew home for Meg's sister's wedding and there were people at the airport waiting for me with signs and cameras. That was before my latest screw up."

"We're talking about women, right?"

West nodded.

"I never saw the hardship before, but I'm sure it's different now."

"It is. She's about so much more than the world I'm in right now. I'd rather let her go than see it hurt her."

"What? That's nuts. Can't your people do anything to settle things down?"

West grunted. "Have they been able to do anything before Meg?"

"No, but aren't there laws now?"

"There are some, but mostly when it comes to children."

"Well, there you go. We've come full circle. You need to marry that woman and have a baby. Why are you standing here with me? Get started," Patrick said, taking West's bottle and depositing them both in a recycle bin as Boyd and Cade walked over to join them.

"I'm sorry, did the break whistle blow, assholes?" Cade said, grabbing a beer for Boyd and himself.

He conveniently forgot to get them another. Typical. Thank God his parents had four boys or West would be more on his own than he already felt. They all stood shoulder to shoulder surveying years of work and the years to come. West missed being part of something, missed working for little or no recognition.

Are you going to marry her? He replayed his brother's question and while his heart was wrapped in the fantasy, he knew what was coming. He'd spent years in the spotlight and watched other actors draw attention to themselves. Any kind of scandal, any vulnerability and rag magazines, along with the public, pounced. He'd messed up, and he had a feeling it was going to cost him a lot more than a slap on the wrist and several thousand dollars.

Meg had to admit, the sight of all four of them standing in the open warehouse of the brewery, jeans and flannels, some with knit caps, and wearing worn-in boots, was more than one woman deserved. She'd been given breakfast and a tour of the vegetable garden behind the McNaughton home before listening to directions to the brewery that now stood in the center of downtown Petaluma. West had been yanked from bed early by his brothers and was "working guilt labor," as his father put it when he gave Meg the keys to his truck so she could drive into town.

She pulled her hood up to the afternoon chill and continued walking toward them. There he was, the man she loved to complete distraction, standing with his brothers. He was one of them, and despite his current furrowed brow, no doubt at something his brother said, he looked happier than she'd seen him since they'd met.

Family did that to a person, allowed for teasing and flaws. Not all families were that way, of course. There'd be nothing good on television or in the movies if families were that simple, but when it worked, as it appeared to work for the McNaughtons, there was nothing like it.

Meg was still unnoticed, so she raised her camera and took a few long shots. By the time she was inside the brewery, they all had their backs to her but she was close enough to hear their voices as she snapped a few shots of the view and then realized what they were talking about.

"A couple called this morning before you came down," Cade said. "I screwed with them, which is a good time. Used the Undead Mortuary, how can I help you? I love the silence while they try to figure it out. Best part."

They all turned when Meg's flash went off. Turned wasn't the right word. People turned to greet a friend, even turned on a dance floor. What the four McNaughton brothers did in greeting to Meg and her camera was almost a pounce.

West grabbed Boyd by the back of his shirt—he'd already taken three bounding steps toward her. The surprise must have registered on Meg's face when she stepped back. All three of West's brothers held up their hands.

"Whoa, whoa. Sorry, Meg. We were... shit. Sorry about that, we didn't see you."

West approached her, smiling, and Meg felt her shoulders ease. Sliding her camera strap over her neck and pushing the camera to her back, she met him halfway.

"I'm sorry. I was taking pictures outside and I..." She glanced up at his brothers, who were now back in their usual relaxed repose. "Sorry."

"We're allergic to cameras these days. Kind of a shame. Hey, if any of those turn out, would you send them to me?" Patrick said. "I can't remember the last time we all had our picture together."

"One of us should get married," Cade said. All eyes were on him. "What? We could get dressed up and take a picture. That's all I was saying. Jesus. Tension, so much tension."

"Hey," West finally said and kissed her. Soft and warm, his tongue dipped between her lips and Meg realized some of their best kissing had been in the past twenty-four hours. Maybe they could buy a place in Petaluma and live happily ever after, her silly heart wondered. By the time all his brothers had joined in the grumbling, West pulled back.

"Who called this morning?" Meg asked.

"You've got to work on your technique, man. A woman should not be asking about paparazzi if you're doing it right."

"Shut it, Cade."

"Why are they calling your home?"

"Because I walked off set. It's kind of a feeding frenzy right now. Who can get the first shot of me post meltdown? Who's going to get the scoop on what happened?"

"Slow news day?" Meg tried to lighten the weight in his expression. She was rewarded with a smile. "Something like that. Hannah sent a car. I'll leave mine here for a while. We need to get back to the house and pack. Vince should be there in about an hour. Did you have breakfast?"

Meg nodded and glanced over West's shoulder. His brothers flashed the half smile of men who knew more than they were letting on. Whatever it was, they'd deal with it. How bad could this frenzy be? If it was anything comparable to what they'd experienced at the smart house, they'd be fine.

"Okay, well I guess we better get going," she said.

After hugging all three of West's brothers, Meg took his hand and they climbed into his parents' truck, but not before Patrick said, "Drive safe. We'll see you at the wedding, Meg."

"Who's getting married?" she asked.

West shook his head.

Chapter Twenty-Nine

By the time they said good-bye to his parents and Vince once again closed them into the backseat, tension had crept into West's body, somehow made worse by the peace and normal of spending time with his family. Worse still by having Meg there, being able to show her what they could be. Although he was certain, now that they were on their way back to the city, that what he'd imagined might work wasn't possible. It wasn't fair. But he had no clue how to prepare his heart or Meg for what he knew was coming next.

He closed his eyes. She had fallen asleep under his arm and there was a part of him, a survival instinct, that wanted to gently set her upright and begin creating distance. He should have done that, but his heart was warm and pulsing in his chest and asking for a few more minutes. So, he pulled her sleeping body closer, stroked her hair, and pretended.

Hannah had called security and texted West that reporters were at Regis's offices in both LA and San Francisco. There was a group outside the hotel and a larger group outside Meg's apartment. *Shit!*

"The ability to contain the situation is far better at the hotel. There are six security guys there, two in the front and two more than your usual at the side entrance. I've asked for a barricade, but I'm not getting a response from local police."

"They probably have a whole hell of a lot more to worry about," West had said.

"I checked with my contacts and one shot of you is going for 15K, you and Meg are up to 30K, and any conflict—listen to me, West—any scene or act of confrontation brings those scumbags one hundred thousand dollars. Please think about that when you emerge from that car. Don't give these bastards a payday. You've never stirred this pot and I'm telling you there will be a wall of them all trying to get a rise. Get into the hotel safely and call me."

West had been to awards shows, movie premieres, and even some pretty crazy parties. Flashbulbs, his name yelled repeatedly, and some heckling were par for the course. He knew the game, but he also knew that any smell of blood turned a manageable pain into a tornado in seconds. He felt trapped and worst of all powerless to defend the woman peacefully sleeping next to him.

He loved her and apart from some macho posturing, there was nothing he could do to keep her life from being turned upside down. He'd never felt the cage of celebrity more than he did when Vince called the security team and he listened to instructions for the simple task of getting them inside safely.

He gently woke Meg as they turned onto Mason Street. As if she sensed the change in energy, she sat up quickly, kissed him, and surveyed their approach to the hotel.

"You're not ready for this, so I need you to listen to me."

"Okay," she said with no trace of humor and a touch of fear. Both squeezed his heart.

"There are paydays for pictures of us. I know that sounds nuts to a normal person, but these guys—"

"And women," Meg added with a tight smile.

"And women, fine. They get a certain amount of money for clear shots of me, you and me, and any kind of conflict or altercation pays big for them."

"Can't we simply get out and let them have their pictures?"

"I tried that. Once. It doesn't work under ordinary circumstances and it definitely won't work now. They want me to lose it somewhere between the car and the hotel because it pays them six figures."

"That's insane."

"It is. So, I need you to put this on." He handed her one of the jackets.

Meg slid her arms into the dark material and was instantly engulfed. West pulled up the hood.

"Do you remember the first time you came back to the hotel?"

"West, I'm not a child. Can't you drop me at home?"

"There's a larger group there."

"At my house?" She pulled the hood off.

He nodded and tried not to lose his patience, but Vince had his blinker on and they needed to be ready.

"Meg, I'm not trying to treat you like a child. I want to get through this. We are going up together. I need you to stay close to me, hood up, and don't look up. Keep your eyes down and whatever you do, do not listen to what they are going to yell at us."

"Okay." She pulled the hood back up, tucked her bag under her arm, and with an eerie sense of calm, turned toward the door. West tugged on his own hood and drew her arm tightly under his.

First they were blinded by a wall of flash, and then all hell broke loose.

◦◦◦

Meg had not gone to a lot of concerts in high school or college. She'd attended the occasional outdoor music festival or the symphony with her dad, but she was not well versed in typical concerts.

The summer before college, she turned eighteen and her friends took her to see Maroon 5. Meg didn't know a lot of their music, but her best friend at the time, Kim, won tickets off the radio, so the four of them went. Meg wasn't the girl to have posters of movies or bands on her walls growing up. She had posters, but hers were of a blue whale breaching or images from photo magazines she followed. Meg liked music, mainly classical. Even as a kid, it calmed her down.

She also listened to her fair share of popular music, but she was never a fan. She didn't understand that kind of adoration. Still didn't.

At the entrance to the concert, two of the doors were jammed. It caused a bottleneck and to this day, Meg remembered the gigantic sway in the shoulder-to-shoulder crowd of screaming girls. She'd held close to her friends, but when she returned home, she told her parents it was the most frightening experience of her life. At the time, all she could do was move with the force, allow herself to be taken one way and then the other. Even after she was older and on assignment in the wild, that concert stood out as terrifying.

By the time West pulled her from the car and held her so close to his body she thought she might stop breathing, that concert, that moment of complete loss of control, seemed like a picnic.

"Hey, West. How are you feeling?" one voice called out as a wall of bodies made it almost impossible to move. Meg kept her head down, focused on all the feet. The security guys in front of them began parting the way through the crowd of flashbulbs.

"Did you bring your girlfriend home to meet the family? Something we should know?"

"Have you been sacked yet, West? *Full Throttle* has gone downhill anyway. You're probably happy to get out now, right?"

Meg could feel the frantic pace of West's chest. His warm breath swept across her face.

"I see your latest conquest is looking good lately. Are you part of her upgrade, West?"

"Does it bother her when those LA women throw themselves at you? Do they bother her?"

The crowd shifted as one of the security guards lifted a guy off his feet. Meg assumed he was set down somewhere else, but she didn't look up. They were moving a little faster now. How the hell far away was the door? It didn't seem this far last time.

West's arm did what seemed impossible and tightened even more around her body.

"We should ask her. Hey, Meg. Does it bother you that your man has slept with most of Hollywood?"

She glanced up a couple of inches and could finally see the white stone of the hotel.

"Hey, West. How does she stack up against all your others? *National Geographic* is a far cry from Victoria's Secret, am I right?"

West shoulder checked a guy who would not budge so hard that Meg heard something clatter to the ground.

"Son of a bitch," West muttered in her ear, head still down. "Please don't listen. They want you to react. Remember what I said. We're almost there."

As soon as the words left his mouth, Meg felt someone pull her up and practically over the crowd. West was right behind her. She could still feel him even if he wasn't touching her anymore. The door slammed and the faint sound of endless clicking was finally muted to bearable. She had loved the sound of her camera for as far back as she could remember. There were times she had been on assignment, waiting for the right shot, with only the hum of her lens near her ear.

The camera was her companion, the tool of her trade, but she'd never been hunted with one. Standing with her back against the cold metal of the service elevator, she wondered if she would ever get that sound, the constant assault at the hands of something she'd loved dearly until that moment, out of her mind.

Chapter Thirty

"I'm issuing a statement," West said, pacing Hannah's office the next morning. "I'm calling them out on that... that assault. That's what it was, an assault. I'm an actor for fuck's sake. You would have thought I was some... I don't know who would be treated that way. She was shaking, Hannah. Catatonic, staring ahead, shaking. She is not built for this insanity. She's still alive on the inside, and I'm not letting them treat her that way. I'm issuing a statement."

"You will do no such thing."

"I will. You can't keep me from issuing a statement. I'm entitled to a life. So is Meg. Stop looking at me like that."

"I'm not looking at you in any way, but you need to relax. We should focus on the fines and your apologies. I've already satisfied the insurance company. You have a perfect history, so they have accepted this as a one-time thing. Have you called Gary?"

West nodded.

"Good. Wonderful. Okay, so I think things will be back to normal by tomorrow." Hannah behind her desk and swiped through her phone. "They need you in wardrobe by eight. Something about refitting for a shirt. Then on set by ten. Do you see any issues with that schedule for tomorrow?"

He shook his head.

"Do you have any questions?"

"Yeah, do you ever listen to me? I mean I'm paying you a percentage of what I make and most of the time, I feel like you're doing me a favor."

"West, what is it you would like me to do for you, for all that money you're paying me, that I'm not doing?"

"I'd like to know you're on my side."

"I am. You are halfway through the last movie in your contract. The studio already wants you for another two installments. If you decide to throw away the twenty million dollars they are going to pay you for those additional films, you can certainly do that. But this movie, the one you are filming now, needs to get made. I know you think I'm a cold bitch, but you don't have time to play angry boyfriend. If she can't handle herself with the rags and celebrity chasers, then maybe she's not the right person for you"—West leaned in to protest, but Hannah held up her hand—"right now. Maybe she's not who you need right now."

"I want to issue a statement."

"No."

"Goddamn it, Hannah! You work for me." West was trapped somewhere between collapsing and punching a wall. He needed to take a breath. He was yelling and he knew it wasn't Hannah's fault, but the bottom was about to drop from a life he desperately wanted. He at least needed to try to fix it, make it work with Meg. He spun away and paced Hannah's office.

When he turned back to her, the expression on her face was unlike anything he'd seen in the twelve years he'd known her. It was pity. Christ, she was looking at him like some poor idiot about to be mauled by a bear. West collapsed into the chair across from her desk.

"I know you are upset, but issuing a statement will do nothing. It's not going to protect her, West."

"She doesn't need my protection."

"Oh, then why are you here yelling at me?"

He took a much-needed breath and said nothing.

"You love her, I understand that."

"Yeah? And how would *you* understand that?"

"Don't be a prick. I'm trying to help you."

After a brief stare down, West nodded and hoped that was enough of an apology. He wasn't capable of much more right now.

"Do you think they are going to read a statement and say, 'Oh wow, we didn't know Westin Drake wanted us to treat him and the ones around him with respect and dignity'? You and I both know that's not how it works. They don't give a shit. They're the downside, the intrusive part of the job. Some statement isn't going to change that, West."

He sat forward in the chair, face in his hands, and accepted defeat as he replayed his conversation with Patrick from the day before. He'd said if it meant letting her go to protect her from the insanity of his life, then that's what he would do. What a fool he'd been saying that with such ease, as if he could somehow turn his feelings for her on and off. Now, sitting across from the woman who had been the cold shower on almost every shred of emotion or compassion he'd ever had, West threw the switch that would break his heart, and Meg's. Standing without another word, he left the office.

He'd fly back to LA in the morning. He'd finish *Full Throttle* and then he'd probably take the $20 million since it was clear no one wanted to see him as anyone other than Nick Shot. He'd fall back into a routine and go right back to where he was before he stepped backstage at the convention center. West had made his choices long ago. He'd tried to change it up, do things differently, and he'd failed. Climbing into the back of yet another black sedan, he heard his Aunt Margaret's words anytime he protested chores or the hand-me-downs from his brothers. "You get what you get, and you don't throw a fit."

West closed his eyes and for the first time in a long time, he cried without the cameras rolling.

Meg woke in the Tony Bennett bed sometime around eleven. The sun was filtered to a soft glow by the heavy curtains, but she could still tell it was almost afternoon. Rubbing her eyes, she reached across the bed for her phone, which she'd left charging on the nightstand, and saw West. He was sitting in a chair on the opposite side of the room watching her.

"What's wrong?" she asked.

It looked as if he attempted a smile, but the weight of his expression barely allowed a twitch of his lips. "Nothing."

She sat up, leaving her phone where it was. After what they'd been through last night, she wasn't sure where to begin. They'd barely said two sentences to one another once they arrived back at the suite. They'd showered, fallen into bed, and clung to one another as if it was the last time they were ever going to make love. From the look in West's eyes, Meg had a feeling they'd been right.

"It's not always going to be like this. Remember, you said that," she said.

"When was the last time you walked down the street, Meg? Remember our first lunch and you wanted to walk?"

"I walked the other... when we were at your parents' house. We walked then. Things will die down, West. We will get moments of normal."

He nodded. "You're right. There will be moments and you'll be fine with those until you want to really walk. You know, until your feet are sore, grab a falafel, and spend the day taking pictures of doors or bicycles. Until you want more than moments. I can't give you normal, Meg. I'm not normal. I made my decisions. No one forced me into my life, but you didn't choose this."

"I chose you." She stood from the bed where she now felt too vulnerable. Scanning the room for her clothes, she thought she might be sick. West rose from the chair and they were a few feet apart, suspended in the inevitability of the situation.

"I know you chose me and I chose you too, but that's not enough. I knew what I was bringing you into, and I did it anyway. It was selfish and I'm sorry."

"What does that mean? You didn't bring me anywhere. I came willingly and what happened last night was part of your life. I'm not some wilting flower, West. I can take care of myself."

She pulled on her clothes, not bothering with her hair, and went to leave the bedroom as if she could somehow outrun the pain. He held her gently by her shoulders.

"You have a whole life, and I won't see that destroyed."

"Then don't. We were fine last night."

"Don't you see? I can't protect you. It's a fundamental part of any relationship. I protect you and you protect me. I can't do that, not against what's on the other side of that door." He closed his eyes, arms dropping to his sides. "I can barely protect myself. I won't survive with my heart out there for everyone to step on until it finally stops beating."

"What are you talking about? I think you do an excellent job of ignoring it. You don't need to—"

"Meg, you are my heart now. You are the best pieces of my life, and I need you safe. I have to know that you aren't always looking at the ground. That you're out in the sunlight taking pictures and protecting the animals you love so much. All of that, all that's good with us, will die in here."

"What about you? Don't you deserve all those things too? Who's going to look after your heart?"

"Mine has been locked away for a while now. Until you."

Meg squirmed from his grasp. She didn't want this, she wasn't going to survive an "I love you, but we can't be together," ending.

"I'll just put my heart back where it was. I'll be fine with the piranhas, but I can't be that person when I'm with you."

She was going to cry. Her heart was sending the rest of her body a warning. Everything was going to break down any minute, but she stood frozen. "I don't want to do all of that without you. Not anymore."

"I'm sorry."

Meg felt as if everything crashed around them and pulled back in shock. "You're sorry? What the hell is that supposed to mean? You've decided you can't protect me or keep me under your wing, so now we're done because you say we're done? Is that like dismissing room service?"

Anger was always better than pain, she thought. Anger was survivable.

He stood in front of her like a child in trouble, and Meg allowed the anger to boil to the surface until she forgot to cry. Moving to the living area, she put on her tennis shoes and laced them so tight her feet would undoubtedly be numb by the time she made it home.

Home. The word echoed in her head like a beacon in the storm of her mind. If she could just make it to her apartment, her life, everything would be fine. She would be on steady ground. He didn't want her. Enough with the fluffy explanations, that's what it came down to and she'd be damned if he got to leave first.

"Well, I guess there's nothing left to say." She grabbed her bag and spun to leave.

"Wait." West put his hand on the door.

Christ, she was so tired of closed doors. He was right. This wasn't her life; she wasn't this kind of person and since he'd chosen his celebrity over his love for her, she would choose too.

"Get out of my way."

"We need to talk about this first."

"You don't want me," she yelled, her voice cracking. "You arrived this morning to tell me that you can't handle the swarm around us and it's time for me to leave. It's like I'm a prop or an extra in the movie that is your life. Who does that? Just decides something like that? We have nothing left to discuss, West. Let me go."

He kept his hand where it was and for an instant, she thought he was going to pull her into his arms, tell her he'd lost his mind, and he would move heaven and earth if it meant they could be together. But, the instant passed and when their eyes met, Meg finally experienced what it was like to act in a scene with Westin Drake. His expression was cold, a mask he could hide behind. In fact, there wasn't one trace of McNaughton left in him at all.

"We are going to go down through the lobby. Towner is waiting, as is extra security. I need you to smack me or finish stomping all over my heart down there."

"For an audience."

His jaw flinched, but he continued as if he were reading her toaster manual. "Some indication of a breakup will make this easier for you."

"And for you. Oh, I'm sure Hannah will want a front-row seat."

"Things will play out in the lobby. My security will then escort you to the car waiting in front. Vince will take you home. I will have plainclothes security outside your apartment until things die down. I'd like you to stay in your apartment if you can for at least a couple of days. You'll have a few rough days and then things will return to normal."

There it was, that word, normal. The memory of them at Anna's wedding slammed right through her aching chest. "Tonight we're normal," he'd said. Meg held the wall as her heart practically tore open.

"I hate you," she cried and wanted to smack him before the lobby.

"I'm sure you do," he said.

"Why does it have to be like this?"

He didn't even acknowledge the question. She was going off script. She could see that now. He had steps and a plan. Meg wondered if that somehow helped ease the sting.

"I'll start dating someone else right away." He wasn't looking at her now.

"You have Victoria's Secret on speed dial? West, what are you doing?" She reached out to touch him, and he recoiled. A tear hit his cheek and he wiped it away so quickly Meg wasn't sure if she'd imagined it.

"I don't know any other way, Meg. Please trust me."

"And leave you."

"Yes."

"What if I don't want to leave?" Her voice was weak now that the pain had traded places with anger.

"Then I'll leave you."

Meg gasped for air and for the last time allowed herself to be guided by security. West stood on the opposite side of the elevator and didn't look up again until they hit the lobby. There, among the buzz and flash, he gave the performance of his life. When it was clear the man she loved had firmly locked his heart back behind his dangerous charm, Meg made her exit. The moment the car door closed she collapsed into a ball and cried.

"Are you okay?" Vince asked form the front, his easy familiar voice seemed out of place.

"I am not." She pulled her body closer as if her heart needed every layer of defense.

Meg never liked romantic movies. Sage and Annabelle were the sappy ones in the family. She preferred comedies and now, sifting through the memories of a man she didn't know how to forget, she knew why. Romantic movies lied and she hated liars.

Chapter Thirty-One

*A*fter what felt like months, but was only three weeks, West sat in the corner booth of the hotel bar. He was approaching drunk when Towner removed his glass, handed it to the bartender, and set a tray in the center of the table.

"It's almost four o'clock. Would you like to join me for tea?" she asked.

He would have cried at the gesture, but the numbness from the whiskey didn't allow the memory to hit him as hard as it might if he were sober. Thankful for small favors, he nodded and Towner scooted in across from him.

"I had a thought," she said putting a cup in front of him. "Perhaps you need some healing time with your family in... Petaluma, is it?"

Through the thrumming single malt buzz, West tried to curb his aggravation at anything remotely happy. "Healing time? What are you up to?"

"I was simply acknowledging that downtime can be healing. Since you've been nothing short of a train wreck since your arrival back at the hotel yesterday, I thought you might need some advice. And, I have this new meditation app on my phone. Twenty minutes a day. The voice that leads the exercises is British, so I imagine I'm greeting the day with Jude Law. Not a bad way to start things off. Shall I pour?"

He nodded again. She served their tea and West added sugar. Aunt Margaret used to add milk and sugar. Towner took hers black. Variations on the same theme, he thought.

"Anyway, Jude Law uses 'healing' a lot in my meditations," Towner continued.

"Huh," West managed to say as he relished the warm tea sliding down his throat. "Wait, it's Jude Law?"

"No. I wanted to make sure you were paying attention."

They sipped tea in comfortable silence, nothing but the occasional voice or pre-happy hour bar sounds surrounding them.

"You've been gone quite a bit," she eventually said. "Is the movie almost finished?"

"Three more weeks starting on Monday, not including ADR," West said, stuck between polite conversation and wanting to be left alone.

"ADR?"

"Audio digital replacement," he said.

Towner still seemed confused, so West added, "There is a lot of loud noise in action movies. Sometimes pieces of the dialogue are lost. They replay the whole movie with the music and sound in and we fill in anything that's not clear."

"Interesting."

He sipped his tea. To be honest, not much was interesting these days, but there was no point in telling Towner that. He was sure she could see it all over his "train wreck" of a life, as she so aptly put it.

"Did I ever tell you about the time I went skydiving?" she asked.

West managed a smile. "No."

"Oh, well, first you don't skydive alone. They strap you to someone more experienced. I did not know that, so I was surprised when they strapped me to this young man with impressive arms." She poured herself another cup of tea, and West felt the tea and her story cutting through the whiskey.

"So, that was a treat, but what I found most interesting was the instruction that when you jump, you need to hold on to your partner and ride the wind. No matter how crazy it seems, you must give in because if you fight it, you can hurt yourself."

"Is there a metaphor in here somewhere?" he asked.

"No. I'm simply telling you a story. Do you see a metaphor?" She pushed up her glasses. She was wearing the blue ones this time.

"No." West added more sugar to his tea. "Okay, so you hold on to your partner while the two of you are plummeting to the earth. Then what happens? Mr. Bulging Biceps pulls the parachute and you two float to earth on a little piece of rainbow?"

"Well, that's the interesting part." She didn't even comment on his snarky response and kept going. "I thought it was the instructor's job to pull the parachute. After all, he's the most experienced, the strongest as I've already pointed out. He should be the one to save us at the pivotal moment, right?"

"Makes sense. That's what you're paying for."

"I pulled the cord."

She glanced at him and West knew the metaphor had arrived. *Christ, what was the name of the meditation app?*

Towner nodded. "It's a trust thing and it builds my confidence. My instructor has faith in me to save us both. I'm given that opportunity and I'm stronger as a result. Kind of beautiful, isn't it?"

Finishing what was left in his cup, West busied himself with a refill. It was either that or admit that he'd screwed up. He realized the mistake about a week after Meg left the hotel lobby in a flurry of dramatics. When they stepped off the elevator, she'd chosen not to smack him for the cameras. Instead, she rose to his ear and whispered, "Take care of your tender heart, Westin McNaughton. I'll keep an eye on mine."

Yeah, he wished she'd slapped him, or punched him even—that would have been easier. He had watched her leave and gone back to a room Towner had arranged since there was no way in hell he was ever setting foot inside the Tony Bennett Suite again. He flew back to LA the next morning and stayed there until yesterday. He needed out of LA but wasn't quite ready to deal with the inevitable questions from his family. He snuck into the Main Building Corner Suite a little after midnight on Friday. No 180-degree view, no iconic song. There was a bed and a wireless Internet connection. He was miserable and now, true to form, Towner was explaining to him exactly why.

"I didn't let her pull the cord," he said running his hands over his face.

"No. No, you did not."

"And because I didn't let her save us, or even help save us, I broke her heart."

"And your own from where I'm sitting."

Saying everything he'd been thinking for the past few weeks was strangely liberating. West could feel his whiskey-soaked mind coming back to him.

"Any idea how I can fix this?"

Towner pursed her lips. "This is a tough one."

"Oh, come on. Don't go all mortal on me now."

She smiled and he sent up a silent prayer that she was Yoda, that she could somehow guide him out of the mess he'd made. West was willing to work for it this time. Turned out the path of least re-sistance sucked.

"Have you tried to contact her?"

"That didn't seem fair."

"Good boy. Do you love her?"

West held Towner's gaze and employed every acting skill he had to keep from crying. "Very much."

"What if she's no longer in love with you?"

"I hadn't thought of that."

"That's the spirit. She's still in love with you."

"How do you know?" He felt a jolt of optimism like a kid being told he wasn't grounded.

"I've seen her heart."

"Okay... is this another metaphor?"

Towner shook her head. "Her heart for the foundation."

"Why haven't I seen it?"

"No one has seen it yet. I mean, I'm sure the VIPs have been given a glimpse, but not the public."

"Then how did you see it?"

"The man I'm dating works as a curator at the art museum. Meg has been working on it there, and that's where it will stay until they move it tomorrow for the unveiling."

"Rewind. You have a boyfriend?"

Towner cringed. "I don't like that word, but yes, I suppose he is that. What did you think, I was some aging widow sitting in the lobby waiting for your next crisis?"

West laughed. His head hurt and his mouth was cotton now, but he didn't care. "Forgive me. I should have known better. Back to my crisis. What does Meg's foundation heart have to do with getting her back?"

"Oh, you'll need to see that for yourself. I'll make a call and Vince can take you by the museum. Now that you're back to being simply another pretty face, I don't think there will be much fuss."

"And then?"

"You'll know what to do."

"Such faith in me."

"From the day I met you, Westin. From the first day." She patted his hand and returned to the concierge desk.

West cleared their tea and left the tray on the bar. If he were a certain kind of guy, he might think Towner was sent to him. He might think that Aunt Margaret somehow lived on through Towner. As he strode to the elevator, Towner texted him.

SFMOM at 7:00. Ask for Mark

West stepped into the elevator and glanced at the concierge desk. She nodded as the doors closed. He looked up, as men do when they're hoping there is something bigger than themselves, and for the first time in days, allowed himself to wonder about Meg's heart: both of them.

Meg returned to her apartment that night following a three-day shoot in LA. Amy had closed the deal with the USC coach. While initially taking pictures of college football players had been almost as intimidating as the Spirit Bears, it was a blast. The guys were respectful and fun to work with. She was given creative freedom to shoot the kinds of pictures rarely seen on college sports websites, and she took full advantage. Lots of variety: different angles, shots with some of the fans, and players' family members too. It was exciting. The first time she'd had fun since picking herself up off the couch after the realization that no matter what he said, West had made a huge mistake. He forgot the barbed wire. That the woman he fell in love with could handle anything if she believed in the cause.

And God, she had believed in him. Still did. She'd allowed the false reality of his world to mix her up too, but she'd never given up on him. He couldn't say the same and while there were so many things that broke her heart when she thought about West, the fact that he didn't even put up a fight was the worst.

After getting into her pajamas and putting in a load of laundry, she sat down with the salad she bought on her way home from the airport and opened her laptop. It had been such a long time since she'd had butterflies about a shoot and she needed to focus on what was working. It had been almost three weeks since what her sisters now termed, "lobbygate." Thanks to her family and a large pity party, Meg had found her way back. Professionally anyway.

Following the drama at the hotel, she had stayed out of sight for almost a week, shut off her Internet service, and watched a lot of documentaries. After consuming her weight in trail mix, Meg decided it was time to hit an actual trail. By the time she reemerged, it was as if a huge storm had blown over, leaving nothing in its wake but fresh air and happy plants.

West's security left his post outside her apartment once the photographers lost interest but not before giving her his number just in case "some stragglers return." She would admit it was bizarre having people outside her home even when West wasn't there, but all of that was over now and Meg was back to her routine. As the days went on, her time with him gently softened into memories.

Still she was approaching fine. That was all she could hope for because much like scar tissue, her heart might heal but it would never be the same.

She'd thought about him while she was in LA. Oh, who was she kidding, she thought about him all the time. Wondered if he was all right and if the movie was going well. Driving around the city during her free time, Meg had enjoyed the warmth and the energy, which somehow made her ache even more. Los Angeles was different than San Francisco. It seemed lighter, sunnier. She was sure West's world was different than the surface scenery she drove by, but it didn't seem all that bad. She had allowed herself a moment to imagine what things would look like if they were together somewhere other than the safe spaces he'd arranged for them in San Francisco and then decided there was no point in reliving a discarded dream.

Meg had learned to appreciate humans since returning from the wild. That didn't mean she was ready for swanky parties and the Hollywood crowd, but he'd never even asked her to try. Being in Los Angeles had pulled the mask off the beast West so often complained about, and Meg found she wasn't all that terrified.

While she waited for the USC photos to load, she thought about the heart dedication the next morning. She'd put the final touches on before leaving for LA. The president loved it and commented that he appreciated her courage to be so abstract. Meg wasn't sure if that was a compliment but they seemed pleased.

For Meg, it wasn't abstract at all. Each image she chose was gut-wrenching and therapeutic at the same time. She could have done anything, selected any topic to share with the city where she grew up. She had always used her photographs to show a side of things others rarely witnessed. It was never about preaching and always about reaching out and allowing her experiences to touch those around her. The subject she chose would not be familiar to the casual observer, but details weren't necessary. Everyone recognized love. There were so many reasons her San Francisco heart was West, not the least of which was the fact that he'd shown her so much. She had learned that losing him didn't change that.

"Are these images all about one person?" the president of the foundation had asked when she'd submitted her work.

"No. It's a compilation of a lot of different pieces, a collection of memories and characteristics that make up a whole heart." She wasn't about to share the intimate details of her experience and honestly the West she knew was a collection of several pieces.

They'd told her they were going to use her explanation in their exhibit materials.

"Do you want to select a title for your work, or shall we simply call it the Meg Jeffries Heart? A lot of our artists want the press exposure."

The last thing Meg wanted was press exposure; besides, it wasn't her heart. She couldn't think of anything in that initial meeting, but in LA it had come to her. The perfect name. She e-mailed the president and now all she needed to do was show up tomorrow for the unveiling.

Meg would admit to fantasies that someday West would be walking down the streets of San Francisco, his head down per usual, but then something would pull his focus and he'd notice his heart out in the open air. Or maybe some other couple finding one another like they had that first night she'd kissed him would understand the romance in the heart. Or someone else going through a rough time, would stop and see the isolation. If his celebrity was overwhelming, maybe that was the best way for people to relate to West was in pieces. If that were possible then she'd given the city a true gift. A man so deserving of love instead of adoration. Meg had spent so much time trying to show people the life and beauty of animals. But now that she'd loved and lost, it seemed important to share that journey too.

Not all stories had a happy ending—she should have known that from her time on assignment—but her heart, the real one, wanted to tell him so many things. That she would be fine in his world if it meant sharing it with him. That everyone had baggage and she was so proud of him and his work. All of it, the good and the bad, had brought him to her.

Meg didn't realize she was crying until the buzzer on the dryer went off. Wiping her eyes, she realized that in the flurry of getting to know each other and herself, she'd forgotten to tell him those things.

Regret was sharp and over the past few weeks Meg had thought about calling him, trying to say some of the things distance made crystal clear, but he'd sent her away. "People show you who they are. You simply need to pay attention," her father used to say. He was right and that's why she never picked up the phone.

Instead she set out to create a secret, something that would show their city the man he was without the polish, who he might have been if he'd stayed in theater or if his beer gut had kept him from *Full Throttle*. No one knew that man, except her and his family. He'd given her so much at an unsure time in her life. Through her work, she wanted to leave the details of the man she would love for the rest of her life.

Her father was right. West had shown her who he was and what he was capable of in no uncertain terms. He may never make it out from behind the dark windows of his backseat, but she still held out hope. Still remembered what it was like to stroll with her hand tucked safely into his. He'd given up on her, on them, but she hadn't given up on him. It was too late to say all of that to his face so she would have to be satisfied letting an abstract heart speak for her.

Chapter Thirty-Two

*W*est called down for coffee when he woke up the next morning. He'd barely slept, but it was refreshing to be exhausted and hopeful again. Last night, Mark had escorted him to the back room and left him alone with Meg's work. There was something so grounding in the silence of a museum. Meg's heart was contained in a clear box, no doubt ready for delivery to the hospital foundation where it would be on display for two months and then placed somewhere in the city. He'd learned all of this when he went to the foundation's website after tea with Towner. It made no sense that they would share pictures of a heart that wasn't unveiled yet, but West had never pretended to be patient.

At seven o'clock sharp, he was standing as close as he'd been to Meg's heart in almost a month. He remembered her saying they wanted her to use Polaroid pictures. The heart, painted a deep purple, was covered in tiny snapshots. West carefully leaned on the glass and as he traveled from one image to the next, his chest tightened. By the time he'd circled the heart once, a lump had grown so large in his throat, he was struggling for a decent breath.

The rumpled sheets of the Tony Bennett bed, a sunset off his Pier 32, a single closed eye he recognized as his own, were mixed in with his mother's hands, flowers from his parents' garden, and an incredible shot of his brothers' boots piled near the front door. No faces or identifying features but endless details of a life he never shared. West wiped his eyes and quickly put his hands back on the glass as if he were some child waiting for a store to open. He circled the heart again and when he noticed the title, he slid to his knees.

A Tender Heart

How was it possible that he'd left her with enough love to create something like this? The display in front of him wasn't born of hatred, so she'd lied again. Yeah, he'd be sure to bring that up as soon as he got her back.

He'd messed up and while it shouldn't surprise him, Towner was right. Twice. A guy only met a woman like Meg once in a lifetime, and now that he was sitting on the floor surrounded by her private pieces of his heart, he did know exactly how to get her back. It might take a few tries, but he knew all about rejection. *Dust yourself off and don't be afraid.* His Aunt Margaret had told him that from the time when he was a little boy. He should have listened to her sooner.

Meg took a taxi to the foundation. She was wearing heels, reasonably comfortable ones she bought recently, but she didn't want to risk falling on her ass the afternoon of the unveiling. Each picture ran through her mind a dozen more times last night, assuring her that she'd given nothing away. Choosing West as the theme of her heart had been simple, but she needed the pictures to be personal, the details no one else would bother to know about him. That was the only way she could shield her work from exploitation.

She had photographed some amazing creatures, been to the corners of the world, and yet somehow this simple project seemed as important. Now all she had to do was shake a bunch of hands, including those of the president of the foundation and the mayor of

San Francisco. Her pulse raced every time she thought about it, but at least she didn't have to speak. Finally, someone had let her pictures speak for her.

The sky was overcast as she climbed out of the taxi. Glancing up, she noticed a podium set outside the entrance and four people positioning a box draped in red cloth. They would remove the heart from the box at the unveiling; that's what Meg had been told, and she hoped the sealant they'd put on it was enough to protect her work from the San Francisco weather. Throwing her bag over her shoulder, she was reminded of the first time a taxi had dropped her off for an event she was terrified to face. Glancing up at the tall buildings, Meg wasn't terrified anymore. She'd faced her fears and come out on the other side. A little damaged, true, but better and stronger for the experience.

West walked to the foundation, pacing himself so he was rarely stuck at a crosswalk, he'd learned that technique recently. After Meg, he found he needed air as if it would somehow bring her closer to him. Collar up and hat pulled low, he'd practiced and eventually to his surprise and complete delight, confrontation was either a friendly wave, or he went unnoticed. The piranhas were down to a few, and while he knew that would pick up in the spring when the movie premiered, he wasn't worried. He was done worrying. After seeing Meg's heart, he'd called Hannah with a list of auditions he'd be going on once *Throttle* wrapped. He'd sign up for another two installments, but he wanted to keep trying for other projects.

"Are you sure you can handle the rejection, West? You're a star, I'm not certain you're ready for the hard way again," Hannah had said.

He assured her he would be fine. He was a McNaughton, tough stock, and it was about time he started working his ass off in addition to the occasional wax. That work started with Meg.

Listening to a morning meditation through his headphones, he approached the foundation from the opposite side of the street and noticed her sitting near a podium, legs crossed and wearing the poncho he'd given her.

She looked better than the last time he'd seen her, but she was staring at the heart, still covered and flanked by crowds and reporters. West had often thought he'd met Meg at a time when he desperately needed to feel. She had given him everything, but watching her now, he realized she needed him too. Even with his baggage and piranhas. He woke that morning thinking there was no way he could live without her. With one glance, he knew neither of them could live without the other. They were pieces of a story that only worked if they were together.

West pulled his headphones out and made his way across the street right as the mayor announced her name and they pulled the red cloth off to reveal his tender heart, their tender heart. The crowd clapped and cameras began clicking. The whole scene should have had him scrambling for a better plan. Yet as the mayor shook Meg's hand, West realized two important things. His life was no longer exclusively about him, and he was far from powerless. In all his years in the spotlight, he'd forgotten Mr. Hernandez's number one rule. "Actors are resourceful," he'd instructed. "They hone their craft until they can take any situation and turn it away from themselves and back to the story. They are sorcerers in disguise."

West took a deep breath and remembered who he was and all the people he'd come from. Standing back a safe distance, he watched as the crowd walked around the heart. It was no longer in a box. Towner would be proud as that metaphor struck him square in the chest. The sun parted a small section of the clouds and for a moment, Meg stood among the applause and he could barely keep it together. Her face was beaming and she was once again giving and receiving praise for her work, but this time he'd been her subject. The honor of that was not lost on him, so as the presentation began winding down, he made his way to her, hoping to honor her as best he knew how.

Whispers started by the time he was halfway through the crowd, a woman stepped in front of him, pen and paper at the ready. West held his hand up to stop her as Meg found him and their eyes met. His entire body seemed to reach for her, but when she smiled with those eyes colored by all the beauty she'd witnessed, West needed her more than he'd ever needed anything.

"Westin Drake, would you mind?" The woman's voice broke through and for a beat of panic, West realized he was about to make a spectacle at an event that was for her. *Actors are resourceful*, he almost said out loud, and then he put his arm around the woman.

"Can I ask you a favor?" He didn't wait for an answer since she was doing that shaking and pseudosquealing thing women tended to do when they were close to the cloak of celebrity. "Do you see that woman up there?" He pointed to Meg and at this point, the crowd was all eyes on him. The woman nodded. "There is no one in this world more important to me than that woman. But, you see, I've screwed things up."

"Typical man," someone yelled from the crowd.

"Right?" West chuckled along with the rest of them. Meg twisted her hands. She was nervous. He knew the feeling. "Anyway, I need her to understand that we can have a normal life together, that I'm the guy that can give that to her. I can't do that if you guys lose it and freak out on me."

The woman nodded as if they were coming up with a top-secret plan.

"I need to walk through this crowd without having to sign anything or smile at anyone but her. Can you help me with that? Because I can't live without her and I'm going to have to get down on my knees and beg her to take me back. I need everyone to keep it together for me. Can you do that?"

She nodded again and West kissed her on the cheek. She smelled like roses.

The crowd parted. He nodded to all the official people on stage when he finally reached Meg and then he took her hands. He knew the crowd was still there, that people were watching, but he also understood no amount of training had prepared him for what came next. No romantic hideaways or hotel suites. This was going to be all him out in the open air, and he hoped like hell it was enough.

࿐

"I'm sorry," West said softly, and the animated crowd that had been buzzing around Meg fell silent. It reminded her of the shutter lag during a nighttime photo. That still between capture and result. Her heart felt hesitant in her chest, but when he touched his lips to her hands, everything snapped back to full speed.

West held her face. His hands were cold and his eyes seemed clear and in such focus, she saw flecks of color she'd never noticed before.

"I need you. You told me once to lead with that so I'm hoping that was good advice. I would give anything to go back to that first night I met you, or the first time you let me in, the first time I touched you, or the instant I knew I'd fallen. If I could go back to any of those pictures." He gestured to the heart. "I would hold you like this. I would sink into your beautiful eyes and tell you that you have saved me, Megara Jeffries."

Life was rarely like the movies, and yet here she was surrounded by people in a busy city with a fantasy she never thought possible playing out as if all it needed was a soundtrack. Now was the moment for her to tell him all the things she'd missed the first time. If this were a movie, she would smile and tell him all the right things. Instead, she opened her mouth and the only thing that came out was, "West."

"Let me finish. Most importantly, if I could go back I would trust you, let you pull the cord."

Okay, maybe this wasn't a movie.

"What cord?" she asked.

"Long story. I'll tell you later. The point is, I love you, Meg. That means I will spend my life protecting you from cameras or whatever else gets in our way."

She put her hand to her chest as if she could somehow keep her heart from leaping for him. It was too late. He drew her into him and kissed her.

The crowd was still silent and when he gently pulled back, the warm tears spilled past Meg's smile. West wiped her cheeks.

"I'll protect you too," she said on a whisper as she kissed him again with the strength and determination coursing through her body. She would always keep him safe. She knew that.

The crowd went crazy. She'd managed to upstage him, which was fun since the man normally caused people to completely lose their minds. Meg had already forgiven him and was suddenly looking forward to a backseat when a lady in the audience said, "Do you want to borrow my ring?" The woman winked at West, and Meg almost lost her balance.

"Thank you, but she's not a ring person. Too many things get tangled on it."

West dropped to his knee and the crowd grew silent again. Holy hell, so much for upstaging him.

"Meg, I like the world through your eyes, your lens. I promise to walk more and traipse through the rainforests with you. Hell, I'll even jump in the freezing water with you. Whatever you want, but from the moment I met you, I've needed to be with you. Please marry me."

It felt like the city itself was holding its breath, which was silly since Meg already had her answer. She wiped her damp cheeks and allowed herself to be in the moment. She wasn't rushing this, wasn't quite ready to move on to the next frame just yet. Maybe one more question. She turned to the crowd. "Was any of that from a movie?"

"Unbelievable," West muttered. "For crying out loud, I'm on my knee and the mayor of San Francisco is six feet away from us. You still have questions?"

All the guys in the crowd shook their heads immediately. Obviously the movies they were watching had more explosions than dialogue. The women appeared to flip through their romantic movie catalogs to see if he'd stolen anything from their favorite romantic lead but finally shook their heads too, some of them sharing Meg's tears.

"Nothing? Original work?" she asked.

They nodded.

"Perfect. Westin Drake McNaughton, I may have loved you from the moment you told me to cross my legs and everything would be okay. You've taught me perspective and taken risks with me. I would love to spend the rest of my life with you. Now, get up here and kiss me again."

West looked to the lady who offered the ring.

"Well, kiss her. Don't screw it up now," she said.

Laughter filled the street and vendors from across the street were now outside and clapping too. West touched the side of her face, and just like he had in dozens of hidden spaces, he kissed her like no one could see them.

Their story was nothing like a romantic movie despite the epic crowd scene. Theirs was a tale of clumsy beginnings, quick getaways, and right when she thought a scary ending was inevitable, he'd managed to swoop in and let her save him. They were all the genres rolled into one.

"I'm wearing underwear," Meg whispered in his ear as they made their way off the stage.

"Well, that's a shame."

West kissed her again and when they reached the street Meg looked for Vince.

"How did you get here?"

"I walked."

"Seriously? The one time I wear heels."

He smiled and pulled her forward. "Toughen up, Poncho. You really need to get out more."

Meg laughed, keeping pace with him as the sun ducked behind the clouds and it began to sprinkle.

Epilogue

Meg straightened the picture above the couch as West stood behind her. It was the one she'd taken on their honeymoon to the Galapagos Islands. Their small coffee table was crowded with marked-up scripts West was reviewing and Meg's laptop, full of images that needed to be reviewed before she sent Amy her proofs for the Sierra Club campaign due the following week.

"It's crooked," West whispered into her neck and wrapped his arms around her.

"No."

"Yes."

"Maybe it's too big for the wall."

"Maybe."

She turned in his arms. "Maybe we need one of those big movie-star mansions."

West smiled, his hair every which way, a look that was quickly becoming her favorite style. "I'm not a movie star anymore."

"Yeah, tell that to the guy going through our trash."

West pulled the blinds up and Meg collapsed on the couch in laughter. Shaking his head, he threw himself on top of her. "You thought that was funny?"

"I did," she barely got out, squashed beneath his weight.

He pushed her hair from her face. "I love you."

"I know," she said and pulled his mouth to hers.

"Are you hungry?" he asked.

She nodded, still relishing the warmth of his body.

"There's this new place two blocks down. Vietnamese, I think." He stood and offered a hand to help her up. "It's a gorgeous day. Want to walk?"

Meg's breath whooshed quickly from her chest and returned with the steady knowledge that life was even better once the cameras stopped rolling. West squeezed her hand and they stepped out into the early afternoon. The sun was shining and the Golden Gate Bridge stood in the distance, the last tendril of morning fog dissolving into a blue sky.

Acknowledgements

I would like to thank:

Katie McCoach for listening to my crazy and helping turn it into something special.

Nikki Busch for finding "because" when it was right in front of my face.

Erin Tolbert for taking care of everything else so I can do what I do.

Those who work tirelessly for the protection and preservation of our earth and the creatures who were here first. Your commitment inspires me to be a better human every day.

My family for putting up with the missed phone calls, imaginary friends, and often absent mind.

Readers for continuing to invite me into your lives. The honor is never lost on me.

Tracy Ewens shares a beautiful piece of the desert with her husband and three children in New River, Arizona. She is a recovered theatre major that blogs from the laundry room.

Exposure is her ninth novel, and the eighth in the *A Love Story* series.

If you would like to keep in touch, you can find Tracy on Twitter at tracy_ewens, or subscribe to her newsletter at www.tracyewens.com.